WRITTEN FOR
HITCHCOCK

WRITTEN FOR
HITCHCOCK

Twenty-five Twisted Tales
of Revenge and Intrigue

by Talmage Powell

RUTLEDGE HILL PRESS
Nashville, Tennessee

Dedication

To the late but eternal Alfred Hitchcock, who created the Hitchcock-genre, and to the television producers and publishers and editors of *Alfred Hitchcock's Mystery Magazine* for their presentations of the author's brain children on so many occasions, and for their co-operation in the preparation of the present volume.

Copyright © 1989 Talmage Powell
Reprinted by arrangement with the author.

Published in Nashville, Tennessee, by Rutledge Hill Press, Inc., 513 Third Avenue South, Nashville, Tennessee 37210

Typography by Bailey Typography, Nashville, Tennessee
Cover design by Harriette Bateman

Library of Congress Cataloging-in-Publication Data

Powell, Talmage.
   Written for Hitchcock: twenty-five twisted tales of revenge and intrigue / Talmage Powell.
      p.   cm.
   ISBN 1-55853-019-3
   1. Detective and mystery stories, American.   I. Alfred Hitchcock's mystery magazine.   II. Title.
PS3566.08345W7   1989   89-3539
813'.54—dc19   CIP

Manufactured in the United States of America
1 2 3 4 5 6 7 8—95 94 93 92 91 90 89

Contents

Acknowledgments

The stories in this collection first appeared in issues of *Alfred Hitchcock's Mystery Magazine,* copyright © the publishers, on the following dates:

"The Second Mrs. Randleman," February, 1969; "Gator Bait," March, 1971; "Reward for Genius," November, 1965; "Mind the Posies," June, 1965; "The Holdup," May, 1979; "The Confident Killer," October, 1967; "Easy Mark," May, 1971; "New Neighbor," October, 1975; "Old Man Emmons," February, 1962; "Jury of One," October, 1959; "Heist in Pianissimo," May, 1964; "Lone Witness," January, 1966; "Trial Run," August, 1971; "Stranger's Gift," December, 1969; "Proxy," June, 1966; "The Vital Element," November, 1967; "The Way Out," July, 1969; "False Start," October, 1964; "A Way with a Will," April 1, 1981; "Money, Murder, or Love," June, 1961; "The Ultimate Prey," December, 1974; "To Spare a Life," March, 1970; "I Had a Hunch, And . . . ," May, 1959; "One Unnecessary Man," February, 1958; "The Five Year Caper," August, 1965.

Introduction

Dear Reader,

I am delighted by your presence in the select circle. Your choice of the devisements presently in hand reveals you as a devotee of the short story. This is to say, in all objectivity, that you are intelligent, witty, an observer of meaningful details that often escape the less discerning, and have little time for nincompoops.

The diamond-like incisiveness of the short story, of course, was an early-on psychic necessity for the earthly creature with the big brain. The teller of tales was honored guest at any primeval campfire. Quite naturally, the yarn-spinner took note of which stories best tapped the audience for a tear, a laugh, a shiver, a lump in the throat. These surely were tales worth repeating around the next campfire that beckoned.

Thus, the anthology came into being, the collection of stories more or less threaded together by common theme, genre, authorship.

About 7,000 years ago the best of the best orally-preserved stories were first written down. The creators of the written anthology were Sumerians who lived in cities along the Tigris and Euphrates rivers in what is now roughly Iraq–Iran territory. The development should not surprise us. The Sumerians birthed the first sciences of engineering, hydraulics, mathematics, architecture, and astronomy, along the way inventing the wheel, the table, and the art of writing. In cuneiform script on tablets of clay—imperishable in the climate—they anthologized tales that astonish the tireless archeologists of the present century.

Greek civilization flowered in large part from Sumerian seeds, and if one among them borrowed the hypotenusal concept and called it Pythagorean, another, Meleager by name, circa 60 B.C. brought method to the anthology, much as we practice it today.

To the present gathering I would suggest that the most cunning anthologist of all was Scheherazade, whose wit matched her incredible loveliness. She was picked as queen, as we all remember, by a king who had the nasty inclination to kill off his wives the morning after the night of nuptial raptures. But she so enthralled him by the nightly telling of tales that by the 1,001st night he yielded to the superiority of her cleverness and knew he could not live without her. Without proof to the contrary, we might suspect that the suspense-fraught biography of Scheherazade was an invention of the late Alfred Hitchcock.

Speaking of whom, the tales in this collection represent a large segment of my pleasurable association with the Hitchcock organization, which, via movies, television, and printed word has so stamped the mystery/suspense story that the "Hitchcock Story" has become a genre unto itself.

Pundits have taken shots at analyzing The Story. Those of us who have actually done it for television and between printed covers are more cautious. The Hitchcock story may go anywhere and do anything. No locale, character, idea, or notion is out of bounds. There are no set rules or guidelines. Certain urges, however, are to be given free rein: to open the forgotten trunk in the dusty attic; to release the skeleton from the closet; to poke a hole in the patina of the jet set; to glimpse the blasé contradictions lurking in a bucolic scene; to catch for a moment the antithetic aspects of behavior required by civilization; to apprehend a micro glimmer of the seethe-and-crackle whereby this planet is simultaneously snake-pit and Eden rubbing shoulders incessantly.

Writing a Hitchcock story is a simple act: When one's mood is so abrasive, one's humor so barbed, and one's preachments so jaudiced that a spouse is driven to serious consideration of "doing a Hitchcock" of her own, the time is propitious to repair to the typewriter or word processor.

Or, as in the present instance, to the nearest campfire where a friendly clan has gathered.

Thank you for inviting me.

Your crony and confidant,
Talmage Powell

WRITTEN FOR
HITCHCOCK

Once Willa realized the futility of her efforts, she decided to take matters into her own hands. . . .

ONE

The Second Mrs. Randleman

Willa Randleman was well along in years when she went through her menopause, at an age when most women have all but forgotten the experience and settled into a comfortable matriarchal phase.

The aftermath for Willa was anything but comfortable. Her system refused to reorganize itself. Migraine headaches blinded her. A kidney ailment was a lurking knife. Food she'd always enjoyed worked in her stomach like undigestible porcupine quills.

Yet Willa was courageous, and resolute. She kept up a cheerful front that fooled her friends. Even George didn't know she had to struggle through hellish shadows just to stir herself of a morning. The tasty breakfasts, served on white linen and right on time, continued to greet him after he'd showered, shaved, and dressed. She remained the usual gentle and cheerful foil for his morning grumpiness and bad temper, and always managed to see him off with a smile. George probably expected her to live forever.

Then to top it all off, Willa was mugged one night. Late in that quiet evening George stopped his incessant pacing in the livingroom and appeared in the doorway to the den, where Willa was watching TV. He stood with his fists mashed against his temples.

"George?" Willa got up quickly.

"One of my nervous spells," he gasped. "I swear I'm going to jump right out of my skull! You've got to get me a tranquilizer!"

He didn't look nervous, but he'd explained countless times that he didn't have a visible affliction, like a boil that could be lanced. ("Merciful heavens, Willa, even the doctors don't really understand this kind of thing!")

He'd had this anxiety neurosis for years; and Willa had tried to understand because, once, she'd really loved George.

She started from the den and George emitted a breath that sounded as if he were smothering. "Where do you think you're going?"

1

"To the bathroom, George, to get your pills out of the cabinet."

"I've already looked. I'm all out."

"But you had a fresh bottle."

"I don't care *when* I had a fresh bottle. Maybe you've been taking them. I haven't any now."

"Then I'll phone—"

"I've already phoned," he practically shouted. "They've no one at the drugstore to deliver at this hour. You'll have to run down and get me some."

"But, George, it's so late, so dark. . . ."

"Willa, what do you want me to do? Beg? Please, please, please." He grabbed her hand. "I'm scared of myself . . . don't know what I might do. Maybe slam my head through the front window and feel the shards of glass—"

"No, no, George," Willa broke in, her lips white. "Don't talk like that. I'll hurry, only be a few minutes."

"God bless you, Willa."

Minutes later Willa was in the all-night drugstore two blocks away. She handed the empty bottle with its prescription number on the label to Mr. Freyling, the druggist on duty. "Please hurry," she said. "George is having one of his spells."

The portly druggist had known Willa for a long time. He lifted a shaggy eyebrow. "Funny," he muttered, turning from the counter, "that he never has them on the golf course, or in a poker game."

"What did you say, Mr. Freyling? You're not out of them . . ."

"I said it's late. Man sending his wife out at this hour. . . . You be careful, Mrs. Randleman."

The pills were in her clutch bag when Willa came out of the drugstore. She paused to look up and down the dark street. When her father long years ago had built the rather sumptuous brick home, which he'd eventually left to Willa, the neighborhood had been upper crust—sweeping lawns, neat hedges, two story houses with rambling porches—but the street hadn't been immune to urban blight. Some of the houses had been chopped into apartments, others torn down to make way for a used car dealer, a plumbing supply company, a mobile home sales office.

Willa's tapping heels broke the silence along the shadowed sidewalk. She crossed the intersection and felt a little less insecure. She thought of George with that tolerant, resigned distaste the years had developed. Could it be that she was subconsciously resentful? Her age was apparent in the gray hair, the small, wrinkled face, the myopic blue eyes, the gnarled hands with the brown blotches on their backs, but Father Time had treated George like a favorite son. Tall, flat-bellied, rangy; youthful, cleanly whittled face under a cap of brown hair, that was George. Other people seemed to inspire him.

For them he always had a big smile, a back-slap, a stockpile of breezy stories. He was actually two years older than Willa, but he looked fifteen years younger.

The darkened office of the used car dealer slid by Willa's left hand. The gaudy streamers and tinsel strung over the car lot rustled in the soft breeze. Willa thought nostalgically of the days when the big Wherry house had stood here, its grounds like a lovely park, so cool in summer. Swings, sliding board, sandboxes, wading pool, Dinky Wherry's playhouse with its windows of real glass . . . Wish I'd had a child or two, Willa mused.

Then Willa's small, reminiscent smile froze as she heard the spurt of gravel under a leather sole. Her heart jumped into her throat. The toes of her shoes seemed to catch against each other. She had the quick thought that she'd surprised young vandals in the process of stealing hubcaps. The trick was to continue on without faltering, giving no sign of having seen or heard anything.

Then she actually felt the shadow fall over her. She tried to turn, hands clenching to fight to the ends of her slender strength.

A vise slammed about her throat as a strong arm choked off her scream. A knee struck her low in the back, driving pain through the top of her head.

Stunned, she struggled as she was wrestled off the sidewalk between two cars. She heard the small, quick grunts of her attacker, felt the powerful animal strainings of his muscles. His arm rose and fell. The bludgeon, jackhandle or whatever, drove splinters of bone to the core of her brain.

A blank nothingness . . . Then Willa had the strange sense of being a little shred of the nighttime darkness, a faint, indefinable quivering at first, then her energy built slowly. The silence was pleasant, like that of a summer night after a cooling rain.

She drifted down toward the crumpled white thing lying at the car lot. This was surely a nightmare. She was looking at herself, at her own frail body! She saw the contorted face, the mouth pulled into a grimace, the eyes jutting, glazed. The silken gray hair above the right temple was matted with a red-gray ooze.

The shock sent her spinning, a tiny vortex in a spatial vacuum. She hurtled up among the gaudy streamers and tinsel before she quite realized she was moving.

She steadied and shimmered briefly over the roof of the car lot office. I'm dead, she decided, killed by a man whose face I didn't even glimpse. That's my body lying there. And this invisible thing up here? *My goodness*, the thought rocked her. *I'm a ghost!*

Mr. Freyling stared at the rows of tall brown pill bottles on the shelves before him. The irritated shake of his leonine head was for himself.

He turned back to the counter to re-read the prescription he was filling. Feeling vaguely uncomfortable and annoyed, as if something were bothering him in the back of his mind, he frowned, tried to concentrate on the words a doctor's hand had scribbled.

He looked up as the front door opened. A pale, jerkily moving George Randleman swept the store with a quick glance.

"Anything wrong, Mr. Randleman?" Freyling called, assailed with the feeling that something was.

"My wife . . ." George hurried toward the counter. "I sent her here more than an hour ago. . . ."

"I know." Freyling dropped the small square of paper he was holding and came around the counter. "She paid for the pills and went out."

The two men traded a look, then both went to the front door. The druggist stepped to the sidewalk and looked along the dark, deserted street.

"You won't see her out there," George said. "I just came that way."

Freyling eased back inside. "I think we'd better call the police."

George brushed past him and dropped a coin in the slot of the pay phone. He lifted his hand, but instead of dialing, his fingers went on up to touch his temple.

"What is it?" Freyling asked, looking at him closely.

"Don't know . . . Strange . . ." George turned his head and stared over his shoulder. "Ever get the feeling you knew in advance what would be around the next blind curve on a road you'd never driven before? Or that a room you walked into for the first time was somehow familiar?"

Freyling thought of the absentmindedness, not at all characteristic, that had assailed him just before George walked in. What the devil was going on?

"Like that now," George said. "Like I've been through this scene before."

"Of course, you haven't," the druggist said with a forced firmness. "You're distraught, that's all. I'll get you a pill. Maybe have one myself. . . ."

Willa hovered above a battered old car in the no-down-payment row and watched the police in action. She'd had more luck communicating with the burly plainclothes detective than anyone else so far. With George and Mr. Freyling the most she'd managed had been vague, subconscious discomfort. She'd focused her willpower on the detective, and when the small search party had reached the car lot, the man, thrusting his flashlight beam about, had unerringly discovered the body. His eyes had veiled with pity and shock. Then he'd called to his partner.

The second detective and George had come running. George had taken one look and slumped in a near faint. The younger detective had helped him to the police car where George had sagged on the rear seat to recover.

The big man (he'd introduced himself as Sergeant Rudy Chizik on arrival at the drugstore) had found Willa's clutch bag, ripped open, stripped of cash, and flung near her body; and the weapon, a rusty old tire tool. Willa had been a roiling disturbance in the void when Chizik's light picked out the weapon. It was nothing less than demeaning to have one's life sacrificed with a piece of junk!

Chizik had talked into the police car radio. A second car, trailed by a black van, had nosed into the scene. A man with a camera had aimed at the body and popped flashbulbs from half a dozen angles. Another had dusted the weapon and clutch bag for fingerprints. Two others had eased the body onto a stretcher, covered it, and loaded the black van.

George was sitting up when Chizik leaned in the open door of the police car. "Feeling better?"

George nodded, his face a gray oval in the near darkness.

"Anything you can add to what you and the druggist told me when I arrived at the drugstore?"

"No," George said huskily. "She just went to the store to get some pills—for me. Then she didn't come back. That's all."

"It looks open and shut," Chizik said. "A punk sees her going into the drugstore, figures she's on an errand and will be coming back the same route. Finds a weapon without trouble in that clutter on the back of the car lot, waits for her."

George covered his face with his hands. "Just for the few dollars in her handbag. . . ."

"He probably didn't intend to kill her, but she was struggling and in the pressure of the moment he struck harder than he meant to."

George uncovered his eyes, his hands slow claws dragging down his cheeks. "That excuses him?"

"Certainly not!" Chizik said, a cold ring in his voice. "But you can see what we're up against: no fingerprints on the weapon or bag; an unknown drifter who could be on a freight train headed in any direction at this moment. . . ." Chizik let out a heavy breath. "It's the toughest kind of case to crack. Nothing but deadends. But if he tries another mugging, we may be able to tie him to this one."

"But you said he would hop a—"

"I said he might," Chizik broke in. "On the other hand, he could have bought him some horse by this time and right now be shooting a vein in a flophouse no more than a dozen blocks away."

"Do you always just hope for luck?" George asked nastily.

Chizik kept his cool. "Only when we have nothing else to go on. The net is always spread. We fine-comb every fish that gets caught. We hope for the best."

During the next seventy-two hours, as mortals in the material realm reckoned divisions of the Endless Moment, Willa observed the fate of her body. The autopsy was simply too gruesome. The fellows at the mortuary prepared her for burial with the aplomb of bakers plopping a lump of dough in the pan. The chapel was banked with flowers, and the service was brief but quite lovely. She was touched by the number of people who showed up. The chapel was filled to standing room capacity. It was such a busy time that she didn't have a chance to get close to George until the ride to the cemetery was over.

Two friends and the Reverend Marchand accompanied George home. The minister got out of the car as George did. They stood looking at the silent, empty house.

"If you'd care to have someone stay with you . . ." Reverend Marchand suggested.

"No," George said heavily, "The quicker I face it, the better. I'll be all right." He shook hands with the men, thanked them for everything, took a long breath, and braved the front walk with a steady stride.

As soon as he was in the house a strange transformation took place. He ducked to the front window, shedding his gloom and long face with the ease of a man tossing off a jacket. He peeped between the slats of the blind, and when he saw the car pulling away, he turned and actually jumped off the floor, clicking his heels together. He rubbed his hands together, the motion somehow reminding Willa of a venomous animal licking its lips. A smile lit the whole of his face.

George swaggered to the kitchen, opened a cabinet, and poured himself a drink. Lifting the glass high before he tossed the liquor down, he boomed a toast to himself, "Here's to success!"

He'd kept himself under very tight control until this moment. Now he was in a state of wildly happy release. Willa recoiled from the evil gloating that flowed from him. She seeped through the ceiling and stopped her flight in the attic, where she was a small, lashing, invisible disturbance in spatial vacancy. What in the world had come over George? Could it mean that he, not an unknown mugger. . . .

No, no! It was too much, thinking such a thing about someone with whom you'd shared the intimacy of a marriage bed. Could he have been such a stranger to her?

Willa remained in the attic while the planet darkened and the night silence deepened. She was clutched with a dread of getting so close to George again.

It was after one o'clock in the morning when she heard George stirring. She flitted across the driveway and perched on the ridge of the garage roof as he took the rear door out of the house.

He crossed the dark yard. Below her the car door closed with a soft click. The starter grunted, and the engine purred, but he didn't use the headlights until he turned into the street. He drove out of the neighborhood at moderate speed. Six blocks from the house, the car accelerated eagerly, although George remained within the speed limit.

His destination was a modest brick apartment building across town. He chose the service alley and parked behind the building where the car was out of sight. He hurried around to the front and dashed up a stairway to the second floor rather than wait for the self-service elevator. At Apartment 2–A he tapped lightly on the door with the knuckle of his forefinger. Almost instantly, the door opened just long enough for George to slip inside.

The girl that George took in his arms was every bit as lovely as Willa had sometimes in fanciful moments wished that she could be. Tall, willowy, she had a creamy face with bold cheekbones and full lips, eyes with shadows like violets in the dusk. Glistening jet black hair swept her shoulders.

The girl and George kissed. Willa, spinning against the ceiling, had the sensation of goggling. Mercy! The way the girl was emphasizing the embrace with sinuous, subtle writhings of her body! The heat of George's lust was a reddish aura.

Then the girl shoved him away. Her moist lips drew into a pout. "You took long enough!"

"Trisha baby." He reached for her, but she slipped aside and went to look out the front window, her back to him. "You didn't even phone me, George. I had to find out from the papers and TV newscasts that it was over and done."

George came up behind her and put his hands on her shoulders. His fingers burned through the thin nylon blouse. He nuzzled her hair and whispered in her ear.

"Baby, staying apart for six whole days has been even tougher for me, but I explained it all. Not a living soul knows about us. No one must—until the time comes to let the world know a widower has picked up the pieces of his life and met a new friend."

The pressure of his hands turned her. He caressed her neck with quick kisses. "Baby, baby . . . . It got so I was revolted every time I had to look at her and thought of you waiting here. . . ." His passionate mumblings became a bit incoherent. "A relief . . . satisfaction . . . to pick up that rusty tire tool and know she was out of the way at last. . . ."

"If they suspect, George. . . ."

"They don't. They won't. Too many cases like hers every day. Not enough cops to do the job. They'll give it the routine treatment while they struggle with the rest of their workload. It's perfect, baby. The case will just slide into the unsolved file until hell freezes over."

The girl relented slightly. Her arms crept up around George.

"Did we get all you said, George?"

"It's in the pot, and the pot's ours when the routine stuff is finished. All those thousands in insurance, as if the trusting, foolish old biddy, alive, was worth a fraction of it! The house and lot to convert into commercial property; the stocks and bonds that have brought her a beans-and-bread income from the day her father put them in the safety deposit box."

"You were happy a long time, George, on that income and what you could pick up when somebody wandered into your real estate office and wanted to buy or sell a house."

"Never happy, baby. Not really. And the last of those years were worse than dull, grimmer than grim. Then you made me know what it was like to come alive."

They stood with faces close. The girl looked deep in his eyes.

"Now what, George?"

"Like we planned. We wait a decent interval. Then we meet, court, marry, cash in, get our passports, and go to see the sights—in the spots where the lights are brightest!"

"Hmmmm." Again the girl disentangled and slipped across the room. She paused at a table, picked up a cigarette and lighter. "I've been thinking, George; alone here, plenty of time for thinking, seeing it in the newspapers and all."

George drifted toward her. "What about, baby?"

"Well," she snapped the lighter. "You do plan to keep coming here every time you get the chance to do so safely."

"What else, baby?" George smirked.

"Meantime is what else," she said, a sudden sharpness in her voice. "Meantine, what if you meet someone else? Meantime, what if you change your mind, before that proper interval, as you put it, has passed?"

"You know I'd never do that!"

"You wouldn't want me like a poor little fish that gets stranded when the tide goes out, George?"

"What kind of crazy question is that?"

"Then you won't mind one slight shift in plans," she said, stabbing out her hardly-puffed cigarette.

"Now, baby, the planning has all been—"

"Changed," she put in. "Changed in one detail. We're going to be married now, George, tonight. We've time to dash across the state line, and return before any callers stop at your house. No one else will know—until you're ready to hint around that you've met a friend. Months from now, if you like, you can confess that we've eloped the previous night. I'll move in openly then. But—and that brings us to the last meantime—we're going to tie a little knot tonight." A sultry smile heated her lips. She pressed herself against George, her body an offering. "While the tide is running. . . . How about it, George?"

His eyes were ravenous. "Okay, grab a coat. We'll wake up a justice of the peace in the first county seat we hit across the line."

The shock of the entire revelation spun Willa into limbo. She struggled out slowly, feeling as if her energies had been scattered all over the cosmos.

The late afternoon was bright and sunny, the city its bustling self. She willed.herself to the modest brick apartment building and noted the mailboxes. 2–A, Miss Trisha Hunter; secretly, Mrs. George Randleman; the second Mrs. Randleman.

Willa happened to notice the date of cancellation on a bill that had been mailed to the box. Good grief! Almost a week of material time had ticked away since her funeral.

She wished herself upstairs, in 2–A. No one was in the apartment. It was stuffy and heavy with the scent of Trisha Hunter's (Randleman's) cosmetics. A few of George's things had been tossed on a chair in the bedroom; undershirt, socks, a pair of pajamas that Willa had washed and carefully ironed just a couple of weeks ago.

The apparel, however, bore popular brands, available in any deparment store and not even identifiable by laundry marks. Might belong to any gentleman caller. Nothing specific to implicate George or offer the first hint toward the whole appalling truth.

If there were clues, that big fellow, the detective named Chizik, would have to find them. . . .

Chizik was red-eyed and haggard the next morning when he came on for the eight to four-thirty tour. He'd nicked himself three times shaving, insulted his wife by eating only two of the four eggs she always coddled for his breakfast, and yelled at his youngest kid without cause.

Hell of a night, went through his mind; cracking up, long before retirement age, at that.

He went to his desk in the squadroom and tried to concentrate on the mimeographed copy of reports that had come off the night shift. After several minutes he threw the report down, lighted his tenth cigarette of the morning, and barged into the office of his superior, Captain Blumengard. The harried brass was barking orders into one phone while another line held.

Chizik lighted cigarette number eleven while he shifted from one tired arch to another and waited. "Captain," Chizik said when the phones were all cradled, "I want reassignment to the Randleman case."

Blumengard rocked back. "What's turned up in the reports on it?"

"Nothing," Chizik said, "but I—"

"Then why such a request? Don't you know the papers are chewing us out on the Abernathy thing? Here we've got the daughter of a councilman, no less, involved in an LSD party that produced one suicide. What are you doing on *that?*"

"Well, I . . . this Randleman killing . . . ."

"Look," Blumengard said patiently, "that one hurts me too. They all hurt me, but you know the score, Chizik. Mrs. Randleman was killed more than a week ago. Routine mugging that ended up in murder. We'll expend all the time and manpower we can, but we'll have to take our chances on that one. You know that we get a workload every twenty-four hours that would keep our available resources busy for ninety-six. Figure it out for yourself, Chizik." Blumengard shuffled some papers on his desk. His gesture was sheer exasperation. "We do a damn good job with what we've got. You're part of what we've got, and I simply can't spare you any longer on the Randleman case."

Chizik knew he'd been dismissed, but a nagging insistence worried at him like invisible gnats.

"Good morning, Chizik," Blumengard said pointedly.

Chizik shook his head. "Captain, don't know what it is or why, but this Randleman thing keeps bugging me. I've got this *feeling.* Can't really describe it or shake it. Last night, it came over me like I got gooseflesh. Didn't get a half-hour decent sleep. Every time I closed my eyes and drifted off, it was like I got . . . well, an intruder in my subconscious giving me nightmares. All night, nightmares."

Blumengard rocked forward, clenched his hands on the desk. "Chizik, don't scare me with sick talk. Not right now. You mark off sick, I'll break your neck. You get hold of yourself. I've got far too few with your experience and know-how."

"That's why I thought—with my experience, I mean—I could maybe wrap this Randleman thing up."

"The record says a mugger killed her in the commission of robbery. One of these days he'll try again."

"But, Captain, if it wasn't—"

The phone screamed an interruption. Blumengard laid his hand on the instrument. Before he picked it up, he speared Chizik with a look.

"The Abernathy case is already forty-eight hours old. I'm giving you and your men exactly twenty-four more to break it. Do we understand, Sergeant?"

Willa drifted over the rooftops and felt the city sinking into ever deeper slumber, including Sergeant Chizik. She'd done all she could with him. No need tormenting the poor man further.

She was drawn irresistibly to the brick apartment building. She swirled along the alley. Sure enough George's car was there.

She lurked over the vehicle for a moment. She had the certainty that she could, with sufficient will and effort, focus her energy and cause the battery to drain itself.

George would come out tomorrow morning and, unable to start the car, would have to call a service station. George would say, "Can't understand it. Battery was almost new too."

And the bored mechanic would mumble, "Yeah, it happens. They just seem to go dead every now and then."

But would it accomplish anything? Beyond establishing an eyewitness that George had been there? Who would question the eyewitness? And would the eyewitness even remember a face at which he'd barely glanced?

Willa flowed through the brick. She hesitated in the girl's snug livingroom. She hated to witness the scene beyond the bedroom door.

If only Chizik could be standing in this very spot, a short walk would reveal George's secret affair. From that point, a detective such as Chizik would surely uncover the rest of it: but Chizik wasn't here. He wasn't going to be here. If anything at all was done, Willa would have to do it herself. She seeped through the door and forced herself to observe.

They slept now, George and the girl Trisha. George with a smug, satisfied smile on his face. He lay on his left side, facing the wall. Trisha slept on her back, one arm curled up around her head. She looked so lovely, innocent, endearing lying there that it was almost impossible to believe the evil that was really in her.

Willa seethed with a violence that knocked a tiny fracture in the cosmic time warp. The injustice of it all was simply unbearable.

But what to do? Trying to get through to people, she'd so far only aroused in them feelings and sensations which they'd dismissed for lack of a ready materialistic explanation—except in the case of Sergeant Chizik. She'd had more luck with him than anyone else. Even if he'd explained her the next morning as a nightmare, she'd for a moment established a brief link, slipping in and feeling the very essence of the man.

The effort had come to nothing, of course, but she had learned from it. Sergeant Chizik had been sound asleep, all his conscious barriers down, unsuspecting, unresisting . . . and Trisha Hunter was in the same state of existence at this very moment.

It's worth a try, Willa decided, and she summoned all the non-spatial forces at her command, gathered and focused them. For the barest instant, Willa was a glint of fiery ectoplasm in the darkness.

Now!

Trisha Hunter reared up and tried to scream as the concentrated essence of Willa Randleman slammed into her unguarded subconscious depths. The blow was a force beyond the atomic, with a velocity, since it was delivered from the non-material realm, surpassing that of light. The unique energies known as the personality of Trisha Hunter were smashed and the particles scattered to the ends of nothingness.

The lovely image sitting on the bed stirred after a moment, clicked on the bed lamp and looked about as if she'd never really seen the room before.

She flipped back the sheet, stood and crossed to the mirror. She began to smile as she turned this way and that, admiring the mirrored image that had belonged to Trisha Hunter. It was not only lovely, but the vibrance of so much health was a sheer delight—no more migraines, kidney pains, or torturing tummy. How wonderful!

Willa turned to the bed and looked with eyes that had belonged to Trisha Hunter. The nature of her smile changed frightfully as she studied unsuspecting George. *You infatuated old fool,* she thought. *I've the weapons now, and before I'm through you'll think of hell as a welcome escape . . . .*

Lefevre should have understood that even a timid boy could only handle so much bullying before striking back. . . .

TWO

Gator Bait

Crouched on the prow of the drifting water sled under a brazen Louisiana sky, Chat felt the old dread pouring through him in sickening waves. It was an icy prickling in his clammy, sun-leathered skin. It blurred his vision so that Fornier's Bayou seemed to swirl about him, the canebrakes, the hummocks of greasy green palmetto and saw grass, the towering fingers of heat-blasted gray cypress with their festoons of Spanish moss.

A thin, stringy-muscled, undersized thirteen, Chat clutched the scabrous, weathered gunwales and wallowed his tongue inside his mouth, wishing he could spit out the dry, cottony feeling.

He shivered, listening to the watery whisper as Lefevre, his stepfather, stood in the stern, poling the craft. They had inched into the bayou under power fifteen minutes ago. Lefevre had cut the throttle, kicking the air propeller to a stop in its wire-mesh cage. The slow, careful search for an alligator den had begun.

Within five minutes, Chat had spotted the wet hump, the protrusion of tangled twigs that meant 'gator. As if in supplication, a nearly naked young figure clad in tattered jeans and dingy sneakers, he'd crouched with his lips forming a silent plea for Lefevre to miss the 'gator sign. More than anything, he'd wanted to go home today empty-handed, without a wetting.

The sled lurched from a hard jab of the pole. Chat slipped a glance over his shoulder. A big, strapping, Cajun figure in the stern, bending his dark, hairy weight against the pole, Lefevre split his tangle of black, wiry beard with a snagtoothed grin.

"We got us a skin, boy! Get ready. That 'gator is going to shed his hide!"

Lefevre's words seemed to hang in the muggy, primeval stillness.

13

Chat closed his eyes, the dread in him sharpening until it felt like fishhooks in his stomach.

"Boy," Lefevre rumbled, "what's the matter with you? Get a move on! We got to wake that old 'gator up and get him mad enough to come roaring out of his den."

"I don't feel so good, Pa."

"Belly hurting again?"

"Yeah, Pa."

"Now, boy," Lefevre growled, "you just cut that sissy stuff out. Hear me? Ain't you ashamed? What's the matter with you, anyhow? Ain't you normal? Toutain's boy, and those twins of De Vaux, they take to 'gator baiting like it was candy. You going to be the only yellow-belly boy in the swamp?"

Chat clutched his stomach. "I can't help it, Pa."

Lefevre cleared his throat, making it a heavy sound of disgust and disparagement. "Boy, you lived on your ma's apron strings too long, just you and a woman. It's time you quit acting like a girl. Why, when I was your age, I couldn't wait to go 'gator baiting. I used to beg my pa. I used to prod them out for the pure hell fun of it. You need to change your attitude, boy. It's the greatest excitement in the world. Running a fox or treeing a coon don't hold a candle to it!"

"Yes, Pa." Somehow Chat managed to rise. His knees were weak with an inner trembling, but they supported him. Sparks of panic misted behind his eyes as he saw how close the sled had moved in.

"That's better," Lefevre said. He steadied the peeled-sapling pole with his left hand, bent down and pitched the coil of slender hemp rope that had lain at his feet.

Chat caught the line instinctively. He felt his hands forming the noose, slipping it about his shoulders, securing it under his armpits.

Then he was powerless to move further. "Pa, I swear I can't—"

"Enough!" Lefevre's voice was a cruel, muted roar, thick with contempt for cowardice. "I've heard all the mealy-mouthing I'm going to! Now you get the hell in the water and roust that 'gator out or I'll whale the tar out of you."

Shivering, Chat slipped into the water. It was about shoulder deep, a turgid swath hampering his movements. He slipped the long wooden rod from its homemade wire brackets on the port side of the sled. He forced himself to move, taking slow steps on the soft bottom while Lefevre played out the hemp line and steadied the sled, elbow crooked about the pole.

The first rancid mustiness of the alligator's den came to Chat, choking his thin nostrils. Hesitantly, he lifted the hard wooden rod and poked in the direction of the den.

"In closer, boy!" Lefevre snarled. "You ain't playing pat-a-cake!"

The merciless sun seemed to hide as Chat edged forward. Holding the long rod with both hands just below water level, he snaked the tip into the barely visible mouth of the den. His heart was a motionless lump of ice as the rod searched and probed. He felt it strike scaly hide. Then a piece of it snapped as saw-toothed jaws clicked.

The water suddenly thrashed and boiled.

"Pa!" Chat screamed. He leaped backward. He felt the noose under his armpits pinch tight as Lefevre hauled in the line, hand over hand. Chat lost his footing, gagging on water pouring across his sun-bleached thatch and into his nose as Lefevre retrieved him like a wriggling minnow.

The man's strength swooped him into the air, dumped him onto the deck. Supporting himself half-prone and blowing water from his lungs, Chat saw Lefevre out of the corner of his eyes. The towering figure was leveling a thirty-aught-six rifle at the charging alligator. The brute came like a half-submerged log fired from a catapult, leaving an angry wake.

Grinning broadly, Lefevre squeezed the trigger. The rifle-crack jolted through Chat. He turned his face away from the sight of the rolling convulsions, the sudden redness in the black-surfaced swamp water, as the 'gator died.

Lefevre slapped his thigh and his happy guffaw rang like a delayed echo of the rifle shot. "Boy, I got me a skin! It'll fetch some fine black-market dollars so's a citified gent can wear hisself a hundred-buck pair of alligator shoes!"

Lefevre usually drank to success, and this night was no exception. In his small room, Chat lay sleepless on his pallet, watching the reflections of a kerosene lamp dance about the doorway as Lefevre sat alone, drinking at the rough plank table in the next room. The man was already talking to himself and singing snatches of old Cajun songs in a broken French patois. Chat could predict the next hours accurately. His stepfather would drink himself into a stupor and brief peace would come to the unpainted, clapboard shanty set high on its stilts beneath a hoary old willow tree.

Chat wanted to sleep, but each time he closed his eyes that moment returned, that harrowing instant when he was sure the 'gator would get him. He'd never heard of a 'gator-baiting kid being eaten up. Their daddies, or uncles, or whoever they were poaching with always snaked them out, but the knowledge didn't stop Chat's imagination from working. He could see the unwinking 'gator eyes, the cotton-like interior of the jaws, the cruel teeth.

He clenched his fists and gritted his teeth. "I swear," he sobbed to himself, "I can't do it again."

If Ma were still here, he wouldn't have to; or Pa. His real pa had died so long ago from cottonmouth bite that Chat could hardly remember him, but he could recall his father's contempt for the poachers, the black marketeers, the easy-dollar men who were killing off the alligators. Pa had been content to fish and hunt and go off for a few days at a time to work in the distant sawmill when he needed a hard dollar for sugar or gingham or coffee.

After Pa's death, there'd just been Chat and Ma. Life had been very hard. There were few people so far back up in Big Shandy Swamp, and little a boy and his mother could do for a hard dollar. Ma's sister, Aunt Mavis, had sent them a little money now and then, and they'd made out.

Then Lefevre had come courting in his secondhand suit and wrinkled necktie in the collar of his blue denim shirt. Chat suspected that Ma had married him because she felt her boy needed a father, a man about the place.

That hadn't worked out very well, either. Ma had got a terrible pain in her side and before they could pack her out to the half-dozen sunbaked, slab-and-tin buildings of Rickel's Crossing, much less a hospital, Ma had died from a ruptured appendix.

Aunt Mavis had come to the funeral, hugging Chat long and hard after it was over. She'd told Chat about the strange world far off yonder beyond the swamp, about Houston, Texas, where she made good money working as a waitress in a nice, clean restaurant, where she figured on marrying a fellow named Jim who drove a big trailer truck.

"He would've come," Aunt Mavis had said, "but he was on a cross-country haul when word reached me about Sis. You'd like Jim, little Chat, and he would think the world of you. So you try and get your stepdaddy to let you come and stay with us a while. Even live with us. You've always got a home with us, Chat."

Lefevre had squelched the idea before it could take root. "No dice, boy. I need you here, helping on the trap lines and fish nets and running of the house. You forget it, boy, quick and for good. This is your home. This is where you stay."

A short time after that, Lefevre had taken to poaching, an activity that made Chat far more valuable than a prime, blooded, redbone hound dog.

The day after his drinking bout, Lefevre stayed in bed, sick, calling out to Chat now and then to bring him endless quantities of drinking water. He was red-eyed and gray-faced beneath his wild bush of black beard. It was no time to cross him, and Chat spent the hours weeding the garden patch where yams, corn, squash, and gourds grew.

The next morning, Lefevre was up and away early. Chat went fishing, content to be by himself, thankful he didn't run into the Toutain or De Vaux boys. They were always up to something, and when their paths crossed Chat's he was always in for some rough teasing.

He much preferred to think about Aunt Mavis, how kind and sweet she'd been, how nice she smelled when she'd hugged his neck. He wondered what her Jim looked like. He must be a fine fellow to rate a woman like Aunt Mavis. Chat suspected that they'd written him, perhaps even sent him a little money, but he had no way of knowing for sure. It was always Lefevre who went into Rickel's Crossing, end of the line for mail.

The following morning, Chat was awakened by the grip of Lefevre's heavy hand on his shoulder. The instant he opened his eyes, Lefevre's face, glowing with greed and excitement, filled his vision.

"Get a move on, boy! We got us a big one today." On one knee beside the pallet, Lefevre rubbed his palms and grinned in high glee. The morning light seemed to make every jet-black, curling hair about his ears, thick neck and heavy-boned face stand out individually. "Cut his sign working the trap lines yesterday. Almost under our noses, boy. Right over there in Berdine's Lagoon. Claw marks and belly drag say he's a whopper, twenty-five feet if he's an inch!"

"Pa, I don't feel so good," Chat managed.

Lefevre's grin faded. His face darkened. "Boy, how come you want to kill the real fine feeling of the day?"

"I can't help the way I feel, Pa."

"The devil you can't!" He grabbed Chat by the shoulder and flung him to his feet. "I've heard the last of this I'm going to, boy! It's time you got over it. You got a job of 'gator baiting to do, and you're going to do it! I'm going to bust the yellow streak—or break you. You understand that?"

"Yes, Pa." Teeth chattering. Chat snubbed the cord that belted his jeans.

"And don't you forget it," Lefevre warned. "Now you get in there and get ready. I've already cooked side meat and grits while you pampered your lazy head. You got exactly five minutes to eat your breakfast."

With pasty grits and greasy sow-belly wadded in his throat, Chat moved through a morning that didn't seem quite real. Details all stood out with a strangely sharp clarity as the sled moved through the trackless, watery wastes. Low-hanging vines swayed, threatening. A curtain of gray Spanish moss clutched like cobwebs as Chat reached out to part them for the sled's passage. Cypress snags reared from the swirling water like sharp, hungry teeth. A five-foot cottonmouth slithered from a mangrove tangle and eeled beneath and past the water sled, a fearsome omen.

Flocks of birds and a long-legged white heron fluttered from jungle growth as the whirring air propeller shoved the sled along over grassy marsh, drawing no more draft than a surfboard.

The early sun was a torment, a glare filling the whole of the cloudless sky and stepping up the tempo of the mallets beating inside Chat's skull.

The lagoon opened before his gritty-eyed gaze, a long stretch of water with a surface like black glass, hemmed by palmetto, wild cabbage palms, high grass, and a few gnarled pines.

Lefevre cut the engine and the sled slipped forward silently as he began poling.

Crouched in the prow, Chat thought desperately: *Maybe we'll miss the den this time. Maybe the big bull won't be in it,* but he knew he was wrong. From the way Lefevre was tracking the water sled, Chat knew that his stepfather had located the den yesterday, when he'd cut the 'gator's sign, and he knew the bull would be here. He was emptily certain of it.

"All right, boy, over the side." Lefevre kept his voice down, but it quivered with eagerness.

Chat stood up, facing the man slowly. Lefevre had picked up the line, was tossing it to him.

Chat caught the thin rope. "Pa, are you sure this is the way it's got to be?"

Lefevre's mustache and beard shifted with the angry twisting of his mouth. "Don't start that again, boy! Fair warning, for the last time!"

"All right, Pa." Chat wriggled the lasso under his armpits, picked up his long prodding pole, and slipped into the water. It was deeper than he'd thought, claiming him to his chin. Pole upraised like a long, thin spear, he worked his way forward, buoyancy pulling the mucky bottom away from him at each step.

The den was straight ahead, just a few yards now. He could see the mouth of the huge nest just under the surface.

He stopped moving, settled his sneakered feet firmly on the bottom. Glancing behind, he saw Lefevre, solid and spread-legged, playing out the line until it dipped into the water.

"Come on, boy!" Lefevre bit out. "Get moving. Take up the slack. You're just about there."

"I can't, Pa." Chat spoke with head lifted, keeping his chin clear.

Lefevre worked the line in his hands. "Boy," he said in a low, deadly tone, "if you ain't moving before I can count to three. . . ."

"You big overgrown fool," Chat said with a heat he'd never before displayed. "There's snags in here. You blind? Can't you see them sticking up here and yonder?"

"Snags in every swamp," Lefevre said. "You just get your foot loose and be quick about it."

Chat ducked, then reappeared with water spilling from his head. He twisted his face once more in Lefevre's direction. "Can't make it. You want your 'gator, you come in and free my ankle."

Lefevre measured the distance to the den with a glance. He hesitated. He cursed the delay. He threw the line down savagely. Then he slipped over the side and labored with slogging steps toward Chat, his eyes despising the boy for his awkwardness. He came to rest beside Chat. Again his small, black eyes flicked in the direction of the den.

"Just free my foot," Chat said, water lapping to his lips, "and then get back and take hold of the line. Please, Pa. Please hurry!"

With a final glower at Chat, Lefevre lowered his bulk beneath the surface. Chat saw his sinking shadow, felt the touch of Lefevre's hands on his leg.

Then, with a release of his hard, stringy muscles, Chat fired himself off the bottom. He stepped on Lefevre, bearing him down, the surprise of the action addling the man for a moment.

The long prod in Chat's hands shot into the den. It lashed the water. He felt it strike the lurking 'gator—once, twice, three times— with all the strength Chat could put behind it.

Lefevre spluttered up to the surface in the same instant the maddened bull charged from his lair with a bellow that jarred trees at the far end of the lagoon.

"Now, big man," Chat screamed, "let's see who's the best man in the swamp. . . ." He gurgled the final word, surface diving with the agility of a young otter.

Lefevre stared into the enormity of cotton-lined jaws. He endured a fear-paralysis for one second before he broke and thrashed toward the water sled. He was one second too late.

Early the following Monday morning, Chat walked into Rickel's Crossing. His jeans and red flannel shirt were washed clean. His freckled, snub-nosed face was scrubbed. His sun-bleached thatch was combed.

The village hunkered in its usual air of desertion, a couple of muddy pickup trucks parked on the narrow, dusty road that petered out here on the swamp's edge.

Chat spotted Mr. Fargo sitting in a cane-bottomed chair on the porch of his weathered general store. Mr. Fargo was dozing in the heat, a big, fat, bald-headed fellow whose short-sleeved shirt looked like an extra skin pasted on with sweat.

Chat halted at the porch rail, where whittlers had carved initials, notches, and little primitive resemblances to human faces.

Chat cleared his throat and Mr. Fargo opened his big, bulbous, blue eyes. "Well, hello there, Chat."

"How are you, Mr. Fargo?" Chat said politely, looking up from his stance in the dust.

"I'm just fine, boy, but I hear you been in a terrible experience. By the time you run and fetched the Toutains, wasn't much of your step-daddy left to bury."

"No, sir." Chat cleared his throat. "But we give him a right fitten funeral. Now I reckon to go to Houston, Texas, and see my Aunt Mavis."

"That's a far piece, boy. You got any money for bus fare, grub, and such like?"

"I figure I can make it." With plenty to spare, Chat added to himself, feeling the three hundred dollars of poacher's money pinned beneath his shirt. Lefevre had kept his treasure trove in a fruit jar buried beneath the old willow tree.

"If you can't hitch a ride, boy," Mr. Fargo said, "you got a ten-mile walk down our back road to the highway where you can flag a bus. And it's a mighty hot day for walking."

"Not to me," Chat said. "I figure it's a real fine day for walking. Good-bye, Mr. Fargo."

"Good-bye, boy, and luck to you."

Chat nodded, turned, and set off down the road. He began whistling as he rounded the first bend in the road, and it was the note of a bird set free.

Although Cletus believed he had discovered the secret of success, he never imagined its unexpected consequences. . . .

THREE

Reward for Genius

Cletus Higgins sampled the glitter of Florida sunlight, unwillingly cracking his eyelids as someone banged on the door of his cottage.

"Hey, Clete! You in there? I got to see you, Clete." The voice from outside belonged to Perky Bersom who knew better than to call during the afternoon hour Cletus reserved for siesta.

Cletus turned on his lumpy daybed, making no movement to rise. "Go away," he said.

"Clete, this is urgent," Perky pleaded from outside. "I haven't a minute to waste. Let me in!"

"You are a boorish bourgeois," Clete said, eyes closed, "and I will have no truck with you."

"But I have a commission for you, Clete. You want to make five hundred dollars?"

Clete's eyes flipped open. He didn't exactly spring to his feet, but there was no hesitancy in his action as he rose from the daybed.

Clothed in barefoot sandals, rumpled cotton pants and dingy T-shirt with a slight rip in the right shoulder, Cletus stood tall and lanky. His face was a weathered collection of aquiline features in a nest of wild, fearsome black beard and hair.

Clete made his way toward the door through a clutter and disarray that would have driven even a Picasso to the chore of housekeeping. Canvasses, paints, brushes, palettes, easels were mingled with pieces of junk, rumpled clothing, dirty dishes, bean cans, bread wrappers; it was as if a capricious wind had stirred the contents of the cottage for days on end and then raced off when nothing more could be misplaced.

Perky was all set to rattle the hinges when Cletus yanked the door open. He lowered his upraised knuckles and shoved into the cottage. Under his left arm, Perky awkwardly carried a package, wrapped in

21

brown paper, that was thin but large in its perimeter dimensions.

Cletus recognized stress when he saw it. Normally, an action such as breaking into another person's siesta would have brought a sheepish grin and mumbled apology from Perky. But not today. Instead, he shoved aside some dirty dishes, dropped his package on the table, and knuckled sweat off his forehead. "Boy, am I glad you were home!"

"What's this about five centuries of bread?" Cletus asked. He regarded Perky remotely.

Perky and his wife, Lisa, lived a few miles down the beach, where the real estate was much less overrun with mangrove and palmetto, and considerably more valuable. Cletus had a private word to describe the pair. Images. Images from perfect little molds. Perky was boyishly handsome, and Lisa was lovely. Their beach house was small, but it was a sterile page from a decorator's magazine. They lived within the limits of the income from a small trust fund which Perky's father had set up. They devoted all their time to sophisticated little parties, sailing, swimming, bridge, teas, and chit-chat. They exercised religiously, dieted carefully, and took their vitamin pills punctually.

For some time now, Perky and Lisa, who had met Cletus when he'd had a one-man show in Sarasota, had frequently included the artist in their guest list. Cletus Higgins was unique; he was atmosphere; he was color. Perky and Lisa were as proud of him as they were of the modest, but shiny cabin cruiser bobbing at their private dock.

To Cletus, neither of the pair was quite real; merely porcelain images incubated in the kiln of an affluent society.

Recovering his breath and containing his anxiety, Perky slipped a Florentine silver case from the pocket of his natty slacks, chose a cigarette for himself, and extended the case.

Cletus helped himself to three cigarettes. Two of the butts almost disappeared in the black mane when he stashed one over each ear. The third he thrust between thin lips that were surrounded by a black thicket and waited impatiently for Perky to offer a light.

"You're taking a long time to get down to cases," Cletus said.

"I'm trying to think how to start. It's the wildest thing ever happened to me." Perky snapped a lighter and held it forward, careful of Clete's beard. "It's—I want you to do a portrait. Without a model. From another portrait that isn't all there."

Cletus gave him a look. Perky took a nervous drag on his cigarette. "Maybe I'd better start back at the beginning."

"Sounds reasonable. By all means proceed. You've ruined my siesta with an offer of five hundred dollars for what sounds like an impossible task."

"I'm sure you can do it. You've got to do it, Clete!"

"Really? While I never sneer at bread, five hundred isn't entirely vital to me."

"I didn't mean it that way," Perky said with alarm touching his voice. "I'm relying on your friendship. You're the only person who can help me."

"Then let us explore your woes," Clete said. He scuffed toward the kitchenette and began rattling dirty pots in the sink as he collected the various component parts of a percolator.

Tagging along, Perky talked while Clete began preparations to make coffee in an old percolator.

"I have a cousin, Clete. She's several years older than I. Her name is Melanie Sutton."

"I've heard you and Lisa speak of her," Clete said. "She's the one who's filthy with boodle."

"She can buy yachts like I would buy canoes."

"Hand me the coffee, will you? Not that can. It's full of secondhand grease. That's the one."

"Cousin Melanie's folks are all dead," Perky said. "I'm the nearest of kin, surviving."

Cletus dumped coffee into the basket and set the percolator on the two-burner hot plate.

"We haven't seen Cousin Melanie in several years," Perky went on. "She was educated in Europe, and has a decided affinity for the continent. She returns to this country only occasionally."

"I take it that one of those occasions is in prospect."

"She phoned us less than an hour ago," Perky said. "She had to fly to New York to talk to some corporation lawyers, and decided it's the right season for some Florida sun. She'll be dropping in on us by the end of the week, which doesn't give you much time, Clete."

"Time for what?"

"I'm coming to that. The minute Cousin Melanie hung up, Lisa and I thought of the picture."

"Picture? What picture?"

"Cousin Melanie's portrait. She sent it to us from Paris three, four years ago. If she paid the artist anything at all, she got rooked. The portrait's an abomination. We never did hang it."

"But now," Clete said, "you decided you'd better hang the rich relative in the choicest spot in your livingroom."

"You're dead right." Perky frantically lighted a fresh cigarette from his first one. "Lisa and I—well, frankly, the way we have to pinch pennies—Cousin Melanie's money. . . ."

"I'm with it," Clete said, "and I can't blame you for stammering, I suppose. You can't afford to do the slightest thing to offend the rich relative."

"I'd take a chance on swimming in sharky waters if she insisted," Perky admitted.

"So why don't you hang her?"

"We can't."

"Why not?"

"She's ruined," Perky said bitterly. "From the day we got it, Cousin Melanie's portrait has been in the storage room adjacent to our carport. These Florida insects and an audacious rodent have dined royally. Maybe there was some glue or sizing in the canvas that attracted them." Perky shuddered and rolled his eyes heavenward. "If Cousin Melanie ever finds out the manner in which we treated her portrait, she'll draw her own strong conclusions about the way we feel about her. We'll never see the first copper of her money. It will all probably wind up in the hands of some Swiss charity!"

Clete shook stale coffee from a cracked cup and poured himself a helping from the steaming percolator. He carried it into the outer room of the cottage with Perky dogging his heels.

At the cluttered table, Clete ripped string and brown paper from the package which Perky had brought with him. The package, Clete noted, contained two likenesses of Cousin Melanie, a nine-inch by twelve-inch photograph and the desecrated two by three feet painting in oil.

While the face had escaped destruction, the portrait showed obvious signs of careless neglect. A mouse had nibbled the corners. Bug and larvae had burrowed into the board. Moisture and mildew had left stained spots.

Clete surmised that Perky had slipped the photograph from a frame prior to bringing it here. The photo held Clete's attention. Cousin Melanie was not a beautiful woman, but she was patrician, with a finely cut face framed in white hair. The features had that small, firm quality that remained tenaciously young looking, making the hair seem prematurely gray, though it was the real key to her years.

The feature that struck Clete's artistic sense most forcibly was Cousin Melanie's neck. It was amazingly long, delicate, even fragile looking, but it held not a hint of stringy awkwardness. Truly, Clete thought, it was a rare neck, the kind that poets of old rapturously called swan-like.

Perky was literally jittering from one foot to the other. "Well? How quickly can you copy the portrait?"

"I don't know that I can," Clete said. "It's an unholy horror as a work of art, flat, two-dimensional. I'm not sure I can paint so badly."

"But you've got to try!" Perky begged. "She's got to believe that her picture has never been off our livingroom wall."

Clette dropped the portrait on the table. He gave a derisive laugh that wasn't directed at Perky. Instead, it seemed to be for himself and his cottage and the years that were behind him.

"At least, Perky, our conspiracy has a new wrinkle. Many artists have copied masterworks, but I'm sure I'm the first to copy, for such a purpose, an artistic abortion!"

Perky yanked out a handkerchief and mopped his face and neck. "I can never thank you sufficiently, Clete, old boy."

"Yes, you can. Just write the check. And understand one thing; I guarantee nothing. I'll do my best, but I can't promise to succeed in reproducing a portrait so lifeless."

Perky had more cajoling words of pep talk, but Clete took him by the arm and ushered him out.

Clete sketched in the background, when he'd set up easel and canvas, in a matter of minutes. The rest became a nightmare. By the week's end, he had ruined three canvasses. But in the fourth, he believed he'd produced a copy that would pass the rich relative's inspection. He phoned Perky Bersom and told him to buy a frame.

Then Clete drank a tenth of Scotch and retired to his daybed to sleep around the clock. His exhausted brain purged itself while he slept. Lifeless portraits slipped and wheeled in and out of his dreams. They overlaid and obscured the image of a long, delicate, swan-like neck.

The party was one of those small, informal, and entirely happy affairs for which the Bersoms had a long-practiced knack. The aroma of fine barbecue wafted across the patio. Excellent stereo music murmured from the tasteful beach cottage. The landscaping of tropical foliage combined with the background of Gulf and Florida sky to make the spot seem enchanted. Perky and Lisa were the perfect host and hostess. They knew how to choose a guest list, whom to mix.

As he walked from his dirty old sedan, Clete was spotted by Perky who rushed to meet him with a big grin. He punched Clete in the ribs with his elbow.

"Clete, old boy, you're a genius."

"I know," Clete said without superiority. "I take it the portrait passed inspection."

"The minute Cousin Melanie arrived," Perky said, "she spotted the picture. She couldn't have missed it, in the spot I'd chosen for hanging and lighting. She was so overwhelmed by the compliment that she got a little misty-eyed. Clete, old boy, we're in solid with her. Real nice and solid."

"I'm glad I was able to help."

"Help? My friend, we'd be sunk without you! Remind me to put another century of bread in your bank account, as a bonus."

"The worker is grateful for his hire," Clete, said in a slightly insulting tone, "but I sure won't forget to remind you."

"Great." Perky slapped him on the back. "Now, how about a drink? Your usual? And this barbecue is the finest the caterers have ever turned for us."

Clete knew most of the guests, beach neighbors of Perky's and Lisa's. He drifted, passing small talk, sipping his drink.

Fifteen minutes later, Cousin Melanie came out of the cottage, entering the patio from the Florida room. She was slim, trim, youthful despite her years, as her photograph had suggested.

Clete's gaze immediately centered on her neck. Wearing a simple cotton dress, with her neck fully revealed, she turned this way and that in her progress across the patio, smiling and speaking to people. She was obscured now and then from Clete's view as Perky introduced her to strangers. Finally, nothing lay between Clete and Cousin Melanie except Perky's shadow.

Perky was leading her forward. He cleared his throat. "And this is Cletus Higgins, Melly, the artist of whom I've spoken."

Clete and Cousin Melanie exchanged helloes.

"Cousin Melly," Perky said, "has an artistic interest."

"How nice," Clete murmured through cold lips. "How very nice."

"I act a bit," she confessed with a smile. "Too often I have to buy a play to find a vehicle, which indicates, I'm afraid, that I'm a very bad actress. But if one has the money, I say, one should make use of it oneself."

"I'm sure one should," Clete said coolly.

Clete's tone brought a briefly worried look from Perky. But Cousin Melanie and Clete were both ignoring him, and Perky drifted with backward glances toward his other guests.

"Tell me about it," Clete suggested.

Cousin Melanie laughed, joining Clete as he seated himelf on a redwood bench beneath a multi-colored umbrella.

"There isn't much to tell, really," she said. "In Italy, Spain, France you can always find money-hungry producers. I enjoy acting, even if I am—lousy, as you would say on this side of the Atlantic."

Clete sat as if hypnotized by the hollow of her throat. "You seem to have a rare honesty," he murmured.

"Why not? If I get a certain satisfaction from my avocation, who gets hurt? No one. On the contrary, each little play in each little theater makes work for a number of people."

Clete picked up her hands, turning them slowly, looking at them. Then his gaze returned to her neck.

"I'm going to paint you," he said.

She was poised for a moment, her pulse beating like a bird's as she tried to study his face, fathom his eyes. Then she relaxed and smiled. "Are you?"

"A portrait," Clete said, "head and shoulders. A real work, nothing like the atrocity Perky has hanging in his livingroom."

"And what is your commission for such a work?"

He pushed her hands away almost roughly. "No commission. I thought you would understand."

She was silent a moment. Then she half lifted her hand. "I'm sorry. I am very sorry. When would you like me to begin sitting?"

"Tomorrow morning at ten o'clock. I live several miles down the beach. Perky will tell you how to get there."

Clete got up, walked directly to his car, and drove away.

The next morning at ten, red-eyed and pale, Clete looked as if he had substituted small, continual nips of Scotch for sleep during the whole of the night. His mass of beard and hair obscured much of the evidence, and his nerveless control did the rest. Cousin Melanie blithely entered the cottage without noticing the clues to his mental state. Instead, the unbelievable disarray of the cottage captured her immediate attention.

"You," she said with a laugh, "have created a room straight from the left bank, here on the sunny shores of Florida."

Clete reached behind himself, flipping the latch, locking the door. "Sit there, please."

She gave him the grin of a gamin on a lark, crossed to a straight chair, and sat down. She was silent as Clete walked around her slowly, three times.

"I didn't believe it at first," he said. "It simply wasn't reasonable. All night long I wrestled with the problem of it."

She began to frown. "What in the world are you talking about?"

"It was as if my artistic senses had gone haywire," he said. "My genius was playing me false. But no! My perceptions are still true."

She came out of the chair slowly. "I think we had better postpone this, or cancel the idea entirely. Perhaps we can discuss it sometime when you haven't been drinking."

"Who are you?" Clete asked.

"I've no earthly idea what you're talking about. Let me pass, please."

"Who are you?" Clete shouted.

Real fright flared in her eyes. She ducked around him and made for the door. Clete caught her before she could reach it. He grabbed her arm and spun her about.

She had an unusual resistance to panic. "You'd better think what you're doing," she said. "Release me and open the door this instant and I won't report you. Otherwise, it will go hard for. . . ."

Clete made an animal sound in his throat, suddenly and without warning twisted her arm. She was wheeled into a helpless position, frozen in a hammerlock. With his free hand, Clete scooped the hair from the side of her face.

"Only a tiny, threadlike scar," he said. "The plastic surgeon didn't have to do much, did he?"

"You're mad!" she gasped. "You shall pay for this!"

He jerked her away from the door and shoved her across the room. She half fell on the protesting daybed and remained there, supporting herself with her hands on the edge of the railing.

"I don't suppose I need to ask you a third time," he said. He loomed over her, hands on hips. "You were probably an understudy, a double to begin with, searched out with her money, through the talent agencies of Europe. Then later, a bit of plastic surgery and you were her identical twin—except for one thing. So the question now is: What happened to the real Melanie Sutton, the rich old babe with the theater bug? How did you kill her? What did you do with her?"

"I don't know what you're talking about! Move aside or I'll start screaming."

"Go ahead and scream," he said relentlessly, "and we'll tell the whole world why. I'll give you three safe seconds in which to scream."

He waited. Both remained silent, the woman crouching on the edge of the daybed.

"Where is the real Melanie Sutton?" he insisted. "At the bottom of an Alpine crevasse? Feeding the fish off the south of France?"

She stirred, finally, "How did you know?"

"Your neck. The conniving, money-hungry plastic surgeon could not very well change the length of your neck, so it is far too short."

"My neck . . ." she raised her hand slowly to her throat.

"Possibly no one else in all the world would ever have noticed," Clete said. "But I labored over the depicted image of Melanie Sutton for endless hours. When I saw you, I knew instantly, even though it took me all night to believe it, to admit it."

"I should never have come here," she said, "but I had to. The corporation lawyers in New York were faintly puzzled by a thing or two I said and did. I was playing the role of ever-loving elder cousin. They would have become downright suspicious if I'd refused the opportunity to drop by and see my closest surviving relative, Perky boy and his wife. So I had to come. I believed I could carry it off here as well as I did in New York. I'd studied Melanie Sutton and her affairs from close range for a long time. I knew everything there was to know about her—except that her cousin had you for a friend."

"Now I shall live and paint," Clete said, "away from all this. I am now a painter with a liberal patroness."

She came to her feet almost shyly. "And if I am to be your patroness, how do I know I can trust you?"

"You'll simply have to take my word."

"Your word—yes, I suppose I must. You wish me to mail you your first check today?"

"And once a month thereafter," Clete said, "for so long as you live. A thousand a month will do nicely."

The woman was quite composed when she stopped her car in the Bersom driveway. Perky came bouncing out to meet her.

"How did it go, Cousin Melly?"

"Not too badly, but I decided not to sit for any more portraits." She remained behind the wheel of the car, giving him such a sudden, intent look that the smile eased from his lips.

"Perky, I know this isn't talked in polite family circles, but I want an honest confidential answer, just between the two of us. In an acute crisis, to what lengths would you go to insure your eventual inheritance of my fortune?"

The thing in her eyes got through to Perky. His playboy aura seemed to fall away. He became bone and sinew, with the eyes of a hungry, prowling cougar. "I think I would even murder," he said with cool honesty.

The woman behind the wheel looked far down the beach. Then she turned, got out of the car. "My dear boy," she said fondly, "your answer couldn't have pleased me more. . . ."

Although Claude thought he had found a new reason for living, he soon discovered he didn't have the heart for it. . . .

FOUR

Mind the Posies

No believer in miracles, Mrs. Hester Bennett could not fully account for her husband's new interest in life.

Claude's heart attack had been severe, and without any prior warning. He had been coming up the front walk late one afternoon, an old man with iron gray hair who still retained some of his earthy, brutish handsomeness. He'd staggered, clutched his chest, crumpled, looked as if he'd died instantly.

But he hadn't. Not quite. For endlessly long hours Claude's life had been measured by the successive weak pulse beats which never quite stopped.

Hester had remained at Claude's hospital bedside, never taking her eyes for very long from the gray face canopied by the clear plastic oxygen tent, until the doctor told her the crisis was finally past.

A man steeped in bitter solitude had come home, shuffling and looking about the solidly comfortable house as if everything were new and strange to him.

To Hester's queries he gave the same, short answer, "I'm fine!"

He took his prescribed rests with the secretive inner rebellion of a small boy. He ate the flat, salt-free food stolidly, cramming it into his mouth as if he had a strange sort of derision and loathing for himself.

The rapport built by thirty-five years of marriage was broken. Unable to communicate with Claude, Hester mechanically continued her routine of flower gardening and conscientious housekeeping.

Once, as she was arranging a vase of yellow roses, Claude had entered the livingroom unknown to her. His voice had startled her. "Why do you bother?" he said. "They'll only die."

He'd turned and left the room without waiting for her answer. And she'd bit her lip, feeling the emptiness and desolation of the house. The attack has left him with traumatic scars as well as physical ones,

31

she'd thought, but they will pass; after all, thirty-five years of marriage does mean something; the scars will all pass.

The passing, when it had come, had been swift, almost as sudden as the attack that had struck Claude a low blow.

He'd returned to the supervision of his small plastics manufacturing plant for want of something better to do. It gave him escape from the house, from windows that seemed to draw his gaze toward a certain spot on the front walk. He came and went, a tall, rawboned giant of a shadow.

And then one afternoon Hester came in from her flower garden and heard Claude humming in the bedroom. She let the basket slide from her hand to the kitchen table. A tremulous expression crossed her faded, wrinkled lips. A light struggled for life in her tired blue eyes. Claude's humming was off-key, but to Hester, it filled the house with a sweeter sound than the singing of the birds who flitted about their bath at the edge of her flower garden.

Controlling the emotion that surged up in her, Hester went casually to the bedroom. Claude was at the dressing table mirror, bending slightly as he knotted a bright, striped necktie, one she had never seen before. He was impeccable in a freshly pressed suit, the iron gray hair brushed against his temples. There was even color in his face, making him look twenty years younger. Something about his appearance and manner disconcerted Hester. She felt drab and old.

"I didn't hear you come in," she said. "Do you want an early dinner?"

His humming broke off. He looked at her reflection in the mirror. He didn't bother to turn, and she had the feeling that the mirrored reflection of her was enough for him.

"I won't be here, Hester," Claude said. "I'm hiring a new man at the plant, a junior exec, and I'll be taking him to dinner. A man reveals himself, you know, in his choice of manner of food and drink."

She didn't know, but she supposed it was true. For thirty-five years she had waxed floors, pressed draperies, seen to the plentiful supply of snowy white shirts, paired socks, and, in accordance with his wishes, left the running of the business to Claude.

Hester drifted to sleep over a book that night, and was awakened by the hissing sound of the shower the next morning. Maudie, the cook-maid, was putting breakfast on the table when Hester went into the nook off the kitchen.

Claude entered, looking fresher and more agile than he had in years. With a nod toward the room in general, he sat down and spread his morning paper.

"Did you hire the new man, Claude?" Hester asked.

"What?" he said behind the paper.

"The fellow you took to dinner."

"Oh. Him. No, I don't think he'll do. Have to keep looking."

"Claude . . ." she hesitated.

"Yes? Well, what is it?"

"Why don't you bring them home? For dinner. The applicants for the executive position, I mean."

The paper rattled as he lowered it. He gave her a brief look, as if she had gone slightly daft. Then he shook out the paper and turned to another page.

"You might think about it," she said.

"Sure," Claude said. "I will. But it would be a lot of bother."

"I wouldn't mind."

"Well, all right," he said shortly. "I told you I'd think about it."

During the morning, Hester kept herself desperately busy plotting a new flower bed. But her thoughts kept returning to Claude's disdainful impatience with her.

In their long marriage, disagreements had been inevitable. But never before had Hester been ridden with this feeling of being shut out, of being a mere nothing in Claude's eyes. The husband she'd known seemed to have passed from her, really, during that frightful heart attack.

Hester looked toward the house, realizing that Maudie had been calling her name.

"'Phone for you, Mrs. Bennett," Maudie said.

Removing her heavy cotton gloves with their earth stains, Hester went into the house. From the livingroom came the whirr of the vacuum cleaner under Maudie's guidance.

The kitchen extension phone was dangling from its cord, as Maudie had left it.

Hester lifted the phone and said, "Mrs. Bennett speaking."

"You don't know me," a thin, taut, male voice said, "and my name's not important. What I've got to say concerns your husband— and a girl."

"I don't believe I understand."

"She was my girl. At least I thought so, until a well-heeled old leech came along."

Hester clutched the phone in a nerveless hand. The sound of the vacuum cleaner seemed to swell to an intolerable roar that filled the house, reverberated from the walls.

"What are you saying?" she said. "How dare you say such a thing!"

"Okay, lady, keep your head in the sand."

"I don't believe you!"

"So don't. But her name is Marylin Jordan, and the leech is fixing a hideaway for her right now on Taculla Lake. The real cool pad on the point."

"You must have made a mistake," Hester said desperately. "My husband is old and dangerously ill. You're suspecting the wrong man."

"It's more than suspicion, lady. She's a hungry, predatory cat, and he's the rat she's been looking for."

"But he. . . ."

"You know the saying, lady. No fool like an old one. Maybe he's just got to burn big before the wick sputters out."

Hester closed her eyes, swayed. "This is the cruelest kind of joke."

"Joke?" the voice became a shallow, humorless laugh. "Maybe so. On the both of us."

The line went dead. Hester lowered the phone slowly and looked at it, as if it were a dream substance that would dissolve from her hand.

Stirring finally, Hester turned and walked to the livingroom. Maudie was rattling venetian blinds with a cleaner attachment and made no sign of hearing when Hester spoke her name in her soft, normal tone.

"Maudie!" Hester repeated in a louder tone.

An amply-fleshed pouter pigeon, Maudie looked over her shoulder.

"I have some shopping to do," Hester said. "I may be gone a good part of the day."

Maudie nodded and returned her attention to her work.

In her light car, Hester drove out of the city without haste. She didn't enjoy driving. And this was all so silly and useless. She really should turn back, she told herself. But the car seemed to have a will of its own. The city limits dropped behind.

Taculla Lake was a full hour's drive, away from civilization, over a secondary road of macadam. While a few families maintained year-round residences there, the lake mainly provided weekend retreats for those who could afford it. The lodges, widely separated to provide privacy, were mostly of an architectural design in keeping with the setting, with vaulted ceilings and long, railed galleries overlooking private docks for cruisers and small boats.

Hester reached the small village above the lake. There was a large store handling general merchandise, a filling station, a glass and brick building, jarringly out of place, that displayed boats and marine gear. And a small log building with a sign on the roof that read: Hiram Hyder, Real Estate.

Hester parked her car on the gravelled area beside the real estate office. She got out, crossed the small porch, and entered a pleasant office panelled in wormy chestnut. The lone occupant was a heavyset man of middle age. In shirt sleeves, he was bent over a slightly cluttered desk. With the forefinger of his left hand he toyed with the few wisps of hair on an otherwise bald head, while he checked figures on an adding machine tape with a pencil in his right hand.

As the screen door sighed closed behind Hester, he glanced up, rose immediately, plucked a suit coat from the back of his chair, and put it on.

"Mr. Hyder?"

"Yes, what can I do for you?" He came around the desk to offer Hester a chair.

"I want to inquire about renting a lake house," she said.

"My specialty, Mrs. . . ."

She ignored the hint to give her name. "I have one particular place in mind. The lodge on the point."

"Oh, you must mean the Thrasher place. Yes, that's a rare property to be on the rental market. Don't get many like that. The Thrashers decided to remain in Mexico City and figure the place would be better off with somebody in it." Hiram Hyder spread his pleasantly chubby hands. "Unfortunately, it's been taken."

"That's too bad," Hester said. "By whom? I may know them."

"A Mr. Joseph Smith. He came with his secretary, quite a lovely young woman." Hyder glanced away, cleared his throat, and moved behind his desk. "But I have one other place at the moment that might interest you."

"This Mr. Smith," Hester said. "A big man? Powerful frame? Slightly gaunt? Iron gray hair?"

Easing a covert look at Hester, Hyder's manner became guarded. "An exact description of the man. Why do you ask?"

There was one more question. Claude, she remembered, had taken pride in the uniqueness of his car. "Driving a convertible with a custom paint job?"

"As a matter of fact, yes. Is there something you wish to tell me about Mr. Smith?"

"No, Mr. Hyder, there is nothing I wish to say about him at all."

"About this other place. . . ."

"I'm sure it wouldn't do at all, Mr. Hyder. Thank you for your time. Perhaps I'll call again." She escaped quickly, with a nod, a turn, a flight to her car.

When Hester entered the house, Maudie was at the kitchen table sipping coffee and munching on a sweet roll. "Mr. Bennett called while you were out. Twice." Maudie lowered her roll without taking a bite. "You feel all right, Mrs. Bennett?"

"A little tired, a bit dizzy; the sun, the exertion of shopping."

Hester continued her flight, from kitchen to den, where she picked up the phone and dialed Claude's office.

"Where've you been?" he asked.

"Out, Just out. . . ."

"Well, I wish you'd be on the ball when I need you."

She half closed her eyes. Thirty-five years on the ball, she thought. Thirty-five years of being in an assigned place and on the ball.

"What was it you wanted, Claude?"

"I'm not happy with Jerry Lawter's reports. I don't like the way things are going in the sales office downstate. I'm going down there myself and put some ginger in Jerry and staff. So pack me a bag, will you?"

"Of course, Claude. What will you need? One day bag? Two days?"

"Two days, at least," he said. "I'll be by in thirty minutes. I don't want to drive all night."

"I'll have the bag ready, Claude."

She had the luggage prepared, set at the foot of the bed, when he arrived.

He began stripping off his shirt, preparatory to showering and donning fresh clothing. She saw the excitement sparkling deep in his eyes, the almost frenzied movements of his hands.

"Haven't you anything better to do," he said suddenly and shortly, "than to stand there and gawk at me?"

A coldness washed over her, settling in her eyes. Looking at her, Claude made a movement expressing discomfort, turning away from her. "Sorry," he said. "But you know how it is, things fouled up in Jerry Lawter's office and all. You do understand."

"Yes, Claude, I understand."

She wandered out of the bedroom, through the house. She was at the livingroom looking out the windows, when Claude paused in the foyer, the packed suitcase in his hand. "Well," he said, a faint note of awkwardness in his tone, "mind the posies while I'm gone."

"Have a good trip," she said.

It was the end of conversation. She heard him go out. From the window, she saw him put the suitcase in the back seat of the car, which he'd parked at the curb. He got in the car and drove off. She stood at the window and watched it out of sight.

Then she turned quietly, went into the den, closed the door, picked up the phone, and dialed the long distance operator.

When his secretary put the call through, Jerry Lawter's voice was filled with concern and anxiety. "Mrs. Bennett? It's not Claude? I mean, the boss hasn't. . . ."

"No, Mr. Lawter. It's still very much touch and go with him. He should avoid undue excitement and alcohol as killing plagues, but as of this moment Claude is all right. The fact is, he just left here, saying he was on his way to see you."

"Fine," Jerry Lawter said more calmly, "I'll be glad to see him."

"You must give him a message, Mr. Lawter, immediately on arrival. He asked me at the last minute to pack for him. And I—I'm afraid I made a dreadful mistake. In the rush, I took the wrong pills from the medicine cabinet. Mr. Lawter . . . Claude is carrying useless headache pellets instead of the nitroglycerin pills so vitally necessary if he should have . . . if an attack . . . Three days . . . He'll be away three days. . . ."

"I understand, Mrs. Bennett. I'll tell him the very instant he gets here."

"Thank you," Hester whispered. "Thank you very much."

She wasn't aware of moving, until she felt the hot afternoon sunlight on her face. She looked about the yard. A faint laugh came from her. Strange, she'd never before noticed how small and cramped the yard really was.

She crossed to the nearest flower bed and deliberately began pulling the plants out by the roots, one by one. She dropped each plant on the moist earth for a quick death in the sun.

When the seedy old lady appeared in Percy Kittridge's office, little did he expect her to return. . . .

FIVE

The Holdup

Percy Kittridge, finance director of Memorial to Mercy Hospital, frowned in sharp distaste as the old woman appeared in his office. Percy was a neat, precise man of little finicky gestures, and the woman was a horrible old wretch. In a seedy greatcoat that hung almost to her ankles, she was like a mass of pillows lumpishly piled together. Her face was a study in wrinkles and tiny wens. Beneath an old straw hat decorated with imitation flowers, her hair dripped like Spanish moss on an ancient tree.

One moment Percy was rocked back behind his desk, looking out the window and comfortably chatting on the phone, the next he was swinging his chair around to hang up the telephone and there stood the old lady.

"How did you get in here unannounced?" Percy demanded in his rather high, impatient voice.

The old woman pointed to the tattered scarf wrapped about her throat. She was wearing cheap cotton gloves—probably, Percy thought, to hide leprous hands.

"Just walked in," she said in a raspy whisper, "when no one in the outer office was paying attention. No trick to it."

"Well, I'm a busy man. What do you want?"

The old woman's right hand was in the side pocket of her bedraggled outer coat. She lifted the hand. It was gripping a deadly looking automatic.

"I want all the money out of the hospital safe," she crackled.

Percy gasped, on the edge of a sudden faint. His thin lips quivered in a fruitless effort to speak. His bright eyes were parallaxed on the gun.

"Be a nice, sensible li'l fella," the crone instructed, "and you can tell your wife about this at dinner tonight. Otherwise, you're on a

DOA all full of bullet holes when they cart you over to the emergency room a few seconds from now."

"I—uh—this doesn't make sense," Percy managed. "People steal drugs from hospitals, not money."

"There's a first time for everything," the nightmare image said. "You have just one more tick of the clock to move it."

Percy flinched back from his desk, tottering to his feet. "Hospitals do most of their business in paper," he said, struggling for courage. "Medicare and Medicaid checks, checks from insurance companies and patients. Wouldn't it be better to rob some other—"

"Can't rob but one place at a time," the old woman croaked. "And I'm here now. You do plenty of cash business. Everybody don't pay by check. And there's the cash flow from your cafeteria, snack bar, gift shop, parking lot, florist concession. I'm sure the safe is stuffed with more than enough for the likes of me." The muzzle of the gun inched up. "Your time has run out, fella."

Kittridge jumped. "Be careful with that thing! I'm hurrying. I'm hurrying!"

The horrid old woman used her free hand to pull a shopping bag from under her coat. "Put the money in this. I want it all, including the silver. The checks you can keep."

A few minutes later, she was shuffling across one of the broad parking lots adjacent to the huge medical complex and Mr. Kittridge was on the floor of the anteroom next to his office, slumped beside the empty vault, a lump on his crown from a tap of the gun barrel.

The old woman paused beside a pickup truck with a camper cover. There were acres of cars but few people on the parking lot. Satisfied that she was unnoticed, the old woman disappeared.

Under the camper cover the crone worked quickly. And, stripping off the thickly padded coat, gloves, hat, wig, and rubberoid face mask, she was transformed into a nice-looking young man, dark-haired and clean-cut, in jeans and a knitted shirt.

He stuffed the accoutrements of his disguise into a foot locker. He would burn the items a little later, in a place even more private than the camper.

Snapping open the stuffed shopping bag, he dipped his hands into the money. He'd estimated it as the finance director had taken it from the safe—twenty thousand at least. Not an earth-shaking haul, but a nice return on the execution of a carefully structured plan.

Slightly short of breath, the young man fashioned a stack of bills from the bag—twenties, fifties, and hundreds. He stuffed the roll into the pocket of his jeans, then he added the bulky shopping bag to the contents of the foot locker and closed and locked it.

Slipping into the driver's seat, he drove the camper carefully from the parking lot to the drive-in window of a nearby branch bank, where he deposited the money from his jeans pocket. Tucking the deposit slip into his wallet, he smiled a good afternoon to the teller and drove back to the hospital. The automatic barricade at the parking lot swung up, admitting the camper as the young man dropped quarters into the parking-fee slot. The camper wended about and finally slipped into a vacant space reasonably close to the main hospital building.

When the young man walked into the business office, he felt the residue of excitement. Employees had vacated desks and frosted-glass cubicles, clustering at the water cooler to exchange strained murmurs. A middle-aged woman spotted him and came over to the counter.

"It's been quite an afternooon," she said. "We had a robbery."

"No!"

"Yes. An old woman, would you believe it? She walked into Mr. Kittridge's office and forced him to open the vault at gunpoint, then cracked him on the head and disappeared. Mr. Kittridge sounded the alarm when he regained consciousness. He gave the police a full description, but I don't know—you know how it is these days. So many unsolved crimes. But an old woman—would you believe it?"

The young man commiserated with a shake of his head.

The cashier drew a steadying breath. "But that's our problem, isn't it? What can I do for you?"

"I came to take my wife home," the young man said. "The doctor said she could leave as soon as I settle the bill. So I guess we can say goodbye and thanks for everything. It's been a long five weeks."

"And after five weeks," the cashier said in sympathy, "quite a bill."

"No sweat," the young man said. "My private hospitalization plan should be adequate. But I'll need to borrow a pen to write the check."

The choicest balm for grief, work becomes particularly rewarding when executed for the right purpose. . . .

SIX

The Confident Killer

Mom Roddenberry took the news of her daughter's death like a durable hill woman. Her sallow, bony face went as gray as fog. Her slate-gray eyes went out of whack as she tried to keep on seeing me. Her gnarled hands lifted and grabbed her wrinkled cheeks, as if she could make a physical pain that would lessen the hellfire scorching her inside. A wail like a cat caught in a steel trap split her thin lips.

Then she steadied, pulled her shoulders together, stood gasping behind the counter in her cafe. "Gaither . . . Jerl Brownlee murdered my girl?"

"That's what I'm trying to say, ma'am."

She took off the clean white smock that she wore over her simple gray dress as her cafe uniform and came around the counter, a small, spry woman that the Smoky Mountain winters and endless toil had whittled down to a collection of hickory sticks and leather.

"Is Pretty at Doc Weatherly's undertaking parlor now, Gaither?"

"Yes, ma'am."

"Will you walk over with me?"

"You know I will!"

"And tell me the whole of it." Her fingers were like wires on my wrist. "Every last detail. You hear me, Gaither?"

She turned over the cardboard sign that hung inside the glass part of the cafe door. The sign said "Closed." We stepped onto the sidewalk. The old lady closed and locked the door, then stood a minute looking up and down the dusty street like she was a stranger, although she'd lived in the town of Comfort all her life.

"Not much here to satisfy a gal young'un who dreamed of fancy clothes and big city excitement, Gaither."

"She wasn't a bad girl, ma'am."

"That she wasn't, Gaither. Just too innocent and ignorant of the ways of the world and too—attractive to men."

With me at her side, Mom Roddenberry thought of the short eighteen years of Pretty's life, I reckon, as she set off with dogged hillwoman's stride. "I'm listening, Gaither," she prodded.

So I told her how Pretty Roddenberry had come to her end, as we tramped toward the old gingerbread house where Doc Weatherly lives upstairs and undertakes on the ground floor.

Pretty had met her death in cruelly simply manner. She'd sneaked up to the Brownlee lodge to keep a date with Jerl. He was the last of the Brownlees, had inherited a timber and tobacco fortune, and figured he was cock of any walk he cared to set foot on.

Jerl didn't show up in Comfort often, preferring to spend his time and squander his money in resorts where fancy women were plentiful. With a bunch of friends, he had boozed it up at the UT–Clemson game last week, which took place in Knoxville. The swanky Brownlee lodge being on a thousand-acre estate across the line in North Carolina, the gang had trekked over and kept the party roaring.

They caroused over land, lake, and mountainside for three days before they fizzled out. Finally Jerl was left alone, surly and restless. He got to thinking of that cute little trick he'd made a few passes at previous when he happened to be in Comfort, so he called her on the phone, and she was dumb enough to sneak up there.

Who knows what went through Pretty's excited mind as she dolled up in her best dress and perfume? Did she think she could tease her way into that rustic mansion and let it go at that? Did she think Jerl would actually take her away from the drabness and boredom of an isolated little mountain town such as Comfort? Did she kid herself into thinking she might even have a chance of marrying into the Brownlee millions?

Ever how her noggin worked, when the showdown came she just couldn't snatch off her clothes and jump into young Jerl's bed. But she'd called her shots all wrong. She hadn't figured on the size of Jerl's spoiled selfishness. His boozing had sharpened all the meanness in him. Even sober, he reckoned that anything he wanted should be his for the taking.

Pretty fought him. It must have been an unholy sight, Pretty struggling and begging for mercy, of which there was none in the inflamed face before her. She barked his shins and scratched his face; then he knocked her down and busted the back of her head. Maybe she struck the big fireplace or a piece of the heavy furniture.

Jerl thought he'd killed her then and there. He dragged her out, put her in his car, got in and drove a ways across the mountain until he was off the estate, then shoved her out. He must have thought he was reasonably safe. Days, even weeks, might pass before anybody found Pretty's body. By then, Jerl figured, it wouldn't matter what folks suspected. Suspecting and proving are two different matters. He'd just deny that she ever had come to the lodge. Nobody, he reckoned, could prove that some hill renegade hadn't seen her walking up the road and got passionate ideas.

Only thing, Jerl hadn't figured on a situation which the Brownlees themselves had set up. For years the Brownlee estate had been posted and the old man, before his death, had kept a mean caretaker up there to enforce the rule. As a result, the thousand acres teemed with game, and a mountain farmer with a taste for fresh meat had set out that morning to do a little poaching, thinking Jerl's drinking party had adjourned to the lowlands and wouldn't bother him.

The farmer heard Jerl's car booming around the curves on the gravel backroad, ducked into the timber, and his popping eyes witnessed Jerl's final act. The minute Jerl got back in his car and rounded a curve, the farmer went sliding and tumbling into the thicketed ravine where Pretty's body had come to rest.

A final flicker of life twitched through Pretty's china blue eyes. Her silken mane of yellow hair was a bloody tangle about her face as she tried to speak. The farmer dropped his ear close to her lips and caught her final words. She told him what had happened, as if there was any doubt in his mind.

The farmer ran a shortcut to the lodge, broke a window to let himself in, and phoned the sheriff's office in Comfort. Sheriff Collie Loudermilk had flashed the word to the sheriffs of neighboring counties. Roadblocks were set up in minutes.

With Jerl Brownlee in the net, Collie had sent me, his deputy, to fetch down the body. I'd brought the poor broken thing to Doc Weatherly's, gritted my teeth, and dragged my feet to Comfort's only decent cafe, wishing it was just for a cup of Mom Roddenberry's good coffee.

Mom didn't interrupt my tale once. She had a good grip on herself now. She took my words like the seasoned willow takes the slashing sleet. Her suffering was too deep to show on the surface.

We stopped in the shadow of the porch that rambled across the front of Doc Weatherly's place. Mom Roddenbery lifted a hand and touched my cheek. "You're a good young man, Gaither Jones, and I'm beholden to you for telling me the straight of it."

"She was a sweet, human girl, Mom. She was tempted. And she tried to overcome. You always remember that."

"Yes, Gaither, I will."

"And be sure we'll get Jerl Brownlee, Mom."

She lifted her eyes slow-like, and they were the hoar frost that rimes distant peaks. "Yes, that is all that's left now, Gaither; justice; eye for eye, tooth for tooth. If Pretty is to rest easy in her grave, Jerl Brownlee must reap his due."

I didn't need to answer that one. We were both hill people.

"Again, I'm obliged to you, Gaither. Now, I know you got work to do. I'll just ease inside alone to spend a last minute with my daughter."

I watched her creep up the porch steps. Each one added about ten years to her narrow, bony shoulders. The door of the undertaking parlor opened, swallowed her. I turned, jammed my hands in the pockets of my tan twill, kicked some hollihocks growing alongside the walk, and cussed my way back up the street to the office.

The short-range walkie-talkie, which the taxpayers begrudged Collie and me out of the mail order catalogue, was crackling when I walked in.

"Gaither, where in dad-blasted thunderation you been?" Collie Loudermilk howled through the static, sounding like a banshee.

"Playing pool and drinking beer," I said sourly, looking across the street at that "Closed" sign on the cafe door. "You bringing in Jerl Brownlee?"

The walkie-talkie like to have spit fire. "He spotted my car blocking Miden Falls road, skidded off the curve, turned over twice, straight down the mountainside."

"He's hurt? Maybe bleeding to death?" I inquired happily.

"He bounced out healthy as a jackrabbit and with the same ideas. I've lost him, Gaither, somewhere in the gorges above Cat Track Holler. If we don't flush him out of this wild country before nightfall, we lose him. He's got the whole compass to aim at, a good chance of making it out of these mountains. If he does that, well heeled as he is, next thing we know he may be playing with them French girls in that Riviera place."

"I reckon you need me and Red Runner and Old Bailey," I said.

"Naw," Collie growled, "I'm just fiddling with this gadget in hopes of communing with a braying jackass! *Will* you stop wasting time?"

"You're doing all the talking," I said, and cut him off.

I grabbed the two dog leashes off the wall peg, and skedaddled out of the office, around the old brick building to the dog lot behind the jail. Old Bailey and Red Runner heard me rattling the gate open. They snuffled out of their kennels, long ears nearly dragging in the dust. Their baggy, forlorn eyes spotted the leashes, and a quiver went through both dogs. They perked up quick. I swear those bloodhounds can even smell out the prospect of smelling out a man.

A setting sun threw streamers of golden fire across the peaks in the west and twilight was settling in the valleys when me and the two dogs homed in on Collie Loudermilk's location.

Collie is a skinny, sandy man who looks like he couldn't last out a mountain winter in front of the fireplace, but he's the kind of gristle that can dull a knife. He's been sheriffing in Comfort for twenty years, and knowing him firsthand, it wouldn't surprise me if it's twenty more before I inherit his job.

While the hounds and I got our breath in the shadows of the gorges, Collie shook out a sports jacket that would have cost me a month's pay.

"Lying loose in the back seat of Jerl Brownlee's wrecked car," Collie said. "Let's hope it's his and that he's worn it recent before he pitched it back there."

Collie squatted before the excited dogs, held out the jacket, and they took a good long whiff. I stayed with them, keeping the leashes slack, as they snuffled around for a few seconds. Then with a howl fair to curdle the blood, both dogs hit the ends of the leashes, almost jerking me off my feet.

We tracked Jerl up a long hollow where the briars were as thick as riled-up bees, and across a long stretch of naked shale, where only a dog's pads had good footing. Collie slipped halfway across. He burned skin off his knees and elbows as he slid and rolled twenty feet down the slope. He got up cussing because I was holding up the dogs, waiting for him to climb back to us.

Beyond the shale, Jerl had jumped a spring-fed creek, which held us up for a good ten minutes, and crossed a soggy meadow. Then he'd stumbled onto the dim remains of an old logging trail and picked that route up through the timber.

I didn't have a dry rag on me by this time, I was sweating so hard from the exertion. The dogs had lather on their flanks and wet tongues hanging from the sides of their mouths. Collie looked as fresh as a new-grown stinkweed, eyes anxious on the purple shadows that closed in about us.

As the dogs tugged me along, I began to lose track of the number of gullies we crossed, the patches of underbrush we slammed through. My legs felt as if they had fallen off, and I looked down in the failing light to make sure they were still there, like a pair of pump handles underneath me.

Then all of a sudden my glazing eyes glimpsed Collie's shadow shooting out ahead of us. I still didn't see the flicker of motion that had caught his attention. He splashed across a seep that would turn into a creek during a heavy rain, and dived into a canebreak. A minor hell erupted in there. Sawgrass and reeds rattled. A covey of birds sprayed out in all directions. Cattail fluff showered into the air.

Collie came out just as the dogs and I cleared the seep. He had Jerl Brownlee by the shirt collar, Jerl draped on the ground behind him.

"Got him, by gum," Collie said, backhanding an ooze of blood off his nose.

"You done all right, Sheriff," I said, nodding, "after me and the dogs cornered him for you."

Jerl was about the most bruised, scratched, begrimed, and generally trail-weary young punk you'd ever want to see. Collie and I and Jerl's rubbery legs finally got him back to the sheriff's car. We put the dogs in front with Collie. I got in back to guard the prisoner, who didn't look much like it was necessary. We'd come back for my car later.

Jerl didn't have a word to say all the way back to town. He was doing plenty of thinking, and by the time I shoved him in a jail cell, he'd about decided he was still Jerl Brownlee, cock of any walk.

He watched me lock the cell door with hooded eyes. Then his battered lips twisted in a sneer. "You yokels don't think for a minute this is going to work out your way, do you?"

"Looks like it might," I said.

"You dumb rube," he said. "With my dough, I'll have the choice of the finest legal brains from New York to Los Angeles. There are jurors to buy, judges for sale. There are a thousand loopholes in the law, and ten thousand technicalities. With my loot, I can fight this thing to the highest courts in the land, no matter how long it takes. So before you wallow in any naive sentiments about the workings of justice or pat yourself on the back, deputy-boy, just answer me one question. Have you ever heard of a millionaire ending up in the electric chair or gas chamber?"

His question was still rattling around in my head a few minutes later as I trudged across the dark street. The "Closed" sign was still on the door of Mom Roddenberry's cafe, but there were lights in the flat overhead where she and Pretty had lived. I fumbled for the bannister of the outside stairway that led up the side of the building to the flat.

The old lady answered my knock, searched my face for a minute, and invited me into a plain, but comfortable and clean parlor.

I sat down on a studio couch. Mom eased to the edge of a chair across from me. A hard stillness came to the apartment.

"Gaither," she said, "you did catch him. He's locked up. I've already heard."

"Yes, ma'am. But I got a dreadful feeling that rich boy will get out of this."

"Why, lad, we *know* he done it! Cold-blooded and mean. Pretty said he did—and she wouldn't tell a lie with her dying breath."

"I know, but we run up the first stump right there. We got a witness that says that she said it. They call it hearsay evidence. The lawyers he can afford will cut our case to nothing."

The old lady thought about it, hands crimping like talons. Then she raised her slaty gray eyes. "Might be a game two can play, Gaither."

I frowned. "What are you talking about?"

"Would a mountain jury convict an old woman if she was temporarily pixillated by the murder of her daughter?"

The hairs stiffened on the back of my neck as I began to get the drift.

She rose slowly. "Mom Roddenberry's cafe always supplies meals for the jail prisoners across the street. Tonight you got a prisoner. I'm going down now, Gaither, and fix his supper. I reckon that's why you came over, to fetch the prisoner his tray?"

I gulped. "Well, ma'am. . . . Come to think of it, yes."

"A real mouth-watering meal for the man. . . ." She patted my shoulder in passing. "But don't you dast get forgetful and throw the scraps to Red Runner and Old Bailey."

"No, ma'am," I promised. "I reckon such a fine pair of dogs deserve better than scraps tonight."

*The two young predators had no way of knowing that they were about to
become the victims of a much more serious matter. . . .*

SEVEN

Easy Mark

The two youths at the front corner table marked me from the moment I strolled into the psychedelic, nether-world decor of the Moons
of Jupiter.

I was surely a sudden out-of-kilter detail on the scene. My appearance stamped me as the most reprehensible of straights: busi-
nessman, establishment man; specter from the far side of the
generation gap. Fortyish, brushed with gray at the temples, lean, conditioned from regular workouts, I was smoothly barbered, tailored in
a five hundred dollar suit of English cut, with coordinated shirt and
necktie.

A cool young hostess, blonde and topless, decided I was for real.
She smiled a greeting to take me in tow and threaded a way through
a dimly lighted, pot-smoke-hazed broken field of tables and hovering,
pale faces. In passing, I drew a few glances, ranging from the sullen to
the amused. Empty, bored young eyes lifted, noted the stranger, and
dropped again to contemplation of existence and a world they had
rejected. I was of no more real interest than the movement of a
shadow—except to the pair at the corner table. They studied every
detail about me as I was seated and ordering a drink.

On the bandstand a four-piece rock group, as hairy as dusty and
moth-eaten young gorillas, suddenly assailed the senses with electronic sound. The lighting came and went like a Gehenna fire, swirling faces from corpse-green to paranoid purple to jaundice yellow,
cycling and recycling until the brain swam and burst from the brew of
shattering sound and color.

Throughout the hard-rock number I had the impression that I was
being discussed by the pair at the corner table. Their faces in the
ghoulish glows turned toward me, turned away, drew close over the
table as words blanketed by the music were exchanged.

The music shimmered to a long-drawn wail against a mad rhythmic background and slipped eerily to silence. The lighting settled to a twilight. There was a shifting of bodies and a ripple of applause.

I lifted my drink, covertly watching the pair rise from the corner table. I sensed a decision, and my palms became a little damp as they came toward me.

Their shadows streamed across my table. Suddenly they stopped.

"Hi, pops."

The taller, huskier one had spoken. I looked up. He was a strapping youth with a heavy-boned face lurking behind a heavy growth of thick black beard and wiry tresses that fell to his thick neck. He wore nondescript poplin slacks, dirty and wrinkled, and a leather vest that partially covered his massive, hairy chest. His swarthy, bare arms were corded and muscled like a weight lifter's.

The companion beside him was as tall, but much thinner, a fine-boned fellow. Tangled, unwashed locks of yellow and a sparse beard graced a narrow, almost delicate face and high-domed head. The smoldering eyes of a decadent poet peered from the shadows of large sockets. The thin-lipped mouth was faintly quirked, as if sardonic amusement was an habitual reaction.

"We sensed a loneliness," the poet said, "and would offer a friendly ear if you'd care to rap. Peace." He had a thin, nasal voice. His jerky delivery and the embers in his eyes were clues to a good high on drugs. Clad in a rumpled tie-dyed gaucho shirt that hung loose about greasy ducks, he slipped with unreal movements into a chair across the table.

"I'm Cleef," he said, "and my boon companion is known as Willis."

Willis wiped a palm across his leather vest and extended his hand. "Into the pudding, man."

I saw no alternative at the moment but to shake his hand. His grip was modestly powerful. He pumped my hand once, then eased into the chair at my left.

"Pudding?" I inquired.

"As your group would put it," Cleef-the-poet said, "welcome to the club."

"I see. Well, thanks. Buy you fellows a drink?"

Willis' heavy mouth curled gently. "You're out of sight, pops. We don't ruin the belly with booze. But you might blow the price of a joint."

He lifted a muscle-lumped arm and signaled a waitress who was moving from a nearby table. She served them joints from an inno-cent-looking package bearing the brand name of a well-known cigarette. As Willis and Cleef fired the reefers, I ordered a second double Scotch. I figured I needed it.

Cleef drew deeply, half closing his eyes and holding the smoke until his lungs burned for air. Willis was a more conservative pothead, less greedy, less desperate for a turn-on. He puffed, inhaled, exhaled.

"What brings you to a place like this, pops?" Willis asked conversationally.

My gaze roamed the unreality of the room, returned to Willis' dark face. My shoulders made a vague movement. "I'm really not sure," I said.

"Hung-up man, ice cream man," the poet suggested.

"Ice cream?" I asked.

"Now and then user of drugs," Willis explained. "Ice cream habit."

I nodded, grinned slightly. "Thanks for the translation, but I haven't an ice cream habit. Just an occasional Scotch does it for me."

"Translate, extrapolate," Cleef rhymed. "Rap across the gap."

Willis reached and patted the back of my hand. "We'll try to talk your lingo, pops."

"Thanks. It would be less awkward."

The waitress came with my drink. Willis elaborately mused on her thin face and slender topless figure. The gesture on his part was almost pathetically obvious, a cover-up for his quick assessment of the thick wallet from which I paid the tab.

I lifted the Scotch. "Cheers." I rolled the first drops under my tongue for the taste. The liquor dispelled a little of the clammy chill inside me.

I set the glass down and studied it a moment. "I guess it was because of Camilla," I said finally.

"Come again?" Willis said.

"The reason I came in here," I said. "Dear Camilla . . . about the same age as some of the young women in here . . . early twenties . . . very beautiful."

Willis chuckled, eyes brightening. "Well, what do you know! The old boy has got himself a chick!"

"Straight man buys anything his little heart desires," Cleef said lazily.

I couldn't help the angry look I shot across the table. "It wasn't that way at all!"

"Easy, pops," Willis suggested mildly.

I lifted the glass and threw the remainder of the drink down my throat. "Well, it wasn't!"

"So okay."

"I want you to understand."

"Sure, pops. Don't blow your mind."

I took out a spotless Irish linen handkerchief and brushed the cold needles from my forehead. "Blow my mind . . . Sonny, that's just what I did, with Camilla. Couldn't eat, couldn't sleep, couldn't live without her. Went crazy if she glanced at another man. Never wanted her out of my sight. . . ."

"Zap!" mumbled the poet. "What a king-sized hangup."

My vision cleared slightly. "At last you have voiced a truth. I became a different man, totally different, a stranger to myself."

"How'd you meet such a chick?" Willis asked with genuine interest.

I drew a breath. "In a place much like this. I—My wife had died. I was, you might say, in loose-ends bachelorhood. One evening I was entertaining a business client and his wife."

"How deadly dull," decided Cleef.

"She, the client's wife, had heard of a place similar to this one," I said, as if the poet hadn't interrupted. "She wanted to see the sights. She insisted we go, as a lark."

"But you, not the fellowship, were the bugs under the microscope," Cleef intoned sagely.

"Shut up." Willis glowered a look at his companion. "Let the man talk. Go on, pops."

"Go on?" I sagged morosely. "Where is there to go, after Camilla? With Camilla you have been all the way."

Willis' eyes glinted with a grain of fresh respect. "Tough, pops."

"Lovely while it lasted," I amended. "I met her that night, on the lark. We grooved, as I believe you would put it." I broke off, numbly, trying to relate the experience in my own mind to the "straight" sitting at the table with Cleef and Willis. "Then she turned me off. It was nightmare. I pleaded. She reviled. I begged—and Camilla laughed. . . ."

"And she split the scene?" Willis finished.

"Yes," I said, squeezing my eyes tight and seeing her face against the darkness; lovely face, mask-like face; face that could become cruel, unendurably cruel. "Yes, she split the scene." I wrapped it up in a whisper.

Willis scratched his beard and gave his head a short shake. "Who'd have believed it?" He lifted his eyes and looked about the Moons of Jupiter. "So it was the thought of Camilla that brought you in tonight?"

"You might say that," I agreed. I washed the final drop of Scotch from the glass against my lips. "You see, after Camilla, my home town was unbearable. I left. I've wandered, for a long way. It hasn't been easy."

"Looking for another Camilla," the poet said. "I should write about you, man, if it all wasn't so corny." Cleef half stood, drugged eyes flicking about the room. "Is she here tonight? Another Camilla? Do you see another Camilla, man?"

"There will never be another Camilla, sonny," I said. "Once is enough."

"So now you wander some more, pops?" Willis asked.

"Perhaps."

"Why don't we wander together, pops? Have a ball? Cleef and I have rapped about blowing this town. We'd like to see California, New Orleans, Miami when the chill winds blow."

"Dust to salve the itch in our feet," the poet supplied.

"That's right, pops," Willis nodded. "We yearn to roam. You got a car and dough."

"Sorry," I said, suddenly very sober, "but I don't think. . . ."

"Man," Willis said, "you just think about Camilla." His heavy face had changed, hardened. He lifted his right hand almost to tabletop level. I saw the glint of dusky light on six inches of gleaming switchblade. I sat very still. This was the decision the pair had made when I'd strolled in and they'd pegged me for an easy mark.

"Let's go, pops," Willis said.

"All right," I swallowed drily. "I won't resist. You won't have to hurt me."

"That's good, pops. We don't want to hurt you. We're not stupid. Just the dough and the car, that's all."

We rose from the table and walked out of the Dantean room and onto a parking lot, Willis close behind me with the tip of the knife against my back.

"It's the sporty little car right over there," I said. "Please . . . . careful with the knife." I eased the wallet from my pocket, stripped it of cash, several hundred dollars, and handed the money to Willis.

His big hand closed over the bread. "Thanks, pops. And look, you ought to be more careful, wandering into places like the Moons of Jupiter."

"Seeking adventure, you found it," the poet surmised.

I handed the car keys to Willis. "That's it. You have got it. You've stripped me clean."

"So long, pops."

I saw the flash of his big fist. Conditioned as I was, even after Camilla, I could have handled him—both of them, Cleef posing no problem in a rough-and-tumble.

I took the punch on the chin, rolling with it just enough to keep from being knocked blotto. My knees crumpled. I fell on the darkly shadowed asphalt, stunned but not unconscious.

I heard Willis say: "That'll hold him while we split the scene."

I heard the poet intone: "Hail the open road!"

I heard the rush of their feet, the starting of the car, the sigh of engine as the car took them from the parking lot.

I got up and dusted myself off in time to see the taillights vanish around a distant street corner.

Good-bye Camilla's car. . . . Bought with my money, but she'd done the shopping, chosen the model. Not even a fingerprint to connect the car to me; I'd wiped them away before entering the Moons of Jupiter.

I strolled to the street in order to find a taxicab several blocks from the scene.

Good-bye, Camilla . . . .

I still had the smallest catch in my throat. I hadn't really meant to kill her when I struck her in that final moment of insane rage.

Farewell, Camilla. . . . It was hard to cover my tracks and get rid of you, the evidence. I wonder when they will find you in the trunk of the car? California? New Orleans? At some service station in Alabama when the attendant moves from gas pump to the rear of the car and catches the first whiff of the ripening smell?

As for you, easy marks, you know not from where I came, or where I go, or even my name.

So enjoy the ride. . . .

When Isadora was unable to deal with the surly youth, she resorted to the only means she knew for solving her problem. . . .

EIGHT

New Neighbor

Each of us lives in one world only," Mrs. Cappelli said, "the singular world within the skull. No two are alike. Who can possibly imagine some of the dark phantasms within the worlds other than one's own?"

Isadora, old, gray, spindly, gnarled, more friend and companion than servant, drifted to Mrs. Cappelli's side. The two women were of an age, in the autumn of their lives, with a close bond between them. The years had touched Mrs. Cappelli with the gentler brush. She was still trim; her face had not entirely surrendered its youthful lines; her once-black hair was braided in a coil atop her head, a silver tiara.

The two stood at the window of Mrs. Cappelli's slightly disarrayed and comfortably lived-in bedroom and looked from the second-story window at the youth in the back yard of the house next door.

"A strange one," Isadora agreed.

He was lounging on a plastic-webbing chaise, indolent, loose, relaxed, calmly pumping a pellet rifle, In scruffy jeans and T-shirt, he was long, tanned and lean, slightly bony. Even in repose he was a suggestion of quick, whip-like agility and power. His face was cleanly cut, even attractive, his forehead, ears and neck feathered with very dark hair. Idly, his gaze was roving the bushes and trees, the pines at the corners of the yard, the avocado tree, the two tall, unkempt palmettos.

He lifted the gun with a casual motion and squeezed the trigger. A bird toppled from the topmost reaches of the taller pine tree, the small body bouncing from limb to limb, showering a few needles, hanging briefly on a lower limb before it struck and was swallowed by the uncut grass along the rear of the yard.

The youth showed no sign of interest, once again pumping the gun and stirring only his eyes in a renewed search of the trees.

57

Mrs. Cappelli's thin figure flinched, and her eyes were held by the spot where the bird had fallen.

Isadora touched her arm. "At least it wasn't a cardinal, Maria."

"Thank you, Isadora. From this distance the details weren't clear. My eyes just aren't what they used to be."

Isadora glanced at the face that had once been the distillation of all beauty in Old Sicily. "I think we could use some tea, Maria."

Mrs. Cappelli seemed unaware when Isadora faded from her side. She remained at the window, as hushed as the hot Florida stillness outside, looking carefully at the young man on the chaise.

Mrs. Cappelli had been delighted when the house next door was rented at last. It had stood vacant for months, a casualty of Florida overbuild. Dated by its Spanish styling, it was nevertheless a sound and comfortable house in a substantial and quiet older neighborhood where urban decay had never gained the slightest foothold.

Mrs. Cappelli had expected a family. Instead there were only the mother and son arriving in a noisy old car in the wake of a van that had disgorged flimsy, worn, time-payment furniture. Mrs. Ruth Morrow and Greg. A lot of house for two people, but Mrs. Cappelli supposed, correctly, that the age of the house and its long vacancy had finally caused the desperate owner to offer it as a cut-rate bargain on the sagging rental market.

After a settling-in day or two, Mrs. Cappelli saw Mrs. Morrow pruning the dying poinsettia near the front corner of the house and went over to say hello.

It was a sultry afternoon and Mrs. Morrow looked wan and tired, with hardly enough remaining strength to snap the shears. Mrs. Cappelli wondered why Greg wasn't handling the pruning tool. He was at home. Who could doubt it? He was in there torturing a high-amplification guitar with amateurish violence. His discordant efforts were audible a block away.

"I'm Maria Cappelli," Mrs. Cappelli said pleasantly. "It's very nice to have new neighbors."

Mrs. Morrow accepted the greeting with hesitant and standoffish self-consciousness. Her glance slipped toward the house, a silent wish that her son would turn down his guitar. She was a thin, almost frail woman. She needs, Mrs. Cappelli thought, mounds of pasta and huge bowls of steaming, mouth-watering *stufato*.

Mrs. Morrow remembered her manners with a tired smile. "Ruth Morrow," she said. She glanced about the yard. "So much to do here. Inside, the place was all dust and cobwebs." Her gaze moved to Mrs. Cappelli's comfortable abode of stucco and red tile. "You have a lovely place."

"My husband built it years before his death. We used to come here for winter vacations. To me, it was home, rather than New York. I love Florida, even the heat of the summers. My son was born in the house, right up there in that corner bedroom." Mrs. Cappelli laughed. "Shortest labor on record. Such a bambino! When he decided to make his entrance, he wouldn't even take time for a ride to the hospital."

Mrs. Cappelli's unconscious delight in her son brought Ruth Morrow's fatigued and hollow eyes to Mrs. Cappelli's face. Mrs. Cappelli was caught, held, and slightly embarrassed. Such aching eyes! So many regrets, frustrations and bewilderments harbored in their depths. . . . They were too large and dark for the thin, heavily made-up face that at one time must have been quite pretty.

"My son is named Greg," Mrs. Morrow murmured.

"Mine is named John. He's much older than your son. He has a wife and five children—such scamps!—and he comes to see me now and then when he can take the time. He is a contractor up north, always on the go."

"He must be a fine man."

Mrs. Cappelli was urged to say something comforting to the wearied mother before her. "Oh, John sowed an oat. I guess they all do, before they settle down. Nowadays John is always after me to sell the old antique, as he calls the house. Come and live with him, he nags. I tell him to peddle his own papers. This is not the old country where three or four generations must brawl under one small roof."

Mrs. Morrow nodded. "It's been real nice of you to say hello, Mrs. Cappelli. I do have to run now. I work, you see. At the Serena Lounge on the beach, from six in the evening until two o'clock each morning. I always have a good bit to do to get ready for work."

"The Serena is an excellent place. John took Isadora and me there the last time he was down."

Ruth Morrow punched the tip of the pruning shears at a small brown twig. "Being a cocktail waitress isn't the height of my ambition, but without professional training, it pays more money than I'd ever hoped to make. And God knows there is never quite enough money."

It might ease the situation, Mrs. Cappelli mused, if her boy dirtied his hands with some honest toil. She said, "The honor of a job is in its execution, and I'm certain you're the best of cocktail waitresses."

The sincerity of Mrs. Cappelli's tone brought the first touch of animation to the tired face with its layered icing of makeup and framing of short, dark brown hair. Before Mrs. Morrow could respond, the front door of the house slammed, and Greg was standing in the shadow of the small portico. Both women looked toward him.

"Greg," Mrs. Morrow called, "this is Mrs. Cappelli, our next-door neighbor."

"Hi," he said, bored. He gave Mrs. Cappelli a single glance of dismissal, dropped to the walk with a single smooth stride and headed around the house.

"Greg," Ruth Morrow called, "where are you going?"

"Out," he said, without looking back.

"When will you be home?"

"When I'm damned good and ready!" He rounded the corner of the house and was out of sight.

Mrs. Morrow's face came creeping in Mrs. Cappelli's direction, but her eyes sidled away. "It's just his way of talking, Mrs. Cappelli."

Mrs. Cappelli nodded, but she didn't understand. How could Mrs. Morrow accept it? Parental respect was normal in a child, be he six or sixty.

A car engine was stabbed to roaring life and Greg raced down the driveway. He cornered the car into the street with tires screaming.

"I really have to go now, Mrs. Cappelli."

"It was a privilege to meet you," Mrs. Cappelli said.

"Well?" Isadora asked as soon as Mrs. Cappelli stepped into the house.

"She is a poor woman in the worst of all states," Mrs. Cappelli said, "a mother with a cruel and unloving son."

Isadora crossed herself.

"He is killing his mother," Mrs. Cappelli said.

Greg was an immediate neighborhood blight, a disease, an invasion. The Ransoms' playful puppy bounded into the Morrow yard and Greg broke its leg with a kick, claiming that the flop-eared trusting mutt was charging him. He hunted chords on the thunderous guitar at one o'clock in the morning, if the mood suited him. Many evenings he was out, usually returning about three A.M. with screaming tires and unmuffled engine. Frequently he filled the Morrow house with hordes of hippies for beer and rock parties.

Neighbors grumbled and swapped irate opinions of Greg among themselves over back-yard fences and coffee klatches. Lack of leadership was a stultifying, inertial force, and nothing was done about Greg until about two o'clock, one morning, when the biggest blast yet hit the peak of its frenzy in the Morrow house.

Mr. Sigmon (the white colonial across the street) decided he just couldn't stand it any longer. He threw back the cover, sat up in bed, turned on the bedside lamp, and dialed Information on his extension phone. Yes, Information informed, a phone had been installed at the

Morrow address. Mr. Sigmon got the number, hesitated for a single minute, then dialed it.

The Morrow phone rang six or seven times before anyone noticed. Then a girl answered, giggling drunkenly. "If this isn't an obscene call, forget it."

"Let me speak to Greg," Mr. Sigmon said, the phone feeling sweaty in his hand.

The girl screeched for Greg, and he was on.

"Have a heart," Mr. Sigmon pleaded. "Can't you tone things down just a little?"

"Who's this?" Greg asked.

"I . . . uh . . . Mr. Sigmon, across the street."

"How'd you like a fat lip, Mr. Sigmon-across-the-street?"

"Now look, Greg . . ." Mr. Sigmon gathered his courage. "All I'm asking is that you be reasonable."

"Go cram it!"

A burst of anger burned the edges from Mr. Sigmon's timidity. "Now look here, you young pup, you quiet down over there or I'll call the police."

For a moment there was only the noise of the party on the line, the wild laughter, the shouted talk, the overpowering background of hard-rock rhythm. Then Greg said, "Well, OK, pops. You don't have to get so sore about it. We're just having some fun."

The party cooled and Mr. Sigmon stretched beside his wide-awake wife with a feeling of being an inch taller for having put a tether on Greg.

Two days later Mrs. Sigmon got out of her station wagon with a bag of groceries, crossed to the front stoop, and dropped the groceries with a thud and clatter. She put her knuckles to her mouth and screamed. Against the front door lay her cat, stiff and lifeless, its head twisted so that its muzzle pointed upward away from the shoulders.

That night Greg hosted another party, the loudest one yet.

To Mrs. Cappelli it was as if a dark presence had come among them. It wasn't the same warmly quiet old street. It was like a sinister urban street where the aura urged the hapless pedestrian to hurry along after dark with ears keened for the slightest sound.

"Perhaps the Morrows will move on," Mrs. Cappelli said at break-fast.

"Yes," Isadora agreed. "They are Gypsies. But when? That's the question. Next month? A year from now? Before the youth does something even more dreadful?"

"That poor mother." Mrs. Cappelli flipped an egg in the pan. "If she moved around the world, she would not have room for her problem."

Later in the day Mrs. Cappelli carried her afternoon tea up to her bedroom. She put the steaming cup on a small table and crossed to the side window. Outside, on a level with the sill, was a small wooden ledge. Two sparrows were hopping about on it, pecking bits of food from cracks.

"Hello there," Mrs. Cappelli said, "you're early for dinner. You must be hungry, going for those leftovers."

She turned to the bureau and picked up a canister. The sparrows fluttered away as she opened the canister and reached out to spread a feast of seeds and crumbs on the ledge feeder.

The sparrows had returned by the time Mrs. Cappelli fetched her tea and settled in the wooden rocking chair near the window. Other birds arrived, more sparrows, a robin, a thrush, a tiny wren. They were a delight of movement, color; they were so naturally happy, so easy to please.

The daily bird feeding and watching was silly, perhaps—the whim of an old woman—but the birds rewarded Mrs. Cappelli with a quiet pleasure in a sometimes endless day. Therefore, she inquired of herself, isn't it a most important thing?

She wondered if the Prince would come; and then he did. Gorgeous. Regal. The most beautiful cardinal since Audubon. He had been a daily visitor a long time now. He always came to rest on the edge of the feeder, proud head lifted and tilted as he looked in at Mrs. Cappelli.

She leaned forward slightly. "Hello there," she said softly. "Is the food up to your kingly taste today?"

She couldn't quite delight in the words or in the sight of Prince and his friends. No, not anymore. She sat back, fingers curled on the arms of the chair. Today, more than yesterday or the day before, she was aware of depleted joy. She'd tried not to admit the awareness, but now, in the ritual of the birds, was a hint of anxiety, even fear in her heart. She couldn't entirely free her mind of the memory of the youth next door with his pellet gun. Pump, pump, pump. . . . His strong hand working the lever while his eyes roamed the trees for an innocent, unsuspecting and helpless target, and a feathered body twisting and turning as it plunged headlong to the ground.

Perhaps, Mrs. Cappelli thought, she should stop feeding the birds while the air gun is over there threatening them . . . .

As the thought crossed her mind, she saw a sudden puff of red feathers on the cardinal's breast. The bird was gone. That quickly. That completely. The other birds scattered in sudden flight.

Mrs. Cappelli sat with a hot dryness blinding her eyes, then she snapped from the chair and hurried down through the house. With late sun searing through the cold film on her flesh, she searched along the driveway and through the shrubbery growing against the house. The cardinal's body was not be seen, and she was sure that Greg had run over and picked up the evidence before she'd got out of the house.

She thought of him watching the ledge, seeing her birds, hearing the sound of her, perhaps, drifting from her open window as she'd chatted at the cardinal. A dark instinct had risen in him, a hunger, and his devious mind with its unknown depths had schemed. He'd waited, like a beast savoring the anticipation of the kill. Then he'd felt the thrill of pulling the trigger at last and seeing the cardinal fall.

Mrs. Cappelli turned slowly, and he was there, standing near the front walk of the Morrow house, the air gun in the crook of his arm. Tall. Lean. Young. Challenging her. Baiting her. His lips lifting in a smile that sent an icy shard through her.

She turned on stiff legs and went into her house.

The policeman's name was Longstreet, Sergeant Harley Longstreet. He was tall, strapping, with a pleasantly big-featured face and lank brown hair.

With the drapery pulled aside in the livingroom, Mrs. Cappelli watched him come from the Morrow house. He stood a moment, looking over his shoulder, a loose-leaf pocket notebook in his hand. Then he came across to the Cappelli front door.

Mrs. Cappelli opened the door while he was still a few feet away and stood aside for him to enter. With a glance at his face, she suspected that he hadn't been very successful with Greg Morrow. He was a nice young policeman. He'd responded quickly to her phone call. He'd heard everything she'd had to say. He hadn't thought a bird's death unimportant—not when it was coupled with the circumstances. He'd attached considerable meaning and importance to it. He had gone over to the Morrow place almost an hour ago. Now he was back.

Mrs. Cappelli stood with her fingers on the edge of the opened door. "I think I understand, Mr. Longstreet," she said with no accusation or rancor.

"He simply denies killing the bird, ma'am. Did you actually see him kill it?"

"I didn't see him pull the trigger."

"Well, you see, Mrs. Cappelli, the law is black print on white paper. Mrs. Morrow isn't home. No one else is out and about the houses close by. Without a witness or some tangible evidence I've done about all I can."

"I appreciate that, Mr. Longstreet."

He hesitated, tapping his notebook on his thumb. "He says you are a crotchety old lady who doesn't want young people in the neighborhood."

"He's a liar. Mr. Longstreet. I delight in reasonably normal young people. Do you believe him?"

"Not for a moment, Mrs. Cappelli. Not one word." He flipped his notebook open. "I checked the records briefly when I got your call, to see if he was in any of the official files. We have computers nowadays, you know. I can push a button and tell whether or not he'd been recorded in any city or county agency."

She closed the door finally and stood leaning the back of her shoulders against it. "And what did your computer tell you?"

His sharp eyes flicked between her and the notebook. "He spent two years, our Greg Morrow, in a correctional institution for maladjusted teen-agers. Committed when he was sixteen. Released on his eighteenth birthday, which was eighteen months ago. Prior to the action that put him away, he had a record of classroom disruption, of vandalism in his schools, of shaking down smaller classmates for their pocket money. He was finally put away after he assaulted a school principal."

"The principal should have given him a sound thrashing with a strong hickory switch," Mrs. Cappelli said. "But in that event it would have been the principal who went to jail."

"It's possible," Longstreet agreed. He tucked his notebook in his hip pocket. "We've had complaints about Greg almost from the day he was let out, in various neighborhoods where the Morrows have lived. But other than a suspended sentence for trespassing, after a house was vandalized, nothing has stood against him in court."

Mrs. Cappelli moved slowly to a large chair and sank on its edge, hands clasped on her drawn-together knees. "Mr. Longstreet, Greg Morrow is not merely a mischievous boy. He is the kind of force and fact from which those fantastic and gory newspaper headlines are too often drawn."

"That's very possible."

His tone caused her to glance up, and she caught the bitterness in his eyes. Her sympathy went out to him for the hardness of his job.

"Don't feel badly, Mr. Longstreet. I thank you for coming out and talking to him. Perhaps it will frighten him for a little while and help that much."

"We simply can't lock them up without evidence of the commission of a crime. Sometimes, then, it's too late."

"After the commission of a crime, Mr. Longstreet, it is always too late." She rose to her feet to see him out.

He stood looking down on her, the small sturdiness of her. "I'll have the police cruiser in this area increase its patrols along your street, Mrs. Cappelli. I'll do everything I possibly can."

"I'm sure of that."

"Good day, Mrs. Cappelli."

"Good day, Mr. Longstreet."

She watched him stride down the front walk and get into the unmarked police car parked against the street curbing. He sat there for a brief time after he started the engine, looking at the Morrow house; then he drove away.

As she turned, Mrs. Cappelli saw Greg. He was standing in the Morrow yard, thumbs hooked in his belt, watching the police car move toward the intersection and turn out of sight.

Mrs. Cappelli started to close the door. Then, with a sudden impulse, she went outside and walked across to the driveway that separated the two properties.

"Greg . . . may I speak to you?"

He moved only his head, turning it to stare at her. "Why should I talk to an old bitch who sics the fuzz on me?"

She whitened, but held back the swift heat of anger. "I thought we might have a civilized talk. After all, Greg, we do have to live as neighbors."

"Who says? Somebody around here could die. Old biddies are always popping off, you know."

She drew a difficult breath. "A bit of reasonableness, Greg. That's all I'm asking. I was happy when you moved into the neighborhood, so young and vigorous. I looked forward to some youthful activity next door."

"Old creep. You called the fuzz."

"You know why, Greg. Somehow I must impress on you that there are limits. Why can't we discuss them? Observe them? Live and let live?"

He looked at her with studied insolence. "You made a bad mistake calling Longstreet, old lady. I don't like it. I don't like it at all. I won't forget it, either."

Her voice rang with the first hint of anger. "Are you threatening me, Greg?"

"Who says? Can you prove to Longstreet that I am? Just your word against mine. I know how the law works. I know my rights."

"I don't think this is getting us anywhere, Greg. I regret having come out and spoken to you."

He drifted a few steps toward her. The dying sunlight marked his cheekbones sharply. His body was tense, as if coiled inside. "You got a lot more regrets in the future, old lady. You better believe it. Think about it. You won't know when, how, or where. But I don't like people trying to throw me to the fuzz."

"I hope this is just talk, Greg."

He laughed suddenly. "That school principal—the one who got me sent up. Know what happened? About a year after I got out, a hit-and-run driver marked up the punk principal's daughter, that's what. She'll be a shortlegged creep the rest of her life. Sure, the fuzz questioned me—but they couldn't prove a thing."

She could bear it no longer. She turned and started toward her front door with quick steps.

"Don't forget to think about it, old lady," he called after her. "And remember—nobody ever proves a thing on Greg Morrow."

Three passing days brought Mrs. Cappelli the faint hope that Greg had thought twice and again. Perhaps his insults and threat had sufficed his ego. Usually, such fellows were mostly talk. Usually.

The fourth night Mrs. Cappelli stirred in her always-light sleep, dreaming that she smelled smoke. She murmured in her half-conscious state; and then she had the sudden, clear, icy knowledge that she was not asleep.

She flung back the sheet, a small cry in her throat, and stumbled upright, a ghostly pale figure in her ankle-length white nightgown.

"Isadora!" she cried out as she hurried into the hallway. "Isadora, lazy-head, wake up! The house is on fire!"

Isadora's bedroom door flung open and Isadora appeared, gowned like her mistress, her iron gray hair hanging in two limp braids across her shoulders.

"What is it? What's happening?" Isadora chattered, her eyes bulging. She glimpsed the faint reddish glow in the stairwell and began crossing herself again and again. "Oh, heaven be merciful! Mercy from heaven!"

Together the two women stumbled in haste down the stairway. The fiery reflection was stronger in the dining room.

"Quickly, Isadora! The kitchen!"

They ran across the dining room, wavering to a halt inside the kitchen. Mrs. Cappelli's quick glance divined the situation. The curtains over the glass portion of the outside door had caught fire first. They were now remaining bits of falling ash and embers. The flames had spread easily to the window curtains along the rear of the kitchen, and were now gnawing at the cabinetwork, fouling the air with the stench of burning varnish.

Isadora dashed into the pantry, knocking pots helter-skelter as she grabbed two of the larger ones. Mrs. Cappelli was more direct. She pulled the sink squirter hose out to its full extension, turned the cold water on hard, and fought the flames back until she had drenched out the last flicker.

With wisps of smoke still seeping from the cabinetwork, Mrs. Cappelli groped for a kitchen chair and sank into it weakly. She matched long breaths with the gulps Isadora was taking, and strength began to return.

"How horrible it might have been," Isadora said through chattering teeth, "If you hadn't awakened."

"Yes," Mrs. Cappelli said.

Isadora gripped the kitchen table to help herself out of her chair. "We must call the fire department to make sure everything is out."

"Yes."

"And the police."

"No!"

Isadora looked at Mrs. Cappelli, wondering at the sharpness of her tone. "Maria . . . we know who did this. We know he has been planning, waiting, thinking and deciding what to do."

"Yes, and tonight he made his move." Mrs. Cappelli's gaze examined the fire-blackened kitchen door and paused at its base. She got up, crossed to the door, and knelt down. She touched the ashes at the base of the door. "And so simply he did it," she said. "Not all these ashes are from burned fabric. Some of them feel very much like brittle burned paper. So easily, without breaking in or leaving marks on the kitchen door, he simply slid strips of paper underneath the door until he had a sufficient pile inside. Then it remains for him but to light the tail end of the final strip and watch the tiny flame creep along the paper under the door and ignite the pile inside. Soon the hungry flames reach up to touch the curtains. . . ."

The two women were an immobile tableau—Isadora standing beside the table, Mrs. Cappelli kneeling at the door, looking at each other.

"Yes, I see," Isadora said. "It's all very clear. It would be clear to the police. But they cannot make the youth confess. They are not permitted. And he will have an alibi, someone to swear that he was far away from this street tonight."

A small sob caught in Mrs. Cappelli's throat. "How much can we endure, Isadora? Call the firemen quickly. Then I want the phone. Late as it is, I want to hear the sound of John's voice."

At ten o'clock the following evening an airport taxicab deposited John in front of the Cappelli house.

"It's he!" Isadora said, watching him pay off the taxi and get out his single piece of luggage.

Beside Isadora, the giddy center of a little vortex of excitement, Mrs. Cappelli nudged hard with her elbow. "Quickly, Isadora! The table . . . the dinner candles."

Isadora darted from the front door, leaving Mrs. Cappelli there alone to watch the approach of her son.

He wouldn't have eaten on the plane, she knew. Mama always had one of his favorite meals waiting, whatever his hour of arrival. Tonight Mrs. Cappelli had centered the dinner around *arosto di agnello,* and already she could imagine him filling his mouth with the succulent lamb and blowing her a kiss of approval from his fingertips.

"Ah, John, John!" Her wide-flung arms enfolded his dark, towering, masculine strength and, as always, she wept joyously.

He picked her up, almost as if he would tuck her under his arm, and kissed her on both cheeks.

"What is that I smell? Not roast lamb as only *mia madre* can make?"

"But yes, John! How was the flight? Isadora, wherever are you? Quickly, Isadora! The most handsome boy on earth is famished!"

Arm linked with her son's, Mrs. Cappelli strolled into the dining room, questions tumbling about her daughter-in-law, her precious grandchildren.

All was well up north, John assured her. All was going beautifully.

He sat down at the head of the old hand-carved walnut table, an inviting array before him, snowy linens, bone china, crystal and sterling, tall candles in beaten silver holders, fine food in covered dishes.

Isadora and Mrs. Cappelli were content to sit on either side, near the head of the table, watching him eat and anticipating his every wish from the serving dishes.

Then at last he could eat no more, and he rewarded his mother with a loving wink and appreciative little belch.

He laid his napkin on the table, pushed back his chair, and lifted one of the candles to light a thin black cigar.

Mrs. Cappelli was at his side as he walked to the windows in the side of the room and stood there looking at the lights of the Morrow house.

"Now, Mama," he said quietly, "What's this trouble?"

She told him every detail from the moment Greg Morrow had moved next door. She acquainted John with Greg's every habit, the identity of Greg's closest friends, the make, model and license number of the Morrow car. It took her several minutes; she had accumulated a great deal of information during the time Greg had been a neighbor.

When Mrs. Cappelli finished speaking, John slipped his arm about her shoulders. "Don't worry, Mama," he said quietly. "It will be taken care of. The young animal will stop killing his mother. He will kill and maim no more animals. He will hit-run no more children. He will light no more arsonist fires. It will all be taken care of very soon, when the first proper moment arrives."

Looking up at him, Mrs. Cappelli knew it would be so. In her, regrettably, Greg Morrow had made the biggest mistake of his life.

She thought of John's grandfather and his father and of Cappelli men from Sicily to San Francisco. In all the Mafia—and it had been so for generations—there were no better soldiers than Cappelli men. They enforced Mafioso law without fear or regard—and none was more stalwart than the loving fullness of her heart, her John.

Although paranoid Old Man Emmons seemed totally incapable, he proved surprisingly resourceful when under assault. . . .

NINE

Old Man Emmons

The feeble outcry from the old man's bedroom penetrated Charlie Collins' slumber. His senses swam back to consciousness. Then a light flashed on and he was aware that Laura was getting out of the twin bed next to his.

"I thought I heard father," she said.

"I heard something myself."

They threw back covers, slipped into robes, and hurried to the bedroom the old man had wanted when he came to live with them, the corner bedroom, the one with lots of windows, cross ventilation.

The old man's bed was empty. He had made his way into the adjoining bathroom. He seemed to be through with being sick, and stood shivering.

Charlie and Laura rushed to him.

"Father," Laura said, "you should have called us."

"I did. You wouldn't answer," the old man said accusingly.

"We came the second we woke," Charlie said.

The old man fumbled for the drinking glass in the porcelain rack beside the medicine cabinet. Charlie grabbed the glass, rinsed it, filled it with water.

The old man washed his mouth out, gargled noisily, his mouth a sunken, wrinkled hole in his face. His skin held a grayish cast. A bundle of dried sticks inside the old-fashioned nightgown, the old man was a terrifyingly cadaverous comment on the mortality of human flesh.

"I'll get the doctor," Laura said.

"I don't want the doctor," the old man said, pulling away from them belligerently and shuffling toward his own bed, across the room.

"It must have been those pickles at dinner," Charlie said.

71

"I've eaten pickles before! I know what made me sick!"

Charlie and Laura looked at each other, then at the old man wavering toward the bed.

"What, sir?" Charlie asked.

"I know," the old man said ominously. "I got a good stomach. I don't get sick easy. I know what caused it."

The old man crawled into bed and pulled the covers over his head. Laura touched Charlie's arm. They slipped out of the room. In the hallway, she whispered, "You can't do much with him when he sets his mind this way."

"How about the doctor?"

"I'm sure he's all right, Charlie. It was those pickles. You go on back to bed. You've got to work tomorrow—today. I'll listen for him."

Charlie didn't think he would get back to sleep. He lay and smoked, thinking of Laura in the chair she'd drawn close to her father's door.

He'd thought he had a full awareness of the circumstances when he married Laura. An only child, she'd cared for her father a long time, since the death of her mother. She'd explained that she wanted to keep her father with her, and Charlie had said okay. It wasn't, after all, as if they were a pair of teenagers running away to get married. Both were in their thirties.

Charlie's first wife had accidentally killed herself nearly ten years ago, rushing home from a bridge game late one icy afternoon. Laura had never married, never had much chance to know men, for that matter.

She and Charlie had met prosaically enough in a supermarket. They were, he guessed, prosaic people. Laura was no raving beauty, though she was well built and had a pleasant face framed in brown hair. Charlie was a tall, pleasant looking man, a little on the thin side, who looked as if he worked long hours at a desk in a large office, which was exactly the case.

The old man's strenuous objections had marred what should have been one of life's more perfect moments. Charlie had regretted this more for Laura's sake than his own. He'd figured he understood the old man and was old enough himself to overlook the shortcomings of a close, demanding in-law.

But now, after only a few weeks of marriage, Charlie wasn't so sure. There was a point where churlishness became too barbed for comfort, where a martyred air of being persecuted permeated the whole house.

Charlie napped finally, awoke too quickly, and dragged through the day. Driving home, he hoped Laura'd had a chance to catch a nap this afternoon. She'd looked plenty bushed when he left the house this morning.

Old man Emmons was in the living room, cackling toothlessly at a TV run of an old W. C. Fields comedy. Charlie spoke cordially, and the old man speared him with a look from his cavernous eyes. "You back?"

Charlie let it pass. "Where is Laura?"

"Gone to the store," the old man said. "Can't you keep still while the movie's on?"

With a sigh and shake of his head, Charlie passed through the house, crossed the rear yard and entered the garage. He was outfitting a wood-working shop, using one side of the garage. The place was chilly. He turned on the butane heater and began to tinker with a drill press, setting it in position and bolting it down.

He was spending more and more time out here, he realized. The thought caused him to drop his wrench, sit on a saw horse, and light a cigarette. He wondered if he were already in the process of becoming one of those hobbyist husbands, shunted out of his own house by an in-law.

He threw the cigarette on the floor and ground it under his heel. Damn it, that old man was going to have to change his ways, and that's all there was to it.

Charlie went back into the house. The living room was empty. Laura was home—there was a bag of groceries on the table just inside the front door.

Then Charlie heard their voices, hers and her father's, in argument, from the old man's bedroom.

"He hid my pills, I tell you!" the old man said.

"No, father," Laura said patiently, "they were right there in the cabinet where you put them—behind the soda box."

"You're working hand in glove with him!"

"Father. . . ."

"I can see it now! He's turning you against me."

"No, father. We both love you and want you to be happy. We want to take care of you."

The old man snorted in disbelief as Laura came into the living room, picked up the groceries, and started toward the kitchen.

"I'll hurry dinner up, Charlie. I was late getting to the store."

Laura's worn look caused Charlie to put off what he'd intended to say.

"I'll give you a hand," he said.

The right emotional distillation didn't again take place inside of Charlie, and he didn't speak his mind during the following week.

Then on Tuesday Laura called him at the office. The old man had fallen down the basement steps and would Charlie please hurry home?

He explained briefly to his boss, ran to the parking lot, and fought traffic out to the development.

Laura met him at the door.

"How is he?" Charlie asked.

"He's all right." She passed the back of her hand over her forehead. "I guess I shouldn't have called you, Charlie, but when I heard him go tumbling. . . ."

"I know. What does the doctor say?"

"That my father is a very lucky man, or indestructible," her face twisted, giving it a strange expression Charlie had never seen before. "The doctor just left."

"Is he coming back?"

"Not today. He wants me to bring father into his office tomorrow morning, just for a check-up."

She'd need the car, then. That meant riding the bus to work. Schedules out here put Charlie either fifteen minutes late or forty-five minutes early to the office.

He sighed. "Well, I guess I better look in on him."

"Charlie. . . ."

"Yes?"

"Don't get him. . . . I mean. . . ."

"I'm the soul of patience," Charlie assured her, a touch of bitterness in his voice.

Charlie opened the old man's bedroom door softly and stepped inside. The old man had his eyes closed. His bones made creases in the covers and that was all.

As Charlie neared the bed, the old man opened his eyes and looked at him.

"How are you, sir?"

"I'll survive," the old man said softly. "I'll survive a long time."

"We hope so. How did it happen?"

"I fell down the basement steps."

"I know. Laura told me that on the phone."

"I could have been killed."

"But you weren't, and we're grateful for that. The doctor said you're fine."

"Could have been killed . . ." the old man said, as if Charlie hadn't spoken. "All because there was a carton of old shoes on the steps. Right near the top."

Charlie tried to understand the old man's feelings. "I meant to take them down last night."

"But you didn't," the old man said in that soft voice that sounded like a whisper from an eternal tomb.

"No, I . . . Laura asked me to. . . . Listen, what am I explaining every detail to you for! . . ."

He caught the glint of warped satisfaction in the old man's eye. He felt awkward and foolish. His quick anger drained to be replaced by something else.

"You hate me," the old man whispered.

And it was true. For the first time, Charlie knew it was true. The old man seemed to have a profound knowledge of it.

"You're a little upset," Charlie said through stiff lips. "You know we care greatly for you."

He turned and went out. He found refuge in the shop, turning on a lathe and letting the chips fly.

Finally, he realized that Laura was calling him from the house. He switched off the lathe, turned off the heater, and hurried across the backyard. He had no right to act childishly toward her, to pity himself because he lacked the manhood to be the head of his own house.

He waited until late that night, until he was certain the old man was asleep and wouldn't come creeping in. He cut the legs for a cocktail table without his mind being on the task. When he came into the house, he washed his hands in the kitchen, thinking of what he would say.

Laura was on the end of the couch, feet curled under her while she watched TV. Charlie felt a great reluctance inside of him as he approached her. The word "showdown" came to his mind, frightening him a little.

He eased down beside her. She looked at him and smiled. He really did love her, he thought. Under different circumstances, with some kids around. . . .

"How's the table coming, Charlie?"

"Fine."

"Can I have a look tomorrow?"

"Sure, if you want. Laura. . . ."

Thundering hooves and banging sixguns filtered into the space between them.

"I wanted to talk to you," he said, his collar feeling tight.

"About father," she said.

"Yes, I guess so."

"You want him out."

"I'm afraid I do," he said.

"Why be afraid, Charlie?" she asked, almost gently.

He stared at her, again with that feeling of strangeness.

"I'm not afraid, Charlie. I'll be glad when he's dead."

"Laura. . . ."

"Why deny it? You feel the same way. I'm not surprised. He taints and kills everything he touches."

"Then we'll put him in a home?" Even with her attitude, which had surprised him so, the words sounded callous, cruel.

"No, Charlie, we won't put him in a home. I knew from the beginning this was something we'd have to discuss."

"But if we keep him here. . . ."

"That's what we're going to do, Charlie."

"But you just said. . . ."

"That I'd be glad when he's dead? I mean it. We're going to keep him right here, right with us, until the day he dies."

"I see," he said glumly, although he didn't see any solution at all.

"You think I'm choosing between duty to a father and love for a husband, Charlie?" She stirred with a faint rustling sound of her clothing against the couch upholstery. Her hand reached to touch his cheek.

"I love you, Charlie. And I don't feel any duty toward him. His miserliness and meanness killed my mother and ruined my childhood. If the question were so simple, there wouldn't be any problem."

"I don't think I understand, Laura."

"Of course you don't. You've never been told that he's a rich man."

"Rich?"

She leaned toward him slightly. "He's worth over a quarter of a million dollars, Charlie."

"But that gloomy old barn you lived in before we were married!"

"I know. But it isn't so strange or unusual. Not as extreme as those cases you read about where some recluse dies in filth, with a million dollars glued under the wallpaper or tucked under the mattress. My father's a miser and always has been. I didn't know he was worth so much myself until my mother died. There were some papers I had to sign. I made inquiries, and when I found out—well, Charlie, right then and there I began waiting for him to die. I'm his only heir, you know. It will all come to me."

The walls seemed to tilt a little, and the TV was a crazy, animated painting by Dali. Charles wiped his hand across his face. It came away wet. The discovery of the old man's wealth was not the real shock. This new side of Laura—that's what took him a moment to absorb.

"You think I'm evil, Charlie?"

"No, I realize. . . . I mean, years of living with him wouldn't endear him to anyone. . . ."

"He's never suspected my feelings. Isn't that a greater, more laudable sacrifice than acting out of pure love."

"Yes," Charlie said, his voice hoarse and quick. "Yes, it is, Laura."

"If we throw him out, there is the chance a nurse will marry him for all that money."

"Yes, there is a strong chance."

"Or out of spite, he'd will the money to some charity. I know he'd do that, Charlie."

"I'm pretty sure of it myself, knowing him."

"So we don't have any alternative, do we?"

"Not that I can see."

She smoothed the hem of her dress over her knees and stared thoughtfully at the carpet.

"A quarter million, Charlie."

"I can't imagine that much honest-to-goodness money."

"Trips around the world. Good clothes. Thumb your nose at the mortgage company. Think in those terms, Charlie. When he is at his most trying."

"I'll do that."

She raised her eyes slowly to his. "We'll earn the money, Charlie."

"I guess we will."

"We must always be kind to him. As long as he lives."

"Yes. Kind."

"Are you afraid, Charlie?"

"Of taking care of an old man until he dies?" he laughed softly. "No, I'm not afraid, Laura."

Charlie felt five years younger when he woke the next morning. He hummed while he shaved. His undreamed-of good fortune caused him to look at himself in the mirror "Old pal," he said to his image, "you're going to be a rich man."

A feeling of love and respect for the old man surged up in Charlie. *When I spend that money,* Charlie thought, *I want it free and untainted. I want you to know that it's mine by right. I want to remember that I eased your last days, Father Emmons.*

The old man noticed the change. Two days later when Charlie brought him a box of his favorite sugar stick candy, the old man's eyes seemed to sink in even deeper depths, cloaked with caution.

They were in the old man's bedroom, the nice, sunny room. "Charlie," the old man said, "what are you up to?"

"I don't know what you mean, Father Emmons."

"This business of holding a chair for me, of calling me father, of bringing me stuff like this candy."

"Why, I. . . ."

"And no accidents, Charlie, for the last couple days."

"Accidents?"

"You know what I mean," the old man said softly. "Nothing in my food to make me sick. No hiding of my pills. No boxes on the basement stairs."

"Just accidents, that's all," Charlie said. "I hope you like the candy."

"Here," the old man said suspiciously, "you eat a piece of it."

Charlie stared at him. Then he took a stick of candy from the box.

"Not that one," the old man said, grabbing the candy away. "I'll eat this one." He pulled a piece from the box and thrust it at Charlie.

Charlie took a bite while the old man watched him closely.

"Is the candy good, Charlie?"

"Sure, but if I had your. . . ."

"What was that? You meant to say something, didn't you, Charlie. If you had my what? My what, Charlie? If you had my what?"

Charlie swallowed. "If I had your taste, I'd try some better candy."

"I like this candy," the old man said.

He remained standing there, just staring, until Charlie finally said awkwardly, "well, it's pretty good candy at that."

He went to his own room and closed the door. He leaned limply against it. The first misgiving since his talk with Laura came to him. *Already he suspects that I'm planning something . . . that I know about his money . . . that I'm going to kill him.*

Kill him.

Charlie put his hands over his ears, went in the bathroom, and took two aspirin. Through the small window, he saw the old man puttering in the backyard, nibbling at his stick candy.

Charlie was in the living room trying to concentrate on the newspaper when the old man came back in. The old man stood holding his candy. He was stringy inside his heavy sweater and baggy pants.

"Have some candy, Charlie."

"No, thanks, I. . . ."

"It's real good."

The overture seemed genuine enough. Charlie took a stick of candy, and the old man went to his room and closed the door.

Charlie carried the candy to the kitchen and dropped it in the garbage can.

"Dinner in a few minutes, Charlie," Laura said, busy at the stove.

"Sure," he said absently.

He stepped out of the kitchen, crossed the yard, opened the shop door, and clicked the light switch.

The small room was full of butane from the heater's open pet-cock. The electric spark and the butane produced a chemical reaction that sent the garage mushrooming into the twilight sky. A piece of the garage knocked down an antenna across the street. A woman in the next block went hysterical when she heard the explosion and screamed something about the Russians. Charlie had barely time for one last thought: "Old Man Emmons had it all worked out, blast him, but he's blasting me right out of his money!"

One woman can be the decisive majority if she's the right person at the right time. . . .

TEN

Jury of One

I knew right away that the district attorney wanted this Mrs. Clevenger on the jury.

Pretending to listen to my lawyer question a prospective male juror, the D. A. studied Mrs. Clevenger, sized her up out of the corner of his eye.

There was a dryness in my throat, a fluttering in my stomach—I was on trial for my life. Murder was a capital crime in this state, and they didn't use anything merciful and clean like a gas chamber. They made you take that last long walk and sit down in a chair wired for death.

It was a nice spring day. The tall windows of the vaulted courtroom were open, letting in a soft, lazy breeze. Speaking quietly and without hurry, the lawyers had been going about the business of picking a jury for a day and a half. The fat, bald judge looked sleepy, as if his thoughts were of trout streams. The whole thing so far had been casual, almost informal. I wondered, considering the difference this day and half had made inside of me, if I was going to be able to sit through the whole trial without screaming and making a break for one of the windows.

To get my mind off myself, I swiveled my head enough to take a new look at Mrs. Clevenger. She was well into middle age, her armor of girdles and corsets reminded me of a concrete pillbox. Her clothing, jewels, and the mink neckpiece draped carelessly over the arm of her chair all added up to a big dollar sign.

I looked at the heavy, blunt outlines of her face which even the services of an expensive cosmetician had failed to soften. You didn't have to know her; just looking at her would tell you she was rich, arrogant, selfish, merciless. Nothing, quite obviously, mattered to Mrs. Clevenger, except Mrs. Clevenger. And as she cast a passing glance in my direction, her eyes were beady and cold. There was no doubt about her being the kind of person who would have her way, no matter what.

I didn't like the way she glanced at me, but the D. A. did. He was the sort who could impress women easing past their prime. He had a tall, rangy, athletic build, a rugged face, sandy hair worn in a crew cut. He'd spotted Mrs. Clevenger already as the key juror, the one he would turn those open, warm, brown eyes on, the one he'd address his quiet, reasonable remarks to—if she were chosen. Win her, and he would have the jury. Win her, and the rest of the jury might as well try to move a mountain.

My lawyer finished his examination of the male juror. "He's acceptable to us, Your Honor," he said.

The judge stifled a yawn, nodded, plunked indolently with his gavel, and told the juror to step down.

Mrs. Clevenger was the next one to be up for examination. Mentally, I squirmed to the edge of my seat.

My lawyer came to the defense counsel table. His name was Cyril Abbott. His given name fitted him very well, perfectly. He was lanky, had a thin face which made his nose look like a big afterthought, carelessly stuck between drooping lips and narrow eyes. A gray thatch of unruly hair completed the rube picture. But if you looked closely into his eyes, you saw he was a tough old fox with wisdom garnered from countless legal battles.

As he shuffled some papers, Cyril Abbott said, "How you feeling, Taylor?"

"Not so good," I said.

"Relax. Everything's under control so far."

"It's getting Clevenger on the jury that's got me worried," I said.

I was more worried on that point than I was about the witness.

The witness had been one of those fluke things. The killing had looked perfectly routine, just another job, though a little out of my usual line.

It was the only time I'd taken on anything outside the Syndicate. I'd been with the Syndicate quite a number of years. I guess I'd grown to take the job for granted. I was never touched by the law. Few professionals are. We're given an assignment, flown into a strange city. Our man is pointed out to us. We choose an immediate time and place. We perform our service and are whisked out of town.

The Len Doty job had seemed simple. A scrawny, down-at-the-heels crook, he'd arrived here recently and taken up residence in a fourth rate hotel.

I'd studied Doty's movements for two days. A thin, harried, nervous man, he'd seemed to have a lot on his mind. He'd been under a strain, as if something big was imminent in his life.

I was the imminent something, only he didn't know it.

I'd tried to approach this job with the same lack of feeling I had on Syndicate jobs. But here I'd been doing my own planning, and not enjoying the security you had when you were a cog in a huge machine.

By the end of the two days, I knew I had to get the job done. I was feeling a growing nervousness. I didn't go for solitude. I wanted to be back in the big town, having a drink with men I knew or stepping out with a particular woman who was gaga over *my* tall, dark ranginess.

I'd kept the thought of fifteen grand—what Doty was worth dead—in the front of my mind. What could go wrong? It was the same as all the others, nothing to connect me with Doty. He'd die, and I'd disappear. The case would eventually slip into the local police department's unsolved file. There may be no perfect crimes, but the records are full of unsolved ones, and the record was good enough for me.

I decided on the time and place. Both nights, late, Doty went from his flea-bag hotel to a greasy spoon far down on the corner for a snack before retiring.

The block was long and dark, with an alley at its midpoint connecting the street with one that ran parallel to it. It's always wise to choose an alley that's open at both ends.

The parallel street was a slum section artery, crowded with juke joints, penny arcades, hash houses. In short, the kind of street to swallow a man up.

I knew the Syndicate big-shots had a rule of planning they tried never to break. Keep it simple.

I kept it simple. The plan was to shoot Doty with a silenced gun in the alley, walk to a garbage can, ditch the unregistered, wiped-clean gun, continue to the crowded street of joints, mingle, catch a city bus to the downtown area. There, I'd return to the good hotel where I'd registered under an alias, take a cab to the airport, and return to the big city fifteen grand richer.

Doty came from his hotel at the expected time. In the mouth of the alley, I listened to his footsteps on the dark street.

When he came abreast of the alley, I said, "Doty."

He stopped.

"Come here," I said, "I want to talk to you." I let him glimpse the gun.

He began to shake. He looked around frantically.

I pushed him twenty feet into the alley. He pleaded for his life.

The sound of the gun was a balloon popping. Doty's knees gave way, and he fell dead.

At that moment, the witness had screamed, long and loud as only a frizzy-headed blonde, in cheap clothes and makeup, can scream. She and her boy friend had decided on the alley as a short cut from one of the amusement places on the parallel street to the tenement where she lived.

Her boy friend was having none of it. He took off on the instant. The girl was right behind him, but just the same she'd glimpsed my face.

Two more balloons had popped in the alley, but in the darkness the shooting was bad. I'd missed her. Then I'd violated another Syndicate rule. I'd panicked—run straight out of the alley almost into the arms of a beat cop who'd heard the screams and was charging up for a look-see.

The cop was no sitting duck. He was big and fast—and armed.

I dropped the silenced pistol and held both my hands up as high as they'd go.

The Syndicate of course had never heard of me. I'd put myself out on the limb. Still, I had dough to hire Cyril Abbott. First day he'd come to jail to see me, he'd asked how much the job had paid. I'd had sense enough to say ten grand. He'd taken the whole ten and told me not to worry.

It was like telling me not to breathe. Maybe a lawyer as foxy as Abbott could cast some doubt on the blonde's testimony. After all, the alley had been pretty dark. I'd faced the street glow only briefly. And everything had happened awfully fast.

The big question—to me—was whether or not this overbearing old lady Clevenger qualified to sit on the jury.

The D. A. buttered her up with those boyish, friendly brown eyes. "Your name please?"

"Mrs. Clarissa Butterworth Clevenger."

"You're an American citizen?"

"Of course."

"Do you have any moral or religious convictions against capital punishment which would disqualify you to sit on a jury in a capital case in this state?"

"None whatever, young man."

I reached for a handkerchief to wipe my face. In my mind I reviewed what little I'd heard of Mrs. Clarissa Butterworth Clevenger. She had lived here twenty years, meeting and marrying one of the town's leading citizens when he was on a Florida vacation. Abbott had mentioned that she'd been boldly, strikingly beautiful in those days, before time, luxury, and her inner self broadened the beam and altered the surface. Her husband had been fifteen years her senior. Three years ago he'd died in a private hospital after a long illness.

The D. A. gave her a considerate smile that silently said he disliked putting a lady of her position through a nonsensical routine. "Do you have any opinions already formed regarding this case, Mrs. Clevenger?"

"None."

"Do you know the defendant, Max Taylor?"

She looked down her nose at the D. A. "Hardly."

"Of course. But this is all necessary, Mrs. Clevenger."

"I quite understand. Get on with it, young man."

"I think we need go no further," the D. A. said. He turned toward the judge. "Your Honor, we find the juror acceptable."

The judge nodded. "Counsel for the defense may question the juror."

Cyril Abbott shuffled a few steps toward the Bench. He stood with that country bumpkin slump and scratched his gray tangle. "Your Honor, I guess the District Attorney has asked the important questions. I don't see any grounds for disqualification of the juror. The Defense accepts her."

I stared at Abbott's slouching back for a moment. Then I sagged in my chair and let a hard-held breath break from my lungs.

As Abbott turned to face me, I'm sure he controlled an urge to wink. For a second I was almost sorry I'd lied to him, hadn't given him the whole fifteen grand.

I don't know what Mrs. Clevenger was before she married old man Clevenger, when she made that trip to a dazzling vacation land in a tropical clime. I don't know what Len Doty had on her when he came looming out of her past. It must have been plenty to cause her to spend a young fortune seeking out a trustworthy name—my name—and making the arrangements to get rid of him.

I'd never know that part of it, and I didn't care. I did know that there was only one thing she could do now, if she didn't want me singing my head off.

I knew how great it was going to be, getting back to the city and telling the boys how I'd been tried with my own client on the jury.

While Judy and Davie planned their perfect crime, they never expected how little their efforts would net them. . . .

ELEVEN

Heist in Pianissimo

Judy put her hands over her ears. "I won't hear another word of it, Davie! We're not criminals, you know."

In the moonlight beside the lake, she was a lovely, petite brunette. I took quick steps after her as she flounced her skirt and moved toward my jalopy, which was parked nearby.

"Okay, okay," I said. "Just pretend I never opened my big mouth."

I held the door for her to get in the car.

"The very idea, Davie, the two of us robbing the bank! Why, we come from decent, respectable backgrounds. We've never had a mark against us, even when we were in our teens. We're about the last pair of young people anybody in town would associate with a bank robbery."

I went around the car and got in. "I know," I said. "So forget it, will you?"

She sneaked a look at me as I started the car, turned it around, and headed back toward town.

"Davie . . ." she said in the murmuring tone that indicated a mountain of thought behind a single word. Davie anticipated it.

"Uh-huh?"

"Whatever gave you the thought?"

"Oh, I don't know. Just wishing you and I could make with life while we're still young, I guess. Maybe it was looking at old man Peterson, your boss at the bank, or Mr. Harper at the hardware store. Tomorrow morning, for example, they'll be standing not six inches from the spot where they started standing thirty or forty years ago."

"Both our bosses are nice people, Davie. They've bought homes, raised families. . . ."

". . . And seen the same faces, talked the same talk, moved through the same routine day after day. They might as well be vegetables, Judy. One day or a million days adds up to the same for them. Because they've never lived. They've just existed in a kind of vacuum. Now it's too late for them. A few more years of the same malarkey and they'll be planted out in a marble orchard and somebody else will have moved into their same dull spots."

"It's best not to think about those things, Davie."

"Sometimes you can't help it," I said. "Not if there is somebody special that you want special things for."

She reached forward and turned on the car radio loud enough to drown out my voice. But we'd ridden less than half a mile when she turned it down again.

"Now mind you, Davie," she murmured. "I'm not planning on doing anything so crazy, but wouldn't it be wonderful if we woke up tomorrow morning or the next day and had fifty or sixty thousand dollars?"

"That's what I tried to point out, there at the lake," I said. "It isn't like we were turning into pathological criminals. We just do this one thing. We keep right on about our business until the furor over the robbery dies down. Then I tell Mr. Harper one day that I've got an offer of a job in California. We get married. Our friends give us a going-away party. We promise to write, but somehow we never do. You know how those things go.

"A few years from now, we won't even remember what this grubby mill town looks like. Instead, we'll have bought a business of our own, worked hard, and retired by the time we're thirty-five. Then we swim in Miami Beach, or play golf in Pasadena.

"I sure don't intend to squander the money, Judy. Just a break, the opportunity to get started, to make it for ourselves while we're young, that's all I was thinking about. It's no worse than the old financial barons who conspired to take oil lands from the Indians, or who entered political deals to use public domain for railroad right of way."

I peeped at her without turning my head, and sighed. "'Course, I guess it was wishful thinking, like we all do at times, and I'm sorry I brought it up."

"It would be nice," Judy said. "Yes, it really would."

"If we had a kid or two, we could give them a decent chance, too."

We rolled through the edges of town, toward Judy's house. Suddenly, she reached and touched my hand. "Don't make the turn, Davie. I don't feel like going in. Let's go to the Jiffyburger and have a sandwich and a malt."

"Okay," I said.

At the drive-in, I found a spot not too close to other cars. We munched on hamburgers without saying anything for a while.

Then Judy stirred in her seat as if her muscles were cramped. "Davie. . . ."

"Uh-huh?"

"It's true that about seventy-five thousand dollars will be in my cage Friday, because of the Landers Mills payday and all their payroll checks."

"I know," I said, "it's one thing that got me thinking."

"Well, I'm certainly not taken with your thieving ideas, Dave Hartshell! But . . . just making believe . . . how would you get the money out of the bank without the guard arresting you before you reached the front door?"

I slouched in the seat and took a big pull at my malt straw. "Oh, I'd pull the heist in pianissimo."

"In what?"

"Pianissimo, Judy. That's a music term. It means very softly. I'd take the money so softly the guard would smile as he held the door for me to leave the bank."

She pulled upright, leaned over to have a closer look at me.

"Davie, how would you go about keeping a bank robbery pian-whatever-it-is."

"I'd prepare the Friday morning deposit from the store a little earlier than usual," I said. "I'd bring it over to the bank just like always, in the leather and canvas money satchel.

"I'd pass the deposit over to you, Judy, like any other morning. Only when you got all through, I'd stroll out of the bank with the satchel crammed with the biggest denomination bills in your cage."

She jerked erect, bumping her head on the top of my jalopy. "Of all the nerve, Davie! Asking me to risk my reputation, everything. . . ."

"You wouldn't risk a thing, honey," I said. "All the tune's in harmony, like in pianissimo. We fix up a note in advance, printed with crayon on a sheet of dime store paper, which we're careful not to get any fingerprints on. Except yours. You'll have to handle it."

"Davie, I do believe you've taken to secret drinking!"

"Just an occasional beer," I said. "This note, which you'll carry into the bank with you Friday morning, says, 'Hand over the money or I'll kill you on the spot.'

"After I'm out of the bank a half hour or so and the place starts getting crowded, you let the note flutter to the floor. Then you keel over in a real bad faint."

She was to the point now where she stared at me like she was helpless to move her eyes.

"I faint," she said finally.

"And right at first when you come around," I said, "you're kind of vague. Then it begins to come back to you. You get excited, and scared, and darn near hysterical. Since I'm young, slender, and dark, you ask them if they caught the middle-age, medium-built, ruddy man. Then they have found the note on the floor of your cage, and they say, 'Which man?' And you say, 'He slipped his coat open to show me a gun he was carrying. I put the money in a sack he handed to me. He slipped it under his coat. I tried to raise the alarm, but a terrible, empty blackness was rolling over me.'"

"A terrible, empty blackness," Judy said.

"You're the one girl I know who can really cool it, Judy. Then you leave it lay at that point. Not too complicated. Not too much description."

"There's just one thing wrong with it, Davie. You remember the bank robbery a few months ago over in Conover?"

"Sure, That's what gave me the idea of. . . ."

"The teller had to take a lie detector test, Davie. It's routine. They've anticipated the kind of thing you're planning."

"And I have anticipated *them*, doll," I said, feeling pretty good at the moment.

"Have you really?" Her voice was cool, and just a little pitying.

I didn't let the womanish attitude nettle me. Merely patted her small, sweet hand. "That's where Mr. Eggleston comes in," I said.

"Eggleston?"

"An old gentleman I met in the Wee Barrel."

"Davie! I've practically *begged* you to stay out of that tavern on your way home from work!"

"This Eggleston is quite a guy," I said, warming to the subject. "Neat, unobtrusive man, with impeccable clothes. Never see him with a gray hair out of place."

"Well, I don't care to know any of the hangers-on in the Wee Barrel." Judy stuck her nose in the air. After a few seconds, it lowered slightly. "When did you fit him into your plan?"

"After I found out he'd once been a metaphysical therapist in Los Angeles."

"Sounds like he was a quack."

"But definitely, Judy. They finally ran him out of town. He's also rigged stock deals, sold salted mines, and headed up drives to raise funds for non-existent charities."

"You seem to know him quite well, Davie," she said, a note of warning in her voice.

"Yeah, we got to be pretty close friends after he found out my girl friend worked in the bank."

"I guess you'll have to get the rest of it out of your system before you start the car, Davie. And it's too far for me to walk home."

"This Eggleston," I said, "when he was in the business of treating nervous and emotionally troubled people, he used a lot of hypnotism. He's really great with it, Judy. You should see some of the stunts he pulls in the Wee Barrel. One night he gave Shorty Connors the post-hypnotic suggestion to stand on his head. And darned if Shorty didn't try to upend himself five minutes after he came out of the trance, just like Eggleston had told him."

"I begin to see the light," Judy said thinly.

"Sure, hon. That silly lie detector machine won't mean a thing. You'll face it under the influence of post hypnotic suggestion. The cops will hunt a non-existent robber and never suspect that. . . ."

"I," she said, "am not the slightest bit interested."

She called me at seven-thirty the next morning, a half-hour earlier than usual.

At five-thirty that afternoon, we entered Mr. Eggleston's hotel room together.

Mr. Eggleston made a small bow when I introduced him. "David, she is every bit as lovely as you stated. It is indeed a pleasure to know you, my dear Judy. May I call room service and get you anything? Perhaps an aperitif?"

"No, thanks."

"No need to be nervous, my dear. The process is painless. You will in fact, feel more relaxed than you have in quite a while."

"Let's just get it over with," Judy said, worrying her small handbag in her hands.

"Quite."

Mr. Eggleston crossed the room, partially closed the blinds, and motioned toward a big easy chair.

Judy sat down like she was forcing her knees to bend. Mr. Eggleston stood smiling and quiet before her.

"To be wholly successful, my dear, I must have your total cooperation. Put yourself in my hands completely."

Judy gulped slightly. I thought she was going to back out. But she must have thought of all the money that would be in her teller's cage tomorrow.

Mr. Eggleston's manner was gentle and comforting. He drew a light occasional chair close to her and sat down. From his pocket, he took a shiny piece of metal about the size of a quarter.

"Focus your eyes on the coin, Judy, and blank your mind. . . .

Relax completely. . . . Offer no resistance. . . . It is so pleasant to relax. . . ."

He continued to talk soothingly. Judy's lids began to droop.

"You are sleepy, my dear. . . . So gently and delightfully sleepy. . . . Sleep. . . . You are going to sleep. . . . How pleasant to sleep. . . . You are asleep, Judy . . . deeply asleep . . . very deeply, Judy."

Mr. Eggleston began to draw away from her slowly. "You are in a deep, deep trance, Judy. You will remain in this trance until I count to three and snap my fingers."

My throat was starting to get a little dry. I evenly shifted from one foot to the other.

Mr. Eggleston glanced at me. "She's a most interesting subject, David. A very wonderful subject. Proof of her intelligence. The moron cannot be hypnotized, you know."

He returned his attention to Judy. "When at last I count to three and snap my fingers, Judy, you will awaken from the trance immediately. Your conscious mind will remember nothing. To your conscious mind it will seem as if you have merely drifted off for a few seconds. But your subconscious will retain everything that is done during the trance to prepare you psychologically and physiologically for what is ahead. Is all this clear?"

"Yes, it is." Judy's voice was so everydayish and normal that I wondered for a second if she was faking the trance. But I knew better. There'd be no point in it. And I remembered how natural Shorty Connors had sounded while Mr. Eggleston had him under.

"Now, Judy," Mr. Eggleston said, "there are a few things we must understand and make clear at the outset. There is nothing magical or supernatural in what we are doing. I can merely assist you. I cannot force you to do anything which you are absolutely determined not to do. For example, I could not force you to remove your clothing in the public square unless you had, in the secret depths of your personality, an exhibitionist urge to do such a thing. Do you understand?"

"Yes."

"If you could stretch a moral point and obtain a great deal of money without injuring anyone, would you do so?"

"Why not?"

"Would you tell a straight-out lie for ten dollars?"

"No."

"A hundred dollars?"

Judy didn't hesitate. "No."

"A thousand dollars?"

Judy hesitated.

"Fifty thousand dollars?" Mr. Eggleston persisted.

Judy rushed the answer: "Any day in the week! Just any old day!"

Mr. Eggleston glanced at me with a satisfied smile, which I returned rather weakly while wiping beads of perspiration from my face.

Then Mr. Eggleston returned to his subject: "Judy, since you are a bright and intelligent girl, I'm sure you know the basic principle of the lie detector. When a person tells a lie, he or she experiences a slight rise in pulse rate, heart beat, blood pressure. The graph registers these changes and the operator of the machine determines if a person has told the truth."

"I understand," Judy said.

"Good. The reason for these physiological changes lie in the psyche, the subconscious. Mind over matter, so to speak."

"I understand," Judy repeated.

"But that is a two-way street, my dear. Isn't it? If the subconscious can control the pulse rate, the subconscious can also ignore it. Tomorrow you will tell a lie in police headquarters. Your conscious mind will recognize it as a lie. But to your subconscious, in that instant, it will not matter: That is the whole crux of the thing, Judy. It's simple. Very simple. Your subconscious will not care one whit whether or not you have told a lie on that single subject." Mr. Eggleston's voice became a soft, but insistent lash. "Your subconscious will experience a momentary moral lapse when you describe the man who robbed the bank. Hence, you will exhibit none of the physiological symptoms for the graph to record. Repeat after me, Judy: It will not matter whether I am lying about the description of the bank robber."

"It—will—not—matter—"

"You must accept this thought in such a way as to be comfortable, Judy. Are you comfortable?"

"Yes."

"Good. Now we shall awaken. One . . . two . . . three. . . ."

I started slightly when his fingers snapped.

Judy opened her eyes, gazed at me blankly a moment, then looked at Mr. Eggleston.

He was paying her no attention. "David, tomorrow night at ten, I shall call at your rooming house for the five thousand dollars you've agreed to pay me."

Judy said, "I must have dozed off a second. When do we begin with this hypnotism?"

"We have finished with it," Eggleston smiled.

She frowned. "Is that true, Davie?"

I nodded.

"But I don't feel any different," Judy said. "Are you sure?"

"Postively," Mr. Eggleston said. He patted me on the shoulder. "And it's a brilliant idea, my boy, one I might have come up with myself!"

I woke the next morning, Friday, with about two hours total sleep during the preceding night. My stomach was jerky, and I nicked myself while shaving. I had a cup of coffee for an indigestible breakfast.

I walked around the block twice, waiting for the hardware store to open. Inside, I had the bank deposit prepared in record-breaking time. I had to kill several minutes arranging a display of fishing gear for the simple reason that I didn't think it wise to be the very first customer in the bank.

Feeling as if every eye in the grubby factory town was focused on me, I forced myself past the glass and brass doors of the bank. The guard, Mr. Sevier, was looking directly at me.

Normally, Mr. Sevier appears to me as a kindly middle-aged man with an elfin sort of face and tufts of white hair in his ears. Today, he grew horns; his skin was a threatening purple; there was brimstone in his slitted eyes.

"Good morning, Mr. Sevier."

"Nice to see you, Davie." He slapped me on the back as I passed.

Behind her teller's wicket, Judy gave me a warm smile. She appeared to have slept quite well, and I wondered if maybe I shouldn't have let Mr. Eggleston put me under also.

I handed the heavy leather and canvas bag to Judy. She opened it, checked the deposit.

Nobody paid any attention to my lingering at Judy's window. There was just enough early business to keep the other employees occupied. Anyhow, everyone in the bank knew that Judy and I were collecting pennies in a joint account toward the day we could be married.

With a nod that no one else noticed, she finally returned the satchel to me.

My heart started going like sixty. I felt as if the weight of the bag were pulling me to one side, making me walk out of the bank at a crazy angle.

I was almost at the doors when Judy called my name quietly.

I had to stop right beside Mr. Sevier.

"Don't forget lunch, Davie," Judy said.

"I won't."

She blew me a little kiss. Mr. Sevier chuckled fondly as he gave me a little punch on the shoulder.

I went to the parking lot half a block away and collapsed in my car.

I tugged my collar with my finger, got a lungful of air, started the car, and drove casually to the hardware store. By the time I parked behind the store, I'd transferred the money to the heavy brown paper bag and stuffed it under the seat of the car. I was practically twitching with nervous eagerness to count the money. Driving along with commonplace innocence, the important work taking place with my free hand below window level, I'd caught only glances of the neatly banded money. But I knew there was plenty. I'd never seen so many stacks of fifties and hundreds in one place in all my life—except in the bank. I was certainly grateful to Landers Mills for paying but twice a month, on the first and fifteenth.

I started to lock the car, then decided against it. So far, everything was perfect. I'd driven directly from the bank, in plain view of the town. Judy and I were experiencing a routine, commonplace day. I wasn't in the habit of locking the jalopy this time of year. The money was safely out of sight. I went into the store.

Fortunately, there were customers to help pass the morning. Even so, I had to make three trips to the gent's room inside of an hour.

Then at ten fifty-six by the clock on the far wall, which had a pendulum behind a fly-specked front that advertised Maney's Merrygrow Manure, the waiting was all over.

Like a well-fed, full-bosomed turkey with a gray topknot, Mrs. Threckle came to the door of the office, spoke my name, and motioned to me frantically.

I hurried to her. "What is it, Mrs. Threckle?"

"Terrible thing . . . ." she gasped, "terrible . . . a bank robbery. . . . They've got Judy at police headquarters . . . ."

I had to grab the office door framing to keep from folding to the floor like a collapsing letter Z. This part wasn't an act, either. I thought wildly: They've caught her, and she's trying to protect me, going it alone. . . .

"You poor, dear boy!" Mrs. Threckle said. "You must get down there right away. I'll explain to Mr. Harper."

I could think of several other directions more preferable. Then Mrs. Threckle saved me from a nervous breakdown.

"She hasn't been hurt, Davie. There was no shooting. They've merely taken her down to get a description of the robber."

Several minutes later, a jalopy full of holdup money was parked in plain view in front of police headquarters. Inside the building there was turmoil. Each time I tried to stop a hurrying policeman, he would jerk his thumb over his shoulder, pointing deeper into the building. "Busy, bud."

Finally I spotted old Silas Garth ambling placidly from a doorway.

Silas has been on the force just about as long as the town has had a charter. He paused in the corridor, more intent on picking something from his teeth than picking up a bank robber.

"Mr. Garth. . . ."

"Oh, hello there, Davie. Guess you're looking for Judy."

"Yes, sir. Is she. . . ."

"Simmer down, son. She's fine. Come on back in the squad room and we'll have a game of checkers until Hoskins and Crowley and that lie detector technician are through with her."

Poor Judy, I thought. Going through hell, that's what.

"What happened, Mr. Garth?"

He shrugged as we walked down the corridor together. "Yegg came walking in, let Judy have a peep at a gun, gave her a second to read the note he shoved in her hand, and walked back out with about sixty-five thousand dollars in a brown paper bag."

"Yowie!" I yelped. "Sixty-five thou. . . . Is there that much money in the world?"

"Shore is, Davie. And I'm feared this hoodlum made it out of town."

"How come you say that, Mr. Garth?"

"Judy—bless her darling heart—was so paralyzed with fright she couldn't give the alarm right away. And when she realized she was in no danger of the gun, she fainted dead away."

"But you said she was fine!"

He laid his hand on my arm. "She is now, Davie. Take it easy, will you?"

"Was she able to give them a description of the robber?"

"General is all. Middle-aged, ruddy, medium height, sort of heavy set. My opinion is, he's an old pro at the robbery game, Davie."

"How come you say that, Mr. Garth?"

The old man started putting checkers in their proper squares on a board that rested on a rickety card table. "We got ways of lifting prints nowadays from surfaces like paper. The note he handed Judy had no prints on it but hers. Reckon he knew his prints would identify him." Mr. Garth shook his head. "Be frank with you, Davie, lots of these yeggs get away with it, at least for one or two outings."

"You don't think they'll catch him?"

"I wouldn't make book on it, son. His chances decrease all the time, of course. Next time out, he may get caught and we'll break our case then."

"Mr. Garth, if you don't mind, I couldn't keep my mind on a checker game right now."

"Sure, Davie." He flung his arm about my shoulders. "We'll go upstairs, son, and see if we can't make it easier on that poor girl."

We went upstairs, and I sought a gent's room while Mr. Garth disappeared into an office. I was pacing the corridor when he opened the office door and came out behind Judy.

She ran straight to me, and I folded her in my arms.

Mr. Garth clucked affectionately. "Judy didn't stretch none of the details of the description, according to the polygraph, Davie. Now you take that girl down the street and buy her a cup of coffee."

I said, "Yes, sir, Mr. Garth!"

Judy and I were still slightly delirious when Mr. Eggleston knocked on my door at ten o'clock that night.

He slipped in quickly, and I closed the door. He looked from me to Judy, a smile dividing his lean, hawkish face.

"Well, kids, we pulled it off!"

"We sure did, Mr. Eggleston, and your five thousand dollars is ready for you."

His eyes went frigid. He pulled a short-nosed gun from his side coat pocket.

"Wh-what is this, Mr. Eggleston?" It was the real thing.

"I've waited all my life for the really big one," he said. "Do you think I'd let a couple of hick kids stand in my way? Now get the money!"

"But Mr. Eggleston. . . ."

"All of it! Now! If it hasn't occurred to you, none of us can squeal without implicating himself."

I was unable to move or think for a second. "But if you shoot that gun, Mr. Eggleston, somebody will hear it."

"And you'll be dead. I'm offering you a deal, Davie. Two lives for the money."

"You're crazy," I said.

"No—and don't let the money destroy your sanity, kid. If I shoot the gun, I'll have a good chance of getting away. You won't have any chances, period. I'm willing to make the gamble, Davie. I'm too old, I've waited too long to let this final chance slip away from me."

His cheekbones began to turn white, and he added: "I'll give you ten seconds to make up your mind, David."

I didn't know Judy had risen. Now I felt her pressing against me. She shivered. "Davie . . . he is a little mad. He means it!"

"Sure I do," Eggleston said cold-bloodedly. "Six . . . five . . . four . . . three. . . ."

"Give him the money, Davie," Judy sobbed, holding onto me wildly.

"In the closet," I said numbly. "The small valise."

Everything around me had a kind of swimming quality. Mr.

Eggleston floated to the closet, the valise floated to his hand. He flipped the catch, peeked quickly inside, pressed it closed with his left hand. The gun still on us in his right hand, he floated out the door.

Judy didn't have to work the next day, it being Saturday. I called the store and reported I was too sick to work.

But I was there bright and early Monday morning. There's no better way to impress an employer than being prompt, when you finally decide you're going to be stuck in a job for a mighty long time.

While gratitude is a noble quality, when too great a demand is made of it other feelings easily take over. . . .

TWELVE

Lone Witness

Marco tingled with excitement and pure delight when Timothy Watkins came to him in a moment of extreme trouble. Marco didn't reveal these feelings. Instead, he ushered a disheveled Timothy into his apartment on a drizzly midnight with a show of concern and sympathy that appeared genuine.

After all, he and Timothy were supposed to be friends. Timothy's money, purchasing a chunk of Marco's foundering business, had bailed Marco out of deep financial difficulty. And like a true friend and honest man, Timothy had come straight to Marco when it appeared Miss Sharon Randall, a lovely brunette, preferred him over Marco.

When he opened his door on the man whom he secretly hated, Marco took in Timothy's appearance at a glance. Timothy was wet and muddy. His face had lost all color. His eyes were glazed, stricken, not quite in complete touch with reality.

Timothy, Marco knew, had had a dinner invitation from Miss Randall. Marco had spent the evening seething at the thought of the two of them alone in the intimate seclusion of her lakeside cottage.

A big, expansive sham of a man, Marco helped Timothy to the couch.

Timothy began mumbling a garbled apology. "No one else I could think of—had to tell someone; better leave. . . ."

Timothy started to rise, but Marco pushed him back. "No nonsense, now," Marco said. He was so eager to know the nature of Timothy's trouble he would have locked the door to keep him here. "You did exactly right. Just relax and tell me what it's all about."

Timothy was incapable of relaxing. Marco crossed the room to the buffet, poured a stiff drink, and brought it to Timothy, who gulped gratefully, shuddered the liquor down straight, and a bit of color came to his face.

"Marco," he said in a whisper of suffering, "I've killed a man."

"What!"

"A stranger. A man I never saw before. Never knew he was there, hardly, until the car hit him."

All the bitterness went out of the evening, as far as Marco was concerned. He put on a front of gravity and trouble. He dropped beside Timothy and put his hand on the wiry, sandy man's shoulder.

"Better tell me about it from the beginning, Timothy."

Timothy was miserably reluctant. "I don't want to involve. . . ."

"More nonsense," Marco said, giving him a slight shake. "What are friends for, anyway?"

Timothy's need was so great and Marco so kind and understanding that Timothy's slate-gray eyes misted. "Miss Randall and I . . . We had cocktails before dinner and a couple drinks afterward. I left there pleasantly mild. Not drunk, but not completely sober either. Not knowing that a man's life would be in my hands. . . ." He closed his eyes and shivered briefly.

"You were returning home from Miss Randall's, Timothy?"

"Yes, driving along, thinking of her, of our evening. I saw the truck stop at the intersection far ahead. It pulled away, and I know now that the driver had let a hitchhiker out. The truck was going no closer to town than the intersection. The hitchhiker was headed on this way.

"I—I didn't see him until I was through the intersection. He was just there, all of a sudden. On the edge of the road, flagging me for a ride.

"I slammed on the brakes and the car skidded slightly. Felt like it was going to flip over. I hadn't realized how fast I'd been driving.

"I jerked the steering wheel. The car slewed off the edge of the pavement, and I heard a bump, exactly like cold metal slapping meat and bone.

"When I managed to get the car stopped, I got out but I didn't see the hitchhiker. It was as if he'd been a mirage in the rainy night, an impression of a thin, slightly stooped guy in jeans and out-at-the-elbows jacket.

"Remembering the sound of that bump, I began to shake all over, I tell you! I grabbed the flashlight from the glove compartment, ran up the road. . . ."

"And found him?"

"Yes," Timothy mourned, his head in his hands. "In a thicket down the embankment beside the road, his head all bloody—I knew he must be dead."

"How did you know? Did you go down and examine him?"

Timothy lifted his head slowly. "No, I—come to think of it, the sight of so much blood—I panicked, I guess. Don't remember anything else clearly until I got here. But he couldn't have been alive with his head battered so badly."

"Did you leave any traces of yourself out there, anything that might link you to him?"

"I—I don't know," Timothy said.

"Then we'll have a look."

"Marco, I don't want to drag you in. . . ."

"Forget it," Marco said, keeping his face averted so Timothy wouldn't see the glint in his eyes. "We're business partners, aren't we?"

Timothy stood up slowly. "You know, I always had the feeling you really didn't like me. Deep down, I mean. Well, after all, you might have felt I stole your girl."

"Come now, Timothy, give me credit for being a bigger person than that."

The highway was a dark, deserted ribbon of slippery black. Timothy slowly stopped his car. "Right over there, Marco," he whispered, although there was no reason for keeping his voice so low. "Across the road. I was heading in the other direction, you know, toward town."

Marco's raincoat rustled as he shifted his bulk out of the car. He had the flashlight in his hand. "Leave the parking lights on, and if you see another car coming, get out and open the hood like you have car trouble."

"Marco. . . ."

"I know. You can thank me later."

Marco went quickly across the highway and started down the slope. He moved below highway level, the flashlight probing a rough, sparsely-grown landscape. His excitement grew higher. Surely, this was the opportunity of a lifetime. He'd get his business and his girl back. Once he went through the motions of friendship, he'd have to go, finally, to the cops, wouldn't he, before Timothy had a chance to move the body? He had conscience, didn't he? He was a law-abiding citizen, wasn't he?

The topping on the cake was the knowledge that if Timothy had played it cool he might have got away with it. Now, he never would.

Irritation began to crowd the elation in Marco. The finger of light became more hurried in its movements. Where in blazes was the guy, the dead man who would return to Marco everything Timothy had taken? The light swung across the heaviest of the thickets. Stopped. Returned.

Marco moved forward, holding the light steady. He cursed under his breath. Clearly, this was the place where the hitchhiker had landed, where Timothy had seen him. There were freshly broken twigs, an impression where a man's body had lain. The wet leaves had been disturbed where the hitchhiker had dragged himself away.

With a growing sense of having been cheated, Marco moved the light slowly. He could see exactly how the man had pulled himself around, groaned his way to his feet. A few feet beyond the thicket was a tattered, soiled handkerchief with a smear of blood on it. The guy had paused there to touch his wounds, steadying, feeling the return of strength.

Marco plunged forward, hoping the hitchhiker had collapsed. Marco's eyes and brain were hungry for the sight of the dead body.

But the hitchhiker had recovered and gone. Marco had to admit the fact. He finally stopped his search and stood overcome by the death of hope. Wouldn't you know it? Those stringy, bewhiskered bums and winos, you couldn't kill them with a meat-axe. A passing motorist had probably picked up the guy. Right now, the bum was no doubt dry and comfortable in a hospital charity bed. The cops would give cursory attention to his accident and invite him to get out of town.

"Marco?"

Marco raised his head. Timothy's shadow was visible up on the highway.

"Marco, what is it? Where are you?"

The sound of the hated voice at this moment put Marco's teeth on edge. He hadn't until tonight known how much he really wanted to remove Timothy, when for a little while it had seemed possible.

And then a thought came to Marco. Timothy had no way of knowing he was down here alone. Without turning on the flashlight, which he'd extinguished when he'd quit searching, Marco called softly, "Get back in the car, Timothy! Trying to attract the attention of anybody who happens to pass? You crazy or something? I'm coming right up."

Chastened, Timothy was under the wheel of the car when Marco returned.

"Let's get out of here, Timothy."

"What took you so long?"

"For pete's sake, I wasn't so long. It only seemed that way to you. I had to find the guy. And then I tried to figure something to do. Thought about moving him. Looked around for a place maybe to hide him."

"Then he's. . . ."

"Deader'n a burned out match, Timothy."

A sob came from Timothy as he hunched over the wheel.

"Look," Marco said, "I'm sorry."

"I'm a murderer, Marco."

"I wouldn't feel. . . ."

"Murderer," Timothy said. He suddenly beat on the steering wheel with the heel of his palm. "I'm a murderer—and the fact can never be changed."

"Hey, now get hold of yourself. We've got to think."

"One second," Timothy sobbed wildly, "I was a decent, law-abiding guy with a business interest and a girl. The next tick of the clock and I'm a killer, and nothing will ever make things exactly the same again."

Marco gripped him by the shoulders. "That's right, Timothy. You have to get used to the idea."

"Marco, I'm scared to face the police."

"No need for you to. Crazy if you do, Pal. You were drinking when you hit that guy. They'll really throw the book at you!"

Timothy shuddered and dropped his forehead on the rim of the steering wheel.

"But cheer up, Pal," Marco slapped him on the shoulder. "There's a way out."

"There is?"

"Sure. I'm going to help you, Timothy."

"How?"

"We'll go back to my apartment. I'll give you all the ready cash I've got. You'll have a long head start before that guy is found. They'll never find you."

"You mean—run away?"

"Any better ideas, Timothy?"

"But I'd lose my share of the business, my girl."

"There are other businesses, other girls. But you just have the next twenty years one time, Timothy. Of course, if you want to throw them away, along with the business and girl. . . ." Marco shrugged. "I'm trying to help you salvage what you can, that's all. I see no other way but for you to get going quick, go far, and never look back. And try not to take it so hard, Timothy. You're not the first guy to have a thing like this happen."

Timothy became quieter. He pulled himself erect, reached to the ignition key, and started the car. Marco was glad he had the cover of darkness to hide his elation.

They rode the self-service elevator up five flights to Marco's apartment. Marco let them in and turned on a light in the living room.

He gripped Timothy's bicep briefly. "Cheer up, Timothy. You'll start a new life under another name a thousand miles away, and all this will seem a bad dream. Now, I'll see how much cash I can rustle."

Timothy moved dully to the window and opened it. He drew in a deep breath of air. The rain had stopped. The night outside was clean tasting and very silent.

Marco returned. "Here's about five hundred bucks, Timothy. Not much, maybe, but used sparingly, it'll take you a long way."

Timothy took the money, looked at it as if he didn't quite realize what it was, and slipped it into his pocket. The lower portion of his face parted in a gray smile. "Murderer. . . ." he mused. "You know, Marco, once you get over the first shock of knowing you're a murderer, it changes your whole outlook."

"Just don't think about it, Timothy," Marco admonished him then.

"Why not? Once you've killed, then human life assumes a completely new value. Or should I say lack of value?"

Marco began to feel uneasy. "Timothy, you ought to use every possible minute to put as much distance. . . ."

"I hate to think of losing the business and my girl, Marco. Really I do, especially since there is only one thing that can definitely link me to the hitchhiker. The rain must have washed the tire tread marks from the shoulder of the road, and I can burn my shoes, in case I left footprints. That leaves just one thing, Marco. You, the lone witness."

Before Marco could speak, Timothy clipped him on the jaw. As he crumpled, Timothy took Marco's shoulders and directed his fall out the open window. Then he kicked back the throw rug from under the window, which made everything reasonably obvious. Timothy would agree with everyone that it had been most unfortunate for the rug to slip.

Once Ethel accepted her mission, she made sure she had what it took to see it through. . . .

THIRTEEN

Trial Run

The three-column heading leaped at Ethel Claridge the instant she unfolded the newspaper that morning:

MOTIVE SOUGHT IN SLAYING

"Would you ever!" Ethel lectured her silent kitchen. "Those nasty newspaper people, doting on death!"

She sank down at the table, blue eyes devouring the story:

A young man who police said was a model citizen was shot to death last night on Sheridan Avenue as he was returning home from the under-privileged youth center where he was a volunteer athletic coach.

Police said the youth's wallet and wristwatch were intact, and ruled out any known motive for the slaying of Allan Zeigler, 22, who resided with his parents, Mr. and Mrs. Edward Zeigler, at 1003 Sheridan Avenue.

Zeigler died instantly from brain damage inflicted by a .32-caliber bullet fired into the back of his head at close range, the medical examiner stated.

Preliminary investigation revealed that Zeigler left the Southside Juvenile Center at the closing hour of 10 o'clock, boarded a municipal bus, and got off at his usual stop six blocks from his home.

Taking charge of the case, Homicide Detective Lieutenant Thomas J. Heim said, "This should shock even a city calloused by violence and crime. Here was a fine young man quietly walking his street from the bus stop to home. Halfway, someone calmly steps up behind him and blasts the life from him with a small-bore pistol, apparently for the sick thrill of killing. But whatever the motive, this is an all-out case as far as this department is concerned."

As police activity and news of the shooting aroused the neighborhood, angered residents described Allan Zeigler as a young man without an enemy in the world, a capable athlete, and an outstanding student who recently graduated from State University and was working an interim daytime job before returning to the university for postgraduate studies toward a master's degree.

Zeigler's mother was taken to City Hospital where doctors reported her in shock and under heavy sedation.

Zeigler's distraught father was unable to provide police with the slightest clue.

"I don't understand. . . ." The elder Zeigler wept as he repeated the words endlessly. "He wasn't just a nice kid, he was a great guy. Everyone felt the same way about him. He liked people, and they liked him in return, respected and trusted him. . . . Those kids on the southside. . . . They'll miss him. We'll all miss him. . . . I just don't understand."

Engrossed in the story, Ethel didn't hear George, her husband, come into the kitchen. She started slightly as his shadow fell across her. She got up and turned toward the stove, clicking a burner to bring water to a boil for instant coffee.

George sat down and picked up the paper without saying good morning, rattling the sports pages open.

Ethel's lips parted on a long-suffering sigh as she separated strips of bacon and stretched then neatly on the broiling pan. She was a tall, strong, spare woman with sallow skin and thin brown hair shot with gray. Her faded blue eyes deepened as she stole a glance at George.

The years had had a curious effect on him. Other men aged; George rejuvenated. At twenty-eight, when she had maneuvered him into marriage, George had the stooped, hollow look of a refugee from a tubercular hospital. Today, the skeletal youth was but a memory. The years had fleshed his frame, filled out the shoulders and cheeks and chased the pallor with the ruddy glow of a robust and virile middle age. Even his drab, mouse-colored hair had gained vitality as the silver claimed it. This morning it was a handsome leonine mane, its tips curling with masculine shagginess from the dampness of his shower.

Looking at him, Ethel was torn by a pang of pity and regret. *But let the head rule, not the heart*, she thought. *The heart is a nest of trickery.*

The bacon was sizzling as she made George's coffee. Slipping the cup on the table beside his elbow, she asked conversationally, "Did you read about the murder, George?"

He rustled the pages to the real estate section. She retreated toward the stove.

"A nice young fellow was killed, George. Named Allan Zeigler. Do you know any Zeiglers?"

He glanced up with irritated eyes. "What? What did you say?"

"I wondered if you know anyone named Zeigler? You know a lot of the businessmen in town."

"Zeigler! There's a Zeigler wholesale paper company."

"Maybe that's Allan's father."

"Allan? Who in blazes is Allan?"

"I just told you, George. The young man who was murdered."

He grunted and flipped to the stock market reports.

Ethel broke a pair of eggs into a warm, buttery skillet. "He was twenty-two, the paper said. Just about the same age as Patti Warren."

Her words brought an unpleasant change to the room. She could feel him looking at her.

"You don't like the setup, you can get out," he said. "I'd welcome a suit for divorce."

"I know you would, George." She stared at the hardening whites of the eggs. "You've made that clear enough."

"Then why don't you have a little pride and quit hanging on this way?"

"Pride, George?" A short laugh gouged through her lips. "Would a divorce heal the terrible way you've wounded me? I took a vow, George—until death do us part."

She heard him fling the paper down and shove his chair back. "I don't care to listen to your broken record this morning, Ethel. I'll breakfast in town."

She flinched when the front door slammed behind him. He wouldn't be here for dinner, she knew. He would return late tonight, befouling the house with the mingled smell of alcohol and Patti Warren's perfume.

Ethel dumped the eggs and watched the disposal gobble them up.

After a breakfast of tea and English muffin, she continued the routine of yesterday, last month, of more years than she could remember: cleaning, dusting, scouring, waxing.

A mist fogged her eyes as she caught the vague, vagrant memory of how she used to hum as she went about her work. She fought the dizzying silence and emptiness of the house with a vigorous assault of her dust cloth on a drum table in the livingroom.

"My, you look nice, Table," she said, stepping back and admiring the soft sheen she'd protected and nurtured for so long. "I've a wonderful idea, Table. We'll dress you up with an arrangement of zinnias from the garden!"

She carried the cloth to the kitchen, washed it at the sink and hung it on the rack above the drain to dry. "There we are, Cloth, spotless as ever."

Glancing at the wall clock, she noted that she'd got rid of another morning. She breathed out a note of tiredness.

"Stove, should we make another cup of tea and rest a bit? Of course we should!"

When the tea was ready, she decided to have it in the den. She padded through the house, carefully balancing cup and saucer.

"Television, have you some news from a vulgar and heartless world? It's that time of day."

She clicked on the set and settled on the edge of the couch. The screen came to glowing life. She watched the last couple of minutes of a network game show. She finished her tea during the commercials. Then she set her cup on a low coffee table and leaned forward as the noontime local newscast came on.

Through the camera's eye, Ethel saw the place where Allan Zeigler had been murdered, the wide, tree-shaded street that looked so serene and secure.

The scene cut to an office in police headquarters, a physically powerful figure standing at a desk. The announcer identified him as Lieutenant Heim, Homicide. They discussed the case, Heim parrying questions cleverly and not revealing much more than the morning newspaper had reported.

Ethel studied Heim throughout the taped interview. Her opinion was expressed with an emphatic nod for this sturdy cut of a man, never the skinny weakling George had once been.

Heim's face was a collection of lumps and bone, but it came to Ethel, a flashing revelation, that the deep, Lincolnesque eyes were capable of tenderness. She was quite pleased with her insight.

"No one but a person with a deep, secret sensitivity of her own would ever see beyond what the mad-mad, rushing world sees," Ethel told the electronically-etched image.

She could imagine Heim's presence warmly filling a modest home when his working day was finished, kissing a happy wife, tumbling with roly-poly children. The images evoked in Ethel a bittersweet sense of being lost that was, somehow, strangely satisfying.

She dried her eyes with the cuff of her blouse, got up, and turned off the TV. Crossing the room, she picked up the phone. She dialed a number that had stamped itself into her mind the one and only time she'd looked it up.

The phone in a distant part of town was lifted. "Hello. Miss Warren's residence."

Ethel gritted her teeth, almost choking with nausea at the sound of the warm, feminine voice.

"Miss Warren, this is a friend," Ethel forced herself to speak quietly, levelly, "of Mr. Claridge. I . . . hate to break the news, but there's been an accident."

Ethel heard the girl—the hussy—catch a breath. "Is George . . . Mr. Claridge . . . badly hurt?"

"I'm afraid so. He's on his way to City Hospital in an ambulance. He was asking for you, begged me to let you know."

"C-can you tell me what happened?"

"He was crossing the street and a car swerved out of control. He needs you—dear—and will you get over there right away?"

"Sure," Patti Warren said in a voice tight with concern. "I'll leave right now. And thanks."

"Not at all, dear. Glad to do anything I can for George."

Ethel hung up, smiling. Then her face almost instantly resumed its grim, angular lines. She dialed George's office, speaking now with her nostrils clamped between her fingers. Her voice seemed to bounce from her sinus passages, disguising itself even from George.

"I'm a maid in Miss Warren's apartment building," she told him. "She fell down and got a nasty gash on the head. The doctor's on his way, but she's calling for you."

George had a moment of stunned shock. Ethel could imagine him bolting upright behind his desk.

"Don't let anything happen to her," he shouted. "Do everything you can for her until the doctor comes! Tell her I'll be right there!" He slammed the phone down with the energy of a leaping tomcat.

Ethel dialed a third number, ordering a taxi. The dispatcher assured her that he would have a cab at her door shortly.

She went from den to kitchen, moving with a vigor she hadn't felt in days. She lifted down her flour canister, opened it, and worked her hand down through the fluffy whiteness. She stirred a small snowy cloud of flour as she pulled a ring of keys from the hiding place. They were exact copies of George's keys.

Last Saturday, while he'd watched baseball on TV, she'd gone into the bedroom where his keys, wallet, book matches, and change lay in the bureau tray. She carried the keys to the neighborhood shopping center. Not knowing which key would fit Miss Warren's door, she'd cleverly had them all duplicated, returning George's set without him ever knowing she'd left the house.

The keys emitted a soft, cold tinkle as she dusted the remaining bits of flour from them over the sink. She turned as the door chimes sounded. Her brows lifted. The taxicab had certainly hurried.

Ethel moved from the kitchen, crossed the livingroom and opened the front door. "I have to get a thing or two from the bedroom and I'll be ready. . . ." Her stream of words evaporated, leaving her mouth hanging. Then her teeth clicked. "Why, you're not the taxi driver. You—You're the detective I read about and saw on TV. You're Lieutenant Heim."

He nodded, mirthless, mountainous, rocky. "Is this the George Claridge residence?"

"Yes, but whatever brings you—"

He was looking at her with such a heavy wisdom that her voice again broke off.

"I take it you're Mrs. Claridge?"

Ethel nodded.

"Does your husband own a .32–caliber pistol?"

Ethel looked at him carefully. The sunlight hurt her eyes. Her faded blue dress seemed to grow a size larger as she shriveled inside.

"Please step in, Mr. Heim. There's no need exposing all this to the neighbors."

He took off his hat in the livingroom, and she closed the door quietly. She looked about the room as if it were strange to her. "It's been so long since anyone but George came into this house. . . . Would you like some tea?"

"No, thank you, Mrs. Claridge."

"Would you like to tell me about it?"

"Why not?" he said. "That's why I came, isn't it? These clueless cases. . . . Sometimes when they start to crack, they break wide open. Last night the crack of the small-bore pistol that killed young Zeigler went almost unnoticed. Almost. But one young woman heard it. She looked from her bedroom window not far away."

"Did she see the murderer, Mr. Heim?"

"Yes, as a shadowy figure. And the car. She saw the murderer get into a car and drive away. She had run out on the lawn by that time and as the car passed a street light, she got a piece of the license number."

Ethel sank stiffly on a chair and stared at a worn place in the carpet that was a dreadful dust-catcher.

"The license had an initial that in this state indicates vehicles used for rental purposes." Heim's voice seemed to ooze from floor, walls, ceiling. "From then on it was routine. Checking the auto rental places in town, eliminating the cars and renters one by one—until we came to a set of circumstances that filled every requirement of the situation."

Heim took a side step, trying to look into Ethel's face. "No wonder young Zeigler didn't try to run or put up a fight. When he heard footsteps behind him and glanced over his shoulder, all he saw was a harmless-looking middle-aged woman."

"George had the gun for a long time," Ethel said. "He kept it in the bedroom, the way a lot of people do. I guess he'd about forgotten it was there. It looked like a toy when I first practiced with it in the basement."

She looked up at last. Her bland, blue eyes were dilated, her mouth pinched at the corners. "George was going to find out too—about the gun not being a toy, I mean. I was on my way to get my hat, purse, and the gun when you rang. I had it all planned and timed. I was going to Patti Warren's apartment while she was on a wild-goose chase to the hospital and let myself in. Fighting cross-town traffic, George would be longer getting there. When he burst in, filled with fears for his adulteress, I was going to shoot him. Shoot him, and leave, and let her come back to find him dead, a memory her depraved mind would hold for a long time to come. And I knew then that I could do it, too. I could see it through."

"But why young Zeigler last night, Mrs. Claridge?" Bewilderment stamped Heim's face with a dullard's look. "Wasn't he a total stranger? Why did you take the gun and rent a car and drive around until you spotted the first person you thought it would be safe to kill?"

"Really, Mr. Heim, I thought you were smarter than that!" She looked at him with mild disappointment as she explained. "The boxer trains. The soldier practices with live ammunition. Each prepares and conditions himself for his ultimate act."

As her meaning slipped through, Heim stood rooted, frozen. He stared in unwilling belief.

She reached and patted his hand, humbly, gently, as if she'd found an understanding friend at last. "I'm glad you see the necessity for a trial run," she said gratefully. "I didn't know how I'd react to the impact of murder. I wasn't at all sure I could see it through—the killing of George, I mean—without some prior conditioning and practice. After all, he's been my husband for a long time, and I had to know I wouldn't get cold feet and panic when George was only half-way dead. . . ."

After frail Miss Nettie had determined to avenge the murder of her sister Lettie, she concocted the ingredients of a perfect revenge. . . .

FOURTEEN

Stranger's Gift

Detective Shapiro took a personal interest in the case from the start. He was mildly surprised by his reaction. A man doesn't stay on the police force for twenty-five years without developing the inner armor necessary for the protection of his own spirit. He had dealt with just about every act of violence the human mind could conceive, and prior to the murder of one of the elderly twins, he believed that he could handle any case with detachment.

Perhaps it was the quiet bravery of Miss Nettie, the surviving twin, that got through to him; or maybe in her gracious and fragile personage he glimpsed the last fragments of a genteel world that existed only in memory or storybooks.

Be that as it may, he was not altogether the tough cop when he escorted Miss Nettie home from the hospital, where emergency measures had failed to keep life from leaking from her sister's skull.

The headlights of his unmarked car picked through a neighborhood of large, once-fine homes now suffering the blight of urban decay. The present dreary reality was one of converted apartment and rooming houses, a junky filling station on a corner, faded signs offering rooms to let, a gloomy little grocery store secured for the night with iron-grille shutters.

With Miss Nettie's tea-and-crumpets presence beside him, it was easy for Shapiro to imagine the street as it had been in forgotten days: well-trimmed hedges, houses proud with paint, limousines and roadsters in the driveways, people enjoying the evening cool in porch swings; here or there a house blazing with light and the activity of a party, with Gene Austin crooning from a Gramophone.

Shapiro could see in his mind's eye a Sunday morning with two little twin girls ready for church in the rambling house halfway down the block, bright-faced and scrubbed in their starched crinolines, white gloves, Mary Jane shoes, and white sailor straws with ribbons spilling down their backs. Now one was dead, beaten to death by a mugger who might occupy the very house across the street, dismal as the neighborhood had become.

"This is our driveway, Mr. Shapiro," Miss Nettie instructed politely.

As Shapiro turned, the headlights swept a two-story frame house with a long front porch. The grounds and structure were in better repair and upkeep than their surroundings. Shapiro's sharp instincts painted in history. He guessed it was the only home the twins had ever known. It had been theirs after the demise of their parents. Dr. Cooksey, whom Shapiro vaguely remembered by repute from his boyhood, had left his maiden daughters modestly fixed, and they had continued on until one day it was too late for them to move, to change, to shed the tiny habits of endless days.

Shapiro braked the car in the shadows of the porte cochere, got out with an energy that denied his bulk, his sleepy-looking, rough-hewn face, his forty-nine years. He hurried around and opened the door for Miss Nettie. She was a soft, decorous rustling as she got out and laid a slender, waxen hand on the beefy arm he offered. He escorted her to a pair of French doors that glinted in the darkness, and followed as she unlocked and went inside.

She turned on a light and Shapiro glanced about a parlor straight out of a yellowed issue of *Better Homes;* velour, velvet, and mohair, heavy, overstuffed couches and chairs, lamps with tassels and stained-glass shades, tables with clawed feet resting on glass balls.

Miss Nettie, trim and girlish as a seventy-five-year-old woman could be imagined, brushed a wisp from her forehead. Her eyes were blue pools of grief in a delicately boned face cobwebbed with fine wrinkles, but her control was superb. She remembered the proprieties. "May I take your hat Mr. Shapiro? Do sit down and make yourself comfortable. Would you care for some tea?"

Shapiro was a coffee drinker, with a cold beer when he was off duty, but he was suddenly aware of the silence and emptiness of the slightly musty house, and of this little woman's determination to bear up, to hold life on a normal keel. "Some tea would go nicely, Miss Cooksey."

She seemed to be grateful for the chance to be doing something. Shapiro sank into a chair as she hurried out. He pulled a package of cigarettes from his suit coat pocket, but his glance didn't locate any ash trays, and he put the smokes back, patted his pocket.

Miss Nettie came in carrying an old and ornate tea service. Shapiro stood up. Miss Nettie placed the tea things on a table before the couch.

As she busied her hands with teapot and cups, she said, "I know there are questions you must ask. Please do so, freely. I'm quite prepared and now in control of myself, Mr. Shapiro."

His preliminary questions established what he had already guessed. Yes, she and Miss Lettie, her twin, had lived here all alone, except for a yardman who came one day every other week. They entertained rarely, a small tea or game of bridge with the two or three old friends they had left.

"Most of the girls with whom we grew up," she explained, "have either passed away, yielded to the care of nursing homes, or live a world away from the old neighborhood. Sugar, Mr. Shapiro? One lump or two?"

When he sipped, his distaste for tea was pleasantly soothed. "I didn't know it could be brewed like this."

"Thank you, Mr. Shapiro."

He cleared his throat. "Now about the events of this evening. . . ."

"It all hardly seems real, Mr. Shapiro. Lettie was so kind . . . so harmless. . . . How could anyone be so bestial as to. . . ." Her cup rattled on its saucer. Perched on the edge of the overstuffed couch, her back stiffened. She looked at her hand as if daring it be unsteady again.

"Nothing that happened during the day warned of what the evening would hold," she resumed, her sweet maidenly-aunt voice only slightly off-key. "In the afternoon I made a batch of coconut bonbons, with freshly grated coconut. Making the bonbons is a now-and-again hobby with me, Mr. Shapiro. Specialty of the house, you might say."

She drew in a shallow breath. "A very poor family lives a couple of blocks west, on the same side of the street. A young mother whose husband deserted her and four children. Two of them twin girls, strangely enough . . . like Lettie and me."

Shapiro nodded his understanding that an affinity might develop between two little twins and two old ones.

"We became acquainted with the family," Miss Cooksey said, "through the twins, whom we saw now and then in the grocery store or playing along the street. During the past year or so, Lettie and I had the privilege of doing little things for the children, assisting the family in some small way."

"That was kind of you," Shapiro remarked.

The eyes in their shadows of translucent blue lifted to his. "Kind? Not at all, Mr. Shapiro. The rewards were ours. We enjoyed the children. And today, when we heard that one of the twins had come down with a little flu bug, I dropped over to make sure a doctor had come. The child was doing nicely, but I noticed an expectancy and then a disappointment in her manner. She was too polite to tell me what was on her mind, but I wormed it out of her. When I'd arrived, she'd thought I was surely bringing her some bonbons."

"So you returned home and made her some," Shapiro said.

"Why, of course. I regretted not having thought of it sooner."

"And Lettie was taking the bonbons to the child this evening?"

She nodded, her slender throat working. The first hint of tears glinted in her eyes. "Lettie never reached her destination, Mr. Shapiro. She intended to deliver the candy, visit briefly, and return right away. Her lengthening absence didn't upset me right away. I assumed she'd got talking with the little girl and forgot the time. But finally I grew uneasy. I called the building super and asked him to step to the apartment and have my sister come to the phone. When he returned, he reported that she wasn't there, hadn't been there."

She lapsed from the present for a moment, her soft mouth drawing into a thin, tortured line.

Shapiro quickly envisoned it, the chill that must have come to the silent vacancy of the house as she'd hung up the phone. She'd probably sat a moment, a cold pulse beginning deep within her, telling herself it didn't mean too much, Lettie was all right and would have an explanation that would make her sister's fears seem silly.

"You went out to look for her and found her . . . in the darkness of the alley beside the grocery store," Shapiro reprised gently.

"Yes, that's right." The teacup began rattling again. This time she had to set it on the table and clasp her hands hard in her lap. They continued to tremble slightly. "I might have gone past without knowing she was there, Mr. Shapiro, but I heard the faint sound of her moan. It was almost the last sound she made. I stopped, listened, edged into the alley. Then I saw the pale shadow of her lying there . . . He had smashed her head, dragged her off the street . . . and gorged on the coconut bonbons while he rifled her purse. . . ."

A hard shiver went through her. "What sort of beast, Mr. Shapiro?" The words dropped to a whisper, "Eating candy while his victim dies at his feet."

"Maybe a drug addict," Shapiro said. "Maybe the craving for sweets suggests a hard-drug user."

"He was young, rather tall and skinny, with a scar on his cheek shaped like a W. Lettie managed to tell me that, Mr. Shapiro. And then she said, 'I won't be able to dust my rose garden tomorrow, sis.' Her last words . . ." She strangled and was very pale.

Shapiro reached and touched the thin shoulder. It made him think of the soft wing of a bird. "Miss Cooksey, let me arrange for you to stay someplace else tonight."

"Thank you, Mr. Shapiro. But no. This is my house and I've no intention of running from it."

"Then at least have someone here. We have police matrons who are quite good company."

"I'm sure they are." She moved a little, as if not to hurt his feelings in casting off the support of his hand. "But I'll make do. The quicker I accept the . . . the silence, the better it will be."

"All right." Shapiro slumped back. "But I must warn you. This is the fourth reported mugging in this general area in the past six weeks. There might have been others we don't know about. Your sister was the first fatality."

A quick touch of color splashed Miss Nettie's cheeks. "All by the same young man?"

Shapiro lifted and dropped his shoulders, standing up as he did so. "We can't be sure. One other woman got a look at his face before she was slugged unconscious. She gave us the same description—including the W-shaped scar on his cheek."

Her eyes reflected the way she was twisting and turning it all in her mind. "Then you've been trying to stop this pathological beast for some time—without much luck."

"Without any luck," Shapiro admitted. He hesitated. "But we try, Miss Cooksey. I want you to believe that."

Her eyes met his. She seemed to sense something of his job, the dirtiness and thanklessness of it, the frustrations that were all too much a part of it.

"The public doesn't always understand," he said. "I'm not complaining, but we're under-manned, always facing a job that grows more impossibly big every day. We can't blanket the city looking for a single mugger. We just have to do the best we can with what we've got."

She touched his hand, gently comforting him. *Even in her own extremity,* he thought.

"Good night, Mr. Shapiro, and thank you for your kindness. You've made it easier for me."

Shapiro drove back to headquarters with the thought of her haunting him, piercing the armor of twenty-five years of being a cop, of seeing it all.

On his way through the corridor to Communications, Shapiro bumped into Captain Ramey. Ramey's eyes widened as he took in the cast of Shapiro's face.

"Wow! Who licked the red off your candy?"

Shapiro steamed a breath. "Don't mention candy to me, Cap! Not right now. And don't ever mention coconut bonbons!"

Ramey scratched his head and stared as Shapiro continued his stormy way to the radio room.

In the den of electronic gear, Shapiro had the order put on the air: Pick up slender man probably in his twenties, W-shaped scar on cheek, wanted on suspicion of murder committed during course of forcible robbery.

He was afraid it wouldn't do any good—and it didn't. He went off duty at midnight, and when he got home and sacked in he kept his wife awake grumbling in his sleep.

Between calls to knifings, shootings, and sluggings, Shapiro's unmarked car cruised the Cooksey neighborhood nightly for more than a week.

His trained eye picked out details, the young girl who was peddling herself; the strident woman who beat up her day-laborer husband when he came home drunk; the broad-shouldered teen-ager who undoubtedly was gang chief of the block; the old grouch who chased dogs and kids from his yard with sticks and rocks.

Shapiro liked least of all the actions of Miss Nettie. Each evening right after dark she came out of the ghostly old house and walked west, past the steel-shuttered grocery, across the intersection, the full length of the next block. Then she turned and went back the way she had come, a fragile, helpless figure. She would pause at her front
'k and look back at the long, dark sidewalk she had traversed.
:n she would slip into her house, and a dim light would turn on behind a curtained window upstairs, and Miss Nettie would be in for the night.

She started the excursions the night after her sister was buried. Nothing discouraged her. She walked if it rained, if the wind blew, if the moon shone. It was as if the void of grief had filled her with a compulsion to retrace the steps and feel the same feelings suffered by that other twin image of herself.

In a corner of his mind, Shapiro knew he was making a cardinal mistake in police work. He'd let Miss Nettie become an entity, someone very personal. She was the memory of the grandmother he'd known in childhood, the echo of lost days buried in the smogs of time when cookies had tasted of a never-again sweetness and a tree house in a back-yard oak had soared over a world without ugliness.

The unseen observer in the shadows of a tree or dark, deserted doorway, Shapiro fretted about her. Her newly developed quirk, he told himself, was the result of her sudden bereavement. It was temporary. It would wear itself out. But if not . . . then he would take an off-duty hour to talk with the department psychiatrist about her.

Three weeks passed before Miss Nettie varied what had come to be her norm. Staked out in the concealment of a peeling billboard, Shapiro watched the opposite sidewalk. The night was gloomy, with low gray clouds. He looked at the luminous dial of his wtach. She was ten minutes behind schedule, then twenty, with no sign of her coming shadow-like along the street.

Shapiro drew a deep breath, but held it suddenly. The familiar, slight figure with the short, graceful steps seemed to flow out of the darkness. Shapiro watched as she neared the shadows of the grocery store across the street. His face drooped with sadness. As much as he disliked the thought of her subjected to psychiatric probing, he knew it must be. He couldn't let her continue this way.

Out of habit, his gaze swept the street as he started to move out and cross diagonally to intercept her. His reluctant journey toward a face-to-face confrontation with her suddenly became a charge. He saw the slender figure of a tall, crouching man resolve from the alleyway darkness and slip up behind her. Unreal and dream-like, the shadow seemed to fold about her as the mugger crooked an arm about her neck and snatched her purse.

"Hold it!" Shapiro shouted the order savagely.

The man threw Miss Nettie to the sidewalk and lunged into the well of darkness alongside the grocery.

Miss Nettie scrambled to her feet, rearing in Shapiro's path.

"Mr. Shapiro!"

She grabbed his arm and fell against him. Her weight, even as slight as it was, and his momentum threw him off balance. He twisted and almost fell, banging his shoulder against the corner of the building.

"You're not hurt, obviously," he said, short-breathed. "Just sit tight. That rat won't find a hole big enough to hold him."

She hung onto him. "I didn't know you there, Mr. Shapiro."

Her thin hands were talons, clutching his clothing. He tried to brush them away. "For heaven's sake, Miss Cooksey, let go! That guy's getting away."

"Don't risk yourself for me, Mr. Shapiro. He may be armed."

"My worry," he bit out, "if you'll let me do my job."

He grabbed her wrist, discovering a surprising strength. The ever-lurking hunting instinct was aware that the fleeing feet had departed the farther end of the alley.

"Miss Nettie!" he snarled in exasperation. He let his hands apply enough pressure to break her grip and shove him free. She stumbled backward and collapsed with a small outcry. Shapiro threw a despairing look down the empty alley as he dropped to one knee beside her.

Her face was a pale, soft etching in white.

"Miss Nettie, I didn't mean. . . ." He slipped a hand behind her shoulder to help her up.

"I know you didn't, Mr. Shapiro." She got up with but little assistance, brushed a wispy spill of white hair from her forehead with her fingertips. "Don't blame yourself. Really, I tripped over my own feet, but I'm quite all right."

"Did you get a look at the mugger?"

Her eyes glinted, blue candles in the faintest haze of street glow. "Not clearly—but enough. He was young, tall, skinny, with the telltale W-shaped scar on his cheek."

Shapiro dropped his hand from her shoulder, muttering an ungentlemanly word under his breath. "Well," he sighed bitterly, "the bird seems to have flown the coop. The best I can do now is put him on the air and hope for a pickup."

"Do you think it will work?"

"I doubt it. He's managed to hole up pretty well so far."

She dropped her eyes, making Shapiro think of a chastised child. "I'm glad you didn't get hurt, Mr. Shapiro."

"You took care of that, Miss Cooksey, delaying me as you did."

She sighed softly. "Please don't be angry with me. Even if you had caught him at the risk of your life, would it have done any good? The court decisions nowadays, the parole system—wouldn't he have been back on the streets in a few years?"

"Maybe so," Shapiro admitted, "but he would have been off of them for a few, too."

Her eyes inched back to his. "Yes, I guess you have to think of it that way, or your lifework would be for nothing."

The words were a gentle mirror held up to him. She had sized up the policeman's one excuse for being with uncomfortable accuracy. By the time he was ready to sign out at midnight, he had a case of heartburn, bloodshot eyes, and a headache that would do for the whole department.

He had showered (without relieving his symptoms) and dressed, and was slamming his locker door when Browne from Communications called his name from the doorway.

"Yeah?" Shapiro growled, glancing briefly across his shoulder.

"Bounced down hoping I'd catch you," Browne, robust and dark and an enviable twenty-seven, said. "The call just came in. I think we've turned up your mugger-killer. Young, skinny—with the cheek scar."

Shapiro whirled toward Browne, his headache dissolving. "Where?"

"Fleabag rooming house. One-one-four River Street. His girlfriend, a late-working waitress, breezed in for an after-work date and came out squalling. She found lover boy on the floor. Dead."

A uniformed patrolman had cleared the curious from the scabby, odorous hall and stairway. Adams and McJunkin had arrived to take charge of the investigation. The lab men and photographer had taken their pictures and samples, and Doc Jefferson, the medical examiner, was snapping his black bag closed when Shapiro's rough-hewn and iron-gray presence loomed in the doorway.

Shapiro nodded at the departing lab men, said hello to his fellow detectives, and crossed the dreary, stifling room to the figure sprawled beside the grimy, swaybacked bed.

"Who is he?" Shapiro looked down at the bony face with its scar and bonnet of wild, long, brownish hair.

"One Pete Farlow," Adams said. "Or maybe it's an alias."

"Whoever, he must be our boy," McJunkin added. He was a stocky, freckled redhead, ambling toward Shapiro's side. "That scar is just too unique. Odds are a million to one against its duplicate in a city this size."

"Drifter?" Shapiro suggested.

"I wouldn't bet against you," McJunkin said, "the way he showed up and took the room, according to the building super. Same old pattern. He works a town until it gets too hot and then drifts on to another room, girl, way of life just like the one he left behind him.

"He seems to be the solution—in addition to the murder of Lettie Cooksey—to a string of muggings, drunk-rollings, and strong-arm robberies we've had," Adams said. He was the tallest man in the room, dark and ramrod straight. He motioned with his hand toward the narrow closet, where the door stood open. "He's stashed enough purses and wallets in there to open a counter in a secondhand store."

"Maybe in his private moments," Doc Jefferson said, "he liked to look in on them, touch them, sort of relive the big-man moment when he had taken this one or that one." Doc shook a fine head of silver hair. "You never know about these guys."

Shapiro drifted to the closet. Which was hers? He tried to remember; a flash of white when the mugger had grabbed it there at the steel-shuttered grocery, but not all white; not large, either—relatively small handbag, black or brown, trimmed in white.

On top of the jumble at his feet, just a little to the left of the door-jamb, lay a woman's purse with its dark blue relieved by a diagonal band of white; a rather old-fashioned purse.

Shapiro hunkered and picked it up. Its clasp was broken. He pulled it open, and stopped breathing for a second. In one corner was a tissue-wrapped ball of candy. As if fearfully, his forefinger inched and pushed the tissue aside to expose the tempting creaminess of a coconut bonbon.

"Doc," Shapiro said in a far-off voice, his broad, bent back toward the room, "what did our killer pigeon die of?"

"I won't have a complete report until after the autopsy," Jefferson said.

"But you could give me a very educated guess right now."

"You birds always want your forensic medicine instant," Doc said. "Okay, for what it's worth, I'll wager McJunkin's freckles against Adams' eyeteeth that the autopsy will back up the symptoms. Our vulture died of poisoning. Arsenic, I'd say. He gulped a walloping dose of arsenic."

"The lab boys found little tissues scattered all over the floor," McJunkin said, "the kind they used to use in the old-fashioned candy stores."

Shapiro mumbled to himself.

McJunkin said, "What'd you say, Shappy?"

"I said," Shapiro bit out angrily, "that I'm never surprised at anything the lab boys find."

Wearing a flannel robe, felt slippers, and a net about her soft white hair, Miss Nettie ushered Shapiro into her parlor.

"I'm very sorry to rouse you at this hour," Shapiro said, "but it was necessary."

"I'm sure it must have been, for you to have done so. Would you like some tea?"

Shapiro gave her a stare and sigh. "Not this go-round. Sit down, please."

She sank to the edge of an overstuffed chair and clasped her hands quietly in her lap.

Shapiro faced her with his hands cocked on his hips. "Was your purse a dark blue, with a white band across it?"

"Yes it was, Mr. Shapiro. And I assume from your question that you have found it."

"In the room of a dead man. A young, skinny dead man with a W-shaped scar on his cheek."

He thought he saw the faintest of smiles on her soft lips.

His hands came loose from his sides. He banged a fist into a palm. "Miss Cooksey, blast you, you've made a total fool of me!"

"Oh, no, Mr. Shapiro! I'm much too fond of you to do anything like that."

Shapiro snorted, kicked a table leg, spun on her again with the mien of a grizzly. "You made bait of yourself, Miss Cooksey. I had told you about the previous muggings he'd pulled around here. You saw a pattern. You hoped he'd return—and take the bait."

"Mr. Shapiro—"

He silenced her with a stern finger waggling in her face. "Don't you open your gentle little peep to me one more time until I'm finished. Do you understand?"

"Yes, Mr. Shapiro."

"You took those nightly walks, waiting for him to return, wanting him to, hoping he would strike again. And when he struck, you threw a veritable body-block at me so he could get away with your purse and everything it contained—maybe a little cash, and a batch of bonbons loaded with arsenic!"

"Where would I get—"

"Don't play innocent with me!" Shapiro almost popped a vein across his forehead. "You have a yardman. Your sister grew roses. Anybody can get arsenic, in plant sprays, insecticides." His teeth made a sound like fingernails scraping across sandpaper. "You pegged him to a T, Miss Cooksey. He gulped the arsenic-loaded candy. Almost all of it."

"Almost, Mr. Shapiro?"

He reached in his side pocket and brought out the tissue-wrapped bonbon he had taken from the rooming house closet.

With exaggerated care, he peeled back the tissue and extended his palm. "It's the one that stuck in the corner of the purse when he dumped it on his bed or dresser. It's the one he didn't eat. Do you deny making it?"

She rose slowly. "It's a lovely bonbon, Mr. Shapiro, although a bit squashed from so much handling."

She peered, lifted a dainty forefinger to touch the candy. She picked it up. Then she popped it in her mouth and swallowed before Shapiro had the first inkling of what she was up to.

Flat-footed and with a dumb look on his face, Shapiro received her soft smile.

"Mr. Shapiro, would I eat poisoned candy?"

He shook off a faintly trance-like state. "Yes," he said. "Faced with a situation of sufficient urgency, I'm beginning to believe you'd have the courage to do anything, Miss Cooksey. I think your question is rhetorical. I think you have already, just now, eaten a piece of poisoned candy. I'm also certain that the amount contained in a single piece is not enough to kill you." He shook his head hopelessly. "Whatever am I going to do with you, Miss Nettie?"

"Arrest me for destroying evidence?" she suggested.

"I doubt that I could make it—or any other charge—stick," Shapiro said. "Even if we could prove you made some poisoned candy, you didn't offer it to anyone. The only shred of evidence we have that involves you, come to think of it, is the purse—evidence of a crime *against* you."

She strolled with him to the front door. "Will you come some afternoon for tea, Mr. Shapiro?"

He studied her a moment. "No, Miss Nettie—I think I never want to see you again."

She nodded and patted his hand with a touch of gentle understanding. Then she turned a little in the dark front doorway, looking from his face to a point far along the sidewalk.

"Given the chance," she said almost in a whisper, "I'd have been the first to warn the young man to mend his ways in time—and never to take candy from strangers."

While the three men scrambled to protect their reputations, they never considered that there was more to William's story than he had told them. . . .

FIFTEEN

Proxy

When I left her apartment, I skedaddled straight to Mr. Friedland's estate. I left the car standing in the driveway and went in the big stone mansion like a coon with a pack on his trail.

I asked the butler where Mr. Friedland was, and the butler said our boss was in the study. So I busted in the study and closed the heavy walnut door behind me quick.

Mr. Friedland was at his desk. He looked up, bugged for a second by me coming in this way. But he didn't bless me out. He got up quick and said, "What's the matter, William?"

I knuckled some sweat off my forehead, walked to the desk, and laid the envelope down. The envelope had a thousand smackers, cash, in it.

Mr. Friedland picked up the money. He looked a little addlepated.

"You did go to Marla Scanlon's apartment, William?"

"Yes, sir."

"She was there?"

"Yes, sir."

"But she didn't accept the money? William, I simply can't believe it."

I couldn't think of any easy way to explain it to him. "She's dead, Mr. Friedland."

He cut his keen eyes from the money to me. He was a lean, handsome man who looked about thirty-five years old in the face. It was just the pure white hair that hinted at his real age.

"Dead?" he said. "How, William?"

"Looked to me like somebody strangled her to death. I didn't hang around to make sure. There's bruises on her neck, and her tongue is stuck out and all swelled up like a hunk of bleached liver. She was a mighty fetching hunk of female," I added with a sigh.

"Yes," Mr. Friedland said, "she was."

"But she don't look so good now."

"Was she alone in the apartment?"

"I reckon. I didn't feel the urge to poke around. Just had a look at her there on her livingroom floor and hightailed it here."

Mr. Friedland absently put the thousand bucks in his inside coat pocket. "She was alive three hours ago. She phoned me, just before I went out. I returned, gave you the envelope, and you went to her place and found her dead. Three hours. She was killed between two and five this afternoon."

"Could have been a lot of traffic in that much time, Mr. Friedland."

"I doubt it. Not today. Today she was expecting a caller with a white envelope. William, you didn't see anyone on your way out of the building?"

"No, sir."

"Phone anyone? Speak to anyone?"

"Not a soul, Mr. Friedland, until I got here and asked the butler where you was."

"Good. You're always a good man, William."

"Yes, sir," I said. "I try to be." Which was no lie. I'm a hillbilly from near Comfort, North Carolina, which is back up in the mountains. It's a mighty poorly place, believe me. Mr. Friedland came up there one summer for a week of fishing. I worked for him that week, and when the week was over he said as how would I like to keep working for him. He said I was intelligent and clean-cut and had respect for other people. He said he needed a chauffeur and a man to do errands and personal chores. He said I would have quarters on a nice estate and steady pay. So naturally I jumped at the chance. That was near five years ago, and I'm glad to say that Mr. Friedland has come to depend on me as few folks can depend on a personal worker. He trusts me and knows I can keep my mouth shut. And that means a lot to a bigshot newspaper publisher and television station owner like Mr. Friedland.

While I was simmering down and losing the shakes from my experience in Miss Marla Scanlon's apartment, Mr. Friedland was busy on the phone. He called Judge Harrison Corday and Mr. Robert Grenick, who is the prosecuting attorney. They were both close friends of Mr. Friedland. He told them to drop everything, he had to see them right away. He said a thing of utmost importance had happened which couldn't be talked on the phone. He asked them to come to his study pronto, which they did.

Judge Corday got there first. He was one of the youngest superior court judges in the state. He liked parties and booze, and it was beginning to show around the softening edges of his face. He was a big, reddish man. He'd been a famous football star in college.

He said to Mr. Friedland, "What's up, Arch? I've got a dinner engagement and. . . ."

"You may not want any dinner when you hear what I have to say," Mr. Friedland said. "To save a lot of repetitions, we'll wait until Bob Grenick arrives."

Judge Corday didn't press Mr. Friedland, knowing it would do no good. He sat down and lighted a dollar cigar and tried to read Mr. Friedland's lean, tight face.

Mr. Grenick showed up almost before Judge Corday got his cigar going good. Bald, chubby, and middle-age, Mr. Grenick had thick, heavy lips and thick, heavy eyes. Both his lips and eyes always looked slightly damp, like a lizard's back that lives in a spring branch.

As soon as Mr. Grenick was in the study and the door safely closed, Mr. Friedland said, "Tell them, William, what you just told me."

"Miss Marla Scanlon is dead," I said.

The judge took it without blinking an eye. The state's attorney, Mr. Grenick, choked, put a hand to his neck, fumbled for a chair, and sat down.

"How?" Judge Corday said, cool.

"Murdered, I reckon," I said.

Mr. Grenick made noises like he was having a hard time getting air.

"By what means?" the judge asked.

"Choked to death, it looked like," I said.

"When?"

"Sometime between two and five," Mr. Friedland put in.

"What makes you think I have any interest until the murderer is caught and I act in official capacity?" Mr. Grenick said raggedly. "I hardly knew Marla Scanlon."

"Oh, come off it, Bob," Mr. Friedland said. "Marla Scanlon worked artfully and most skillfully. One by one she compromised the three of us. She didn't stretch her luck. We three were enough. She had her gold mine. She was content. She didn't intend to incur further risk by developing, in a manner of speaking, a source of silver."

Mr. Grenick got half out of his chair, gripping its arms. "I deny any. . . ."

"Please shut up," Mr. Friedland said quietly. "None of us is on trial, not yet. But we're the three who might have killed her. It's reasonably certain that one of us did. She's milked you the longest, Harrison. I was next. Bob, you're her third and final golden goose. Between us, we've contributed, over a period of time, something like a total of sixty thousand dollars."

"Too bad we never reported all that stashed cash to the income tax people," Judge Corday said. "They might have taken her off our backs."

"And the hides from our backs right along with her," Mr. Friedland said.

"How'd you find out all this?" Mr. Grenick asked. "About me, I mean?"

"That's a rather silly question, Bob," Mr. Friedland said. "I'm still a top reporter when it comes to digging out the facts. And I have the resources of a metropolitan newspaper at my disposal, don't forget."

"All right," Judge Corday said, like he was on the bench considering a motion by a lawyer. "It's laid out between us. We three were her patsys. Each had the same reason to dispose of her. We're cruising, in a word, in the same leaky boat. Now it remains to determine whether or not we have a paddle. Unfortunately, I have no alibi for the three hours between two and five this afternoon. Have you, Bob?"

"What?" Mr. Grenick was looking sort of gray, like a prospect for a dose of calomel.

"Where were you between two and five this afternoon?"

"I was. . . ."

"Yes, Bob?" Mr. Friedland prompted.

Mr. Grenick lifted his eyes and looked at his friends. "I didn't go in, understand. A block away, I turned the car. I didn't go all the way to her apartment."

"You were going to see Marla?" the judge asked.

"Yes. I was going to appeal to her, to prove to her that I couldn't afford the blackmail tariff any longer. I was going to convince her that she'd have to be satisfied with less—or nothing more at all. I simply couldn't rake up the money, I tell you. I'm not as well heeled as you two."

"But you got cold feet," Mr. Friedland said. "You didn't actually see her?"

"That's right, Arch, and you've got to believe me."

"Whether or not we believe you," the judge said, "cuts little ice. The important thing is that you have no alibi. How about you, Arch?"

Mr. Friedland shook his head. "I got a call from her at two o'clock. She reminded me that William was due at five with a thousand dollars. I drove out for a quiet, private look at some acreage I may purchase. I came back in time to send William on his errand."

"So any one of us might have killed her," the judge said.

"Listen," Mr. Grenick said in a tight voice, "I didn't do it. But if a scandal of this sort brushes off on me, I'm ruined. The three of us," his eyes looked wetter than usual, "are ruined. There are too many people in city hall and police headquarters who'd like to collect our scalps. We can't hush up a thing as big as murder, not even if Arch does control the press and TV."

"Precisely," Mr. Friedland said. "Sometimes, Bob, you almost convince me you have a mind, in addition to the cunning you've shown in the political jungles. We cannot cover this thing."

"So what do you propose?" Judge Corday asked.

"An unbreakable gentleman's agreement," Mr. Friedland said. "Whichever of the three of us is nailed, he must bear the entire thing alone. He must not turn to his friends for help or implicate them in the slightest. He must stand firm on the statement that he, and only he, was involved with Marla Scanlon. Whichever of us is doomed will at least have the satisfaction of knowing that he shielded his friends."

"It might be rough," the judge said. "When a man's slapped in the face with murder, the natural reaction is to name others, to confuse the issue, to point suspicion elsewhere."

"I know," Mr. Friedland nodded, "and that's my reason for calling you here. We must decide in advance. We must agree that the two who escape will, throughout the future, stand by the loser's loved ones in any crisis, any trouble, as if the loser himself were still here."

"Mr. Friedland," I said.

He turned his head in my direction. "Yes, William?"

"All the time you been talking," I said, "I been thinking. I got a idear."

"William," Mr. Grenick said in a sore tone, "we've far more important things to consider than any ideas you. . . ."

Mr. Friedland shut him up with a motion of his hand. "I don't think we have anything to lose by listening to you," Mr. Friedland said. "Go ahead, William."

"Thank you, sir. You see, Mr. Friedland, you've been real nice to me, giving me a chance to live like I never knowed people live, when I was a hillbilly back up beyond Comfort, North Carolina."

Mr. Grenick groaned. "This is no time for asinine, emotional speeches."

"Yes, sir," I said. "Anyhow, I'm all through speechifying. I just wanted Mr. Friedland to know one of the reasons I'd be willing to do you-all the favor of standing trial for Miss Marla Scanlon's murder."

I had their attention now, believe me. Right then, you could have heard a mouse crossing the attic, only of course there wasn't none in Mr. Friedland's attic.

"William," Mr. Friedland said finally, "I'm touched. But I suspect that you haven't quite finished."

"No, sir, Mr. Friedland. Not quite. All three of you have society wives and fine kids and fancy homes and just everything to make life good. You stand to lose a real passel. But me, I got nobody but myself. And I never before had a chance to get me a stake together."

"How much?" Judge Corday asked.

"Well, you been paying Miss Marla Scanlon plenty. One final payment—to me—will finish it for good. Just chip in five thousand dollars apiece, and I'll protect you all from the aftermath of this terrible thing."

"I won't do it," Mr. Grenick said, "not five thou—"

"Yes, Bob, I think you will," Mr. Friedland said. He eased his backside to the edge of his desk and brought his eyes back to me. "How do you propose to do it, William?"

"It ought to be simple as picking corn when the sun ain't hot," I said. "With your newspapers and TV on my side, and Judge Corday on the bench, and Mr. Grenick handling the case for the state, I ought to come off all right. I'll say that I had been hanky-pank with Marla Scanlon. I'll say she was giving me the boot. I'll say we got in a big fight and I lost my head and killed her without really meaning to. Nobody in this town really cares that she's gone, nobody to question or suspect what you do. I figure the judge should give me about three years for manslaughter. I'll behave good and be on parole inside of a year."

"And then?" Judge Corday said.

"I'll just take my fifteen thousand and go back to Comfort," I said. "None of us has got to worry about any of the others going back on the contract, account of we're all in this together and we sink or swim together."

"William," Mr. Friedland said, "I think you've got a deal. How about it, friends?"

Both the judge and Mr. Grenick were quick to nod.

"I suggest," the judge said, "that you and William contrive to rehearse a bit in private, Bob."

"A good idea," the prosecutor said.

"And you've fine material to work with here," Mr. Friedland said. "You won't have to worry about William botching his part."

"Well, gentlemen," I said, "let's get finished up here with the practice questions and all, soon's we can. I reckon I ought to get to police headquarters in a reasonable time. It'll look better if I surrender myself and show them how sorry I am for what I done to that girl."

"Excellent, William, excellent," Mr. Friedland said.

I got to admit it looked pretty excellent to me too. I'd go back to Comfort a little over a year from now with over fifty thousand dollars, counting the fifteen thousand these men would cough up.

Miss Marla Scanlon, in life, had had an eye on the future. When I'd made her open the wall safe in her apartment before I strangled her. I'd picked up a little over forty thousand.

Folks around Comfort, North Carolina are all eligible for this poverty program the government is running. It'll sure be nice, going back and being the richest man in the whole durn town. The air is clean, the scenery eye-popping, the likker mellow, and the girls all corn-fed beauties. I might even hire myself a chauffeur and personal errand boy—only I'll make sure his name ain't William.

While every link in a chain is important, that one may be vital may be an expensive lesson to learn. . . .

SIXTEEN

The Vital Element

I would never again love the warm water of the Gulf of Mexico . . . never find beauty in its blue-green color . . . never hear music in its rustling surf . . .

The dead girl had been hurriedly buried in the Gulf. She was anchored in about thirty feet of water with a hempen rope that linked her lashed ankles to a pair of cement blocks.

I'd stirred the water, swimming down to her depth. Her body bobbed and swayed, with her bare toes about three feet off the clean, sandy bottom. It was almost as if a strange, macabre, new life had come to her. Her long blonde hair swirled about her lovely gamine face with every tremor of the water. A living ballerina might have enjoyed her grace of motion, but not her state of being. I wept silently behind my face mask.

A single stroke sent me drifting, with my shoulder stirring silt from the bottom. I touched the rope where it passed into the holes in the cement block and out again. A natural process of wear and tear had set in. The sharp, ragged edges of the blocks were cutting the rope. In a matter of time, the rope would part. Her buoyancy would drift her toward the sunlight, to the surface, to discovery.

I eeled about, careful not to look at her again, and plunged up toward the shadow of the skiff. My flippers fired me into open air with a shower of spray and a small, quick explosion in my ears.

I rolled over the side of the skiff and lay a moment with my stomach churning with reaction. Sun, blue sky, the primitive shoreline of mangrove and palmetto, everything around me was weirdly unreal. It was as if all the clocks in the world had gone *tick*, then forgot to *tock*.

"You're a too-sensitive, chicken-hearted fink," I said aloud. I forced myself to peel out of my diving gear, picked up the oars, and put my back into the job of rowing in.

133

I docked and tied the skiff, then walked to the cottage with my gear slung across my shoulder. Sheltered by scraggly pines, the lonely cottage creaked tiredly in the heat.

I stood on the sagging front porch. For a moment I didn't have the strength or nerve to go inside. The cottage was its usual mess, a hodgepodge of broken down furniture, dirty dishes, empty beer bottles and bean cans, none of which bothered me. But *she* was strewn all over the place, the dead girl out there in the water. She was portrayed in oil, sketched in charcoal, delicately impressed in pink and tan watercolors. She was half finished on the easel in the center of the room, like a naked skull.

Shivering and dry-throated, I slipped dingy ducks over my damp swim trunks, wriggled into a tattered T-shirt, and slid my feet into strap sandals. The greasy feeling was working again in the pit of my stomach as I half-ran from the cottage.

Palmetto City lay like a humid landscape done with dirty brushes as my eight-year-old station wagon nosed into DeSota Street. Off the beaten tourist paths, the town was an unpainted clapboard mecca for lantern-jawed farmers, fishermen, swamp muckers.

I angled the steaming wagon beside a dusty pickup at the curb and got out. On the sidewalk, I glimpsed myself in the murky window of the hardware store: six feet of bone and cartilage without enough meat; thatch of unkempt sandy hair; a lean face that wished for character; huge sockets holding eyes that looked as if they hadn't slept for a week.

Inside the store, Braley Sawyer came toward me, a flabby, sloppy man in his rumpled tropical weight suit. "Well, if it ain't Tazewell Eversham, Palmetto City's own Gauguin!" He flashed a wet, gold-toothed smile. "Hear you stopped in Willy Morrow's filling station yestiddy and gassed up for a trip to Sarasota. Going up to see them fancy art dealers, I guess."

I nodded. "Got back early this morning."

"You going to remember us country hoogers when you're famous, Gauguin?" The thought brought fat laughter from him. I let his little joke pass and in due time he waddled behind the counter and asked, "You here to buy something?"

"Chain." The word formed in my parched throat but didn't make itself heard. I cleared my throat, tried again, "I want to buy about a dozen feet of medium weight chain."

He blinked. "Chain?"

"Sure," I said. I had better control of my voice now. "I'd like to put in a garden, but I have stump problems. Thought I'd dig and cut around the roots and snake the stumps out with the station wagon."

He shrugged, his eyes hanging onto me as he moved toward the rear of the store. "I guess it would work—if that bucket of bolts holds together."

I turned and stared at a vacant point in space as the chain rattled from its reel. "Easier to carry if I put it in a gunny sack, Gauguin," Sawyer yelled at me.

"That's fine." I heard the chain clank into the sack.

Seconds later Sawyer dropped the chain at my feet. I paid him, carried the gunny sack out, and loaded it in the station wagon. Then I walked down the street to the general store and bought a few things—canned goods, coffee, flour, and two quarts of the cheapest booze available, which turned out to be a low-grade rum.

I'd stowed the stuff beside the gunny sack, closed the tailgate, and was walking around the wagon to get in when a man called to me from across the street. "Hey, Taze."

The man who barged toward me looked like the crudest breed of piney woods sheriff, which is what Jack Tully was. Big-bellied, slope-shouldered, fleshy faced with whisky veins on cheeks and nose, his protruding eyes searched with a sadistic hunger. His presence reminded me that not all Neanderthals had died out ten thousand years ago.

He thumbed back his hat, spat, guffawed. "Kinda left you high and dry, didn't she, bub?"

An arctic wind blew across my neck. "What are you talking about, Sheriff?"

He elbowed me in the ribs; I recoiled, from his touch, not the force behind it. "Bub, I ain't so dumb. I know Melody Grant's been sneaking out to your shack."

"Any law against it?"

"Not as long as the neighbors don't complain." He gave an obscene wink. "And you got no neighbors, have you, bub?"

His filthy thoughts were written in his smirking, ignorant face. No explanation could change his mind, not in a million years. Might as well try to explain a painting to him.

"Maybe she ain't told you yet, bub?"

"Told me what?"

"About young Perry Tomlin, son of the richest man in the county. She's been seeing him, too, now that he's home with his university degree. Going to marry him, I hear, honeymoon in Europe. Big come-up for a shanty cracker girl, even one as pretty as Melody. I reckon that shack'll be mighty lonesome, knowing you'll never see her again."

"Maybe it will, Sheriff, maybe it will."

"But . . ." We were suddenly conspirators. He gloated. ". . . there's one thing you can waller around in your mind."

"What's that, Sheriff?"

"Son of the county's richest man is just getting the leavings of a ragtag artist who's got hardly a bean in the pot." Laughter began to well inside of him. "Bub, I got to hand you that! Man, it would bust their blood vessels, Perry's and the old man's both, if they knew the truth."

Raucous laughter rolled out of him, to the point of strangulation. When I got in the station wagon and drove off he was standing there wiping his eyes and quaking with mirth over the huge joke.

Back at the cottage, I opened a bottle of the rum, picked up a brush, and stood before the easel. I swigged from the bottle in my left hand and made brush strokes on the unfinished canvas with my right. By the time her face was emerging from the skull-like pattern, the rum had begun its work. I knew I wasn't cut to fit a situation like this one, but the rum made up a part of the deficit.

I dropped the brush and suddenly turned from the canvas. "Why did you have to leave me? Why?"

She was, of course, still out there when the gunny sack dragged me down through thirty feet of water. Her thin cotton dress clung to her as she wavered closer. Behind and beyond her a watery forest of seaweed dipped and swayed, a green and slimy floral offering.

I felt as if my air tanks were forcing raw acid into my lungs as I spilled the chain from the gunny sack. My trembling hands made one . . . two . . . three efforts . . . and the chain was looped about her cold, slender ankles.

I passed the chain through the holes in the cement blocks, and it no longer mattered whether the hempen rope held. The job was done. No risk of floating away.

In the cottage, I picked up the rum jug and let it kick me. Then I put on a clean shirt and pants and combed my hair nice and neat.

I went to the porch and took a final look at the bloodstains on the rough planking. My eyes followed the dripping trail those blood droplets had made down to the rickety pier and the flatbottom skiff. Before my stomach started acting up again, I dropped from the porch, ran across the sandy yard, and fell into the station wagon.

I pulled myself upright behind the wheel, started the crate. Through the non-reality of the day, the wagon coughed its way over the rutted, crushed seashell road to the highway. Trucks swooshed past and passenger cars swirled about me.

On the outskirts of Palmetto City, I turned the wagon onto the private road that snaked its way across landscaped acreage. The road wound up a slight rise to a colonial mansion that overlooked half the county, the low skyline of the town, the glitter of the Gulf in the far distance. A pair of horse-sized Great Danes were chasing, tumbling, rolling like a couple of puppies on the vast manicured lawn.

A lean, trim old man had heard the car's approach and stood watching from the veranda as I got out. I walked up the short, wide steps, the shadow of the house falling over me. The man watched me narrowly. He had a crop of silver hair and his hawkish face was wrinkled. These were the only clues to his age. His gray eyes were bright, quick, hard, as cold as a snake's. His mouth was an arrogant slit. Clothed in lime slacks and riotously colored sport shirt thirty years too young for him, his poised body exuded an aura of merciless, wiry power. In my distraught and wracked imagination he was as pleasant as a fierce, deadly lizard.

"Mr. Tomlin?"

He nodded. "And you're the tramp artist who's become a local character. Didn't you see those no trespassing signs when you turned off the highway?"

"I've got some business with your son, Mr. Tomlin."

"Perry's in Washington, tending to a matter for me. He flew up yesterday and won't be back for another couple days. You call, and make a proper appointment. And get that crate out of here—unless you want me to interrupt the dogs in their play."

My stomach felt as if it were caving in, but I gave him a steady look and said in an icy voice, "If Perry's away, you must be the man I want to talk to. Sure. Perry wouldn't have killed her, but you didn't share your son's feeling for her, did you?"

"I don't believe I know what you're talking about." He knew, all right. The first glint of caution and animal cunning showed in his eyes.

"Then I'll explain, Mr. Tomlin. Yesterday I went to Sarasota to try to interest an art dealer in a one-man show. When I got back this morning I found some bloodstains. They led me to the water. I spent the morning diving, searching. I found her in about thirty feet of water."

I expected him to say something, but he didn't. He just stood there looking at me with those small, agate eyes.

"It wasn't hard to figure out," I said. "She'd come to the cottage to tell me it was all over between us. The shanty cracker girl was marrying the richest son in the county. But you didn't cotton to that idea, did you?"

"Go on," he said quietly.

"There's little more. It's all very simple. You sent Perry out of town to give you a chance to break it up between him and the cracker girl. Not much escapes your notice. You'd heard the gossip about her and the tramp artist. When you couldn't find her in town, you decided to try my place. I guess you tried to talk her off, buy her off, threaten her off. When none of it worked, you struck her in a rage. You killed her."

The old man stared blindly at the happy Great Danes.

"Realizing what you'd done," I said, "you scrounged a rope, couple of cement blocks, and planted her in thirty feet of water." I shook my head. "Not good. Not good at all. When the blocks sawed the rope in two, a nosy cop might find evidence you'd been around the place; a tire track, footprint, or maybe some fingerprints you'd left sticking around."

He studied the frolicking dogs as if planning their butchery. "You haven't named the vital element, artist; proof of guilt, proof that I did anything more than talk to her."

"Maybe so," I nodded, "but could a man in your position afford the questions, the scandal, the doubts that would arise and remain in your son's mind until the day you die? I think not. So I helped you."

His eyes flashed to me.

"I substituted a chain for the rope," I said. "The cement blocks will not cut that in two." I drew a breath. "And of course I want something in return. A thousand dollars. I'm sure you've that much handy, in a wall safe if not on your person. It's bargain day, Mr. Tomlin."

He thought it over for several long minutes. The sinking sun put a golden glitter in his eyes.

"And how about the future, artist? What if you decided you needed another thousand dollars one of these days?"

I shook my head. "I'm not that stupid. Right now I've caught you flat-footed. It's my moment. Everything is going for me. You haven't time to make a choice, think, plan. But it would be different in the future. Would I be stupid enough to try to continue blackmailing the most powerful man in the county after he's had a chance to get his forces and resources together?"

"Your question contains a most healthy logic, artist."

"One thousand bucks," I said, "and I hightail it down the driveway in the wagon. Otherwise, I'll throw the fat in the fire, all of it, including the chain about her ankles and my reason for putting it there. And we'll see which one of us has most to lose."

Without taking his eyes off my face, he reached for his wallet. He counted out a thousand dollars without turning a hair; chicken feed, pocket change to him.

I folded the sheaf of fifties and hundreds, some of them new bills, and slipped it into my pocket with care. We parted then, the old man and I, without another word being spoken.

The station wagon seemed to run with new life when I reached the highway. I felt the pressure of the money—the vital element—against my thigh.

The chain on her ankles had lured Tomlin, convinced him that he was dealing with a tramp interested only in a thousand bucks, so he had signed his confession of guilt by putting his fingerprints all over the money.

I didn't trust the gross sheriff in Palmetto City. I thought it far better to take the vital element and every detail of the nightmare directly to the state's attorney in St. Petersburg.

I was pretty sure the battered old station wagon would get me there.

When the self-important advocate found the perfect loophole, the murderer moved quickly to close it. . . .

SEVENTEEN

The Way Out

Stanley didn't bother to stir on his bunk when he heard the guard rattling keys in the cell door.

"Mr. Graves," the bulky guard said in a polite tone that even a civilian review board would have approved, "you have a visitor. Fellow wants to talk to you."

"Tell him to see my secretary for an appointment," Stanley grunted, his eyes remaining closed.

"That's pretty good, Mr. Graves," the guard chuckled courteously. "But this fellow is a lawyer. He wants to take up your case. He arranged his appointment through the judge."

Stanley lifted the long, thin arm draped across his face. He cracked one eye against the bands of sunlight streaming through the cell window.

Pushing past the uniformed guard was a plump, earnest young man in a gray suit cut in the latest Madison Avenue fashion. He brought into the antisepsis of the cell a hint of good cologne. His necktie, shirt, and shoes were carefully coordinated. His face was round and pink, the kind that men ignore when replaying a golf match at the nineteenth hole. Behind heavy, square-rimmed glasses, his china blue eyes beamed at Stanley with a consciously summoned vitality, optimism, and determination.

The gray-suited figure cleared its throat in a good imitation of a masculine rumble. "Tough spot, eh, Graves? Convicted of a capital crime, gas chamber the next stop, cards all stacked against you. One lone man against the massive Establishment." The rosebud mouth curled in the best Mittyish mimicry of a John Wayne grin. "But the ball game isn't over, even in the ninth inning. Right, Stanley? We're not licked yet. We'll find a way out."

Stanley raised his head a few inches from the lumpy pillow to study

141

the stranger. Even with the prison haircut, Stanley managed a hippie look. His sprawled body suggested ennui. His gaunt, hungry-looking face hung in lines of self-sorrow. His large brown eyes, in the shadows of cavernous sockets, were depthless pools of soul. "Go away," he muttered. "I didn't smoke any signals. I got no bread to fee a lawyer."

"That doesn't matter," the lawyer said generously. "You're in trouble. Forty-three days from today the state is going to gas the life out of you for the crime of murder. Nothing else counts."

"You're telling me?" Stanley said. He fell back and stared at the ceiling light in its wire-mesh cage. "Why come in here and rake up old leaves, Mr. Whoever-you-are? What is your name, anyway?"

"Cottrell," the plump young man said. "Leonard Cottrell. Of the SPCD."

"Never heard of it."

The guard coughed politely. "Take all the time you need with your client, Mr. Cottrell." The turnkey eased from the cell, locking the door.

Leonard Cottrell frowned at Stanley's indolent form. "We're quite well known, Stanley. Society for the Protection of Civil Dissent. Nonprofit organization. Funded with a trust set up by an old lady who lived alone with three cats."

Stanley shifted on the thin mattress, facing the bleak stone wall a few inches away.

Leonard studied Stanley's curled spine and bony shoulders. He shook his head slowly. "Monstrous—the way a heartless society can break a man's spirit. But cast off this despair, my friend. Yours is exactly the type of case that interests us most. Come on, Stanley, where is the old pepper?"

"Ohboy, ohboy, ohboy," Stanley muttered. "Get a load of this guy."

Leonard looked about for a place to sit down. The only seat was a wooden stool of questionable size for his ample bottom. He eased onto it, still looking at Stanley's back.

"We've reviewed your case, Stanley, but a legal record skims the essence of man. Right? It would help if I knew everything there is to know about you as an individual, a man, a suffering human being."

Stanley said nothing. Leonard waited, gradually pursing his lips. "Hmmmm. Just as I suspected. This job has many facets. They've really crushed your personality, haven't they, Stanley?"

"Mr. Cottrell," Stanley said to the wall, "why don't you just split? It wouldn't be like you were copping out. You don't owe me anything."

Leonard's brows escalated. "That's where you're wrong, Stanley. 'Think not for whom the bell tolls' . . . If for thee, then also for me."

"Yeah," Stanley said. "I know."

Leonard reached out to pat the knifeblades of Stanley's shoulders. "Buck up, old man. You'll feel better as we talk. Believe me, we have a Sunday punch, a way out."

Stanley inched his head to look at Leonard over his shoulder.

"Ah, ha!" Leonard grinned. "I thought that would bring a reaction."

Stanley's head dropped back. Again, he was staring at the wall.

"I see," Leonard murmured. "They've so desecrated the inner man that he no longer believes in Sunday punches."

"Okay," Stanley sighed. "What's the Sunday punch?"

"Not so fast." Leonard waggled a breakfast-sausage finger. "Let's start at the top. I'm sure your parents are much to blame for your present plight."

"Yeah," Stanley said. "They gave me birth."

"And they were so grossly involved in material things they never had time for you."

"Nope," Stanley told the wall. "My mother kept house and darned my socks, and my old man took me fishing and to ball games."

"Yes . . . well. . . ." Leonard was wordless for a moment, growing a silent frown. Then he brightened. "Then they spoiled you, smothered you with attention, never gave you a chance to develop in your own way."

"They treated me like family," Stanley said. "I was neither spoiled, nor a whipping boy."

"But surely," Leonard pleaded, "they scarred your psyche in some way."

"I don't think so. I'm the one who left the scars."

"So that's it!" Leonard almost tipped his stool over. "In its early contacts with a hostile social environment the organism developed a guilt complex! When did you first start feeling guilty, Stanley?"

"I don't. Never have."

"How about the murder of Dominic Asalti?" Leonard prodded.

"He was a sick old man," Stanley yawned against the wall. "He's better off."

Leonard sat plucking the lobe of his ear, looking at Stanley's back. "I really must understand you, Stanley, if I am to help you. It's my duty to help, whether you think you need it or not. My duty, my job, my dedication." His voice notched on an angry twinge. "You've no right to spurn me, Stanley."

"Man, I am so loaded with rights they're breaking my back."

Leonard pinched the bridge of his nose. "The higher the obstacle, the greater the sense of fulfillment," he sighed. He drew in a long breath. "Now let's get some building blocks in a row, shall we? When did you leave home, Stanley?"

"Four years ago."

"Couldn't stand the communication gap any longer, of course."

"Nope. I just packed up one day and left."

"But why, Stanley?"

"I didn't like the taste," Stanley said.

"Taste?"

"Of life. I thought at first I was looking for something. I mean, I kidded myself by pretending I was looking. Later, I knew the truth. I just couldn't stand the taste of life. I went a little empty and sick inside every time I thought of the long years ahead. Years of what? Routine. Sticking to a job. Taking the lumps and being satisfied with the re- wards. Getting old and full of pain, and then dying, like I had never been. When I was finally honest with myself, I just wanted to spit out the taste."

Leonard was glowing, fascinated. He stared at the prone figure as if stripping the flesh naked and the flesh to the bones. He was digging into the problem at last. "Where were you when the self-confronta- tion took place, Stanley?"

"I dunno," Stanley said. "I guess I placed myself by degrees. No blinding light. No sudden revelation. I drifted out to L.A. first and joined a hippie colony. I listened to the talk, but they didn't have the answers. They were all ducking, scared of the taste, just like me."

"Did you have lots of girls, Stanley?"

"Sure. All the same, like programmed dolls on which somebody had turned a switch, all as tired as I was. So I bummed to New York and the east side. Might as well have stayed in L.A. Faces the same. Words the same. The winter was a little colder, that's all."

"Drugs, Stanley?"

"Sure. The route. The in thing. Part of the scene, man. Pot, LSD, the hard stuff. But none of it killed the taste."

"How did you get money to live, Stanley? Steal?" Leonard's words were eager, dissecting knives. His eyes sparkled. What a case history to mull over and discuss!

"I padded with a runaway chick from Scarsdale," Stanley said. "She had plenty of bread. She turned on the gas one night while I was out. I came back as the ambulance was hauling her away. Later, I tried the same trip, but I couldn't cut it. I was running to open the windows before the room was half full of gas. I just couldn't stick it out."

Leonard breathed in tremulous excitement. "Was that the only time you tried to kill yourself, Stanley?"

"You kidding? I tried to fall in front of a subway. Couldn't move, glued to the spot. Went up to a roof top in Atlanta. Couldn't step over the edge. Peeled a razor blade in New Orleans, but my fingers wouldn't take it to my wrist."

Leonard's head made small movements of incredulity. How warming the knowledge that he was not like this caricature on a jail cell bunk.

"From New Orleans you drifted here, didn't you, Stanley?"

"It's all in the record."

"But I want the little things that aren't there, Stanley."

"You're a sick, meddling old maid, Mr. Cottrell."

Leonard whitened, then steadied himself. "I understand, Stanley. You've been through a horror. You're facing a worse. Take it out on me, if you like, if it will help."

"Just go to the record," Stanley said. "It's all there. Old man Dominic Asalti wanted to help, too. A real square. He didn't know anything about the nothingness, the emptiness that even an LSD trip doesn't fill for long. He had some dough, not much, so I beat him to death and the cops came to my room and found the piece of bloody pipe. The state provided a judge. My folks hired a lawyer. Nobody beat a confession out of me with a rubber hose—but I'm here. And what else .did you expect?"

Leonard rose to his full height and shoved the stool back with his heel. In his best stentorian tone, he said, "Truly you are here—but neither forsaken nor forgotten, Stanley. Have faith, the doors will open shortly."

"Doors of the gas chamber," Stanley said.

"Never!" Leonard cried. "We shall succor you!"

"But I'm guilty. . . ."

Leonard broke his brisk pacing. "What's that got to do with it? Guilt or innocence is beside the point." Leonard's face flushed even pinker with a sense of impending victory. "The record, you said—and it's there, in the record—the way out. The fact remains that the officers who came to your room and arrested you entered without your permission and found the murder weapon."

Stanley began turning slowly on the bunk. Leonard nodded with delight at the first small show of animation.

"That's right, Stanley, the arresting officers were guilty of illegal entry—not in arresting you, mind you, but in searching your room."

Stanley stood up, eyes glazed, as if trying to comprehend all that was being offered to him.

"You mean," Stanley said, "the technicality will put the gas chamber on the moon as far as I'm concerned?"

Leonard looked as if he were about to dance a jig and click his heels. His smile was radiant. "I mean exactly that, Stanley, fellow human being, victim of a vicious society."

"How about that?" Stanley said. His hands thrust out, and before Leonard knew what was happening, Stanley's hands were on his throat.

Leonard emitted a single muffled scream as Stanley cracked his head against the wall.

Stanley was still beating Leonard's head against the stone when the guard rushed in. Glimpsing the guard's movement, Stanley quietly turned loose of Leonard's neck and let the dead plumpness collapse to the floor.

Stanley looked at the guard's ashen face and noted the trembling in the hand that held the drawn gun. The guard was terribly upset, and Stanley was coldly impersonal about that.

"This time," Stanley said, "I want you people to be very careful. Don't make any technical mistakes!"

Then with very tired movements he crossed to the bunk, settled himself, and lay staring at the wall.

There are times when even a suitcase full of money is more trouble than it's worth. . . .

EIGHTEEN

False Start

In our suite at the Diamond Shores on Miami Beach, Gervasi packed the money, two hundred thousand dollars of it, in an innocent-looking overnight case.

He snapped the case closed and lighted a cigar. Trim and excellently tailored, his careful Florida tan contrasting with the snow white hair, Gervasi looked like the titular head of a very wealthy old family.

He handed me the overnight case. "Call me immediately from Dallas, Nick."

"It goes without saying," I said. I paused at the mirror to adjust my necktie as Gervasi and I strolled toward the door. I had an excellent tan of my own. The face in the mirror was clean-cut, with friendly eyes of brown. If Gervasi looked like the titular head, I gave the appearance of the bright young scion who would one day traditionally fill his shoes. Actually, there was no blood relationship between us. Merely the relationship in business, in the similarity of desire to have the best in life that big money can buy. Perhaps this was the strongest kind, after all.

Gervasi opened the door, laying his other hand on my shoulder. "Have a good trip, Nick."

"Thanks. I will."

I crossed to the elevator and rode down to the plush lobby. Through the tall glass doors I saw my car pulling up under the outside canopy.

Johnny, the bellhop, leaped out of the car and held the door for me when I came out. He'd already brought my twin suitcases down and stowed them in the car trunk.

He glanced at the overnight case in my hand. "Would you like that in the trunk also, Mr. Ramey?"

"You needn't bother."

147

I handed him a dollar, and he thanked me with a short bow. I got in the car and Johnny closed the door gently but firmly. He stepped clear of the car, just a hotel fixture, like the plumbing.

The morning was a monotony of endless miles of flat terrain. I was impatient to get through with the Texas trip and back to Miami for the opening races at Gulfstream. But I kept my foot lightly on the accelerator, never exceeding the speed limit. I certainly didn't want a nosy, rube cop stopping me.

Shortly after mid-day, I drove into a sun-baked town in central Florida which offered no likely place to have lunch, so I continued driving.

On the northern outskirts, I saw a fresh, new motel with spacious, landscaped grounds, swimming pool and restaurant. I turned in and found a spot in the crowded parking area near the restaurant. I guessed that this was the favorite eating place for the local business gentry.

I carried the overnight case inside. With the case securely wedged between me and a wall of the booth, I lunched on an excellent shrimp creole.

With the overnight case firmly in my grip, I paid the check, went out of the restaurant, and moved the short distance to my car. With my free hand, I was reaching in my pocket for the car keys when a hard object jabbed me unpleasantly in the back. It felt exactly like the business end of a gun barrel, an item with which I'd had previous experience.

"Easy! I'm not resisting," I said with dry-throated candor. My gaze flicked to the surrounding cars. All were empty, their occupants inside eating, talking insurance and real estate and fishing and bird hunting.

"How about we use my car, Mr. Ramey?" the man behind me said.

The voice was vaguely familiar. I turned my head slowly, looking over my shoulder. I saw—really saw—the face of Johnny, the bellhop, for the first time. It wasn't a bad-looking face at all, even features, dark hair growing to a slight widow's peak over a high forehead. But the dark eyes were too calm, too quietly determined to quench the acid of alarm that was stinging through me. The face reminded me a great deal of my own.

The eyes went a shade colder. He was carrying the gun in his jacket pocket. He nudged me with it. "This way, Mr. Ramey."

The primary moment of nauseating surprise had passed. The eruptions of the shrimp creole became less violent. I made a casual move to drop the overnight case into my car.

He laughed thinly. "No, Mr. Ramey. We'll take the case along— and keep the other hand in the pants pocket until the gun is safely out of the shoulder holster."

"All right, Johnny," I said pleasantly. "We'll do it your way, for the moment."

"I won't need many moments, Mr. Ramey."

"You may not have many," I reminded him.

Herding me toward a five-year-old Ford a short distance away, he said, "I've thought about it, waited for it a long time. I'm willing to take the gamble. It's a big country. I can lose myself easily."

He reached cautiously around my body, lifted my gun. A prod from his weapon forced me into the car on the righthand side.

"Now slide across the seat," he instructed. "You'll drive, while I have a look at the case."

I started the car. It was as clean inside as a new one. The engine hummed with vibrant, leashed power. It was evident the car had received meticulous care from hands with an aptitude for mechanics.

"Drive north," he said, resting the overnight case on his knees, while he held his gun steadily on me.

I eased the car onto the highway. Traffic northward on the two-lane macadam was just about nonexistent. Insects hummed over the palmetto fields. In the distance, tall pines and cypress stood lonely and gaunt against the backdrop of glaring, tropical sky.

"I assume," I said, "that you located me simply by following me."

"Right," he said. "I had the horse waiting near the employees' entrance at the Diamond Shores. All I had to do was fall in behind you."

"Maybe you were spotted."

"You kidding?" he laughed. "Who sees the coming and going of a bellhop? It'll take awhile for even the bell captain to realize I'm not around the hotel. You know, it was good of you to drive sensibly this morning."

"Watchfully, too, Johnny," I said on a hollow note.

"Sure," he grinned, "but not for an old car that showed behind you a time or two. Guess you figured it was a farmer's car."

My reply was a bleak silence. The truth is, I hadn't noticed the old Ford at all. Nobody who was questionable to Gervasi and me in Miami, or anyplace else, drove an old Ford.

"Don't let it get you down, Mr. Ramey," Johnny said in enjoyment. "We all make mistakes now and then."

"A good point for you to remember, Johnny."

"Thanks, I will. But up to now I haven't made any. I had plenty of time to change from the monkey suit in the back seat of the car, while you were having lunch. It was really simple. I just sat on the rear bumper of the car next to yours and rested until you came out."

"It will get less simple, Johnny."

"Oh, sure," he patted an imitation yawn.

My hands were in hard knots on the wheel. A drop of sweat crept into the corner of my eye and began stinging and making me blink.

"Johnny, you're very young to start out like this."

"Younger the better."

"You ought to think of the years ahead."

"Now you dig, pops," he said warmly. "Now you're getting with it. I've thought of nothing else for a long time."

"You're a nice, clean-cut young man, Johnny, with a future. Unless you. . . ."

"This?" he said in mock horror. "This? Coming from you?"

"Why not from me, Johnny?"

"Oh, nuts!" he said, slouching slightly against the car door. "Now don't start boring me."

"What do you think you know about me, Johnny?"

"I don't *think*. I know. I know that I know! Most all of us know."

"Most all of us, Johnny?"

"You wouldn't dig. You've never been a hotel employee. We're not quite real people. Never really there. You know? Like unseen hands keeping a big, luxury palace afloat. Like spooks with a world all our own, the bellhops, cooks, waitresses, linen women, maids, maintenance men. We eat together, talk together, party together, live together. We got bitter enemies and bosom pals in our own ranks. You know?"

"I don't think I ever really thought anything about it, Johnny."

"Who does?" he asked. He was silent a moment; then he laughed softly. "Sometimes we know more about you than you know yourselves. Waitresses overhear those bitter, whispered arguments of elegant people at dinner. A switchboard girl knows the origin of a secret phone call. A swimming pool attendant knows why a wife swims every afternoon while her husband is looking after his stocks. A bellhop delivers hangover medicine or more liquor to a falling-down, talkative drunk. Now do you know, Mr. Ramey?"

My vision reddened slightly. Gervasi and I were going to take a certain hotel apart, if and when I got back.

"How did you find out what's in the overnight case, Johnny?" I asked thickly.

"I don't know. Not yet."

I gave him a quick frown.

He returned a smile. "I know about you and Mr. Gervasi," he said. "I know about the phone calls to certain people in Dallas. I know you've hung onto the case like you were a bleeder and it held your spare blood. Finally, I know that you, personally, Gervasi's top dog, are making the trip. It all adds up to something very big. Big enough for me."

"I have to admire your nerve," I admitted, although with reticence.

"Not nerve," he shook his head slowly. "I'm not so long on nerve. Just hungry, Mr. Ramey. I ache with the hunger. I wake up at night thinking about it. I just can't live with it any longer. I'm hungry, Mr. Ramey, for a place in that world I and the other spooks help keep afloat."

"And you think the case is full of bread?"

"I'm absolutely sure of it," he said. "Bread in one form or another. Bread I'll never again have the chance to pick up so easy. What is it, Mr. Ramey? Drugs? Hot jewels? Dough for a big gamble that's been rigged? How about the key?" He snapped his fingers. "Give me the key, Mr. Ramey."

"I don't have a key, Johnny. Gervasi has one. There is another in Dallas."

"Okay," he said. "That makes sense. So I'll have to blow the lock with the gun."

"Johnny, there's two hundred thousand in that case."

His face went blank for an instant. Then a laugh of pleased surprise ripped out of him. "Even better than I thought!"

"Johnny. . . ."

"Oh, no!" he said. "No deals. You're not buying me off with peanuts. I'm a pig, Mr. Ramey. And my risk is no greater if I take it all."

"We'll hunt you down, Johnny."

"Where? Hong Kong? Paris? Rome? Rio? Don't talk crazy and spoil the picture I've always had of you, Mr. Ramey."

"There is something I must say. . . ."

"Please, please," he gestured with his hand. "You're spoiling that picture of a man who set his sights and never let anything stand in his way. Why, Mr. Ramey, you've been my idol, my inspiration! I wouldn't think of harming you, unless you forced me. I'm not dumb enough to kill somebody and get the cops after me. After all, their organization is a little bigger than yours. They make it tougher for a man to hide."

"When you take the money at the point of a gun. . . ."

"When I take the money," he said, "I'm damned sure you and Gervasi won't go to any cops. If your deal was honest, you wouldn't be taking the risk of transporting the money this way."

"You got it all figured, Johnny."

"I sure have. And we've talked more than plenty. I want to open the case. I want the fine, slick feel of the money against my fingers. I want to go someplace private and count it a couple dozen times before I start spending it."

He held the overnight case as if he were hugging it. "There's a side road turning into those pines up ahead," he said, giving the road a long look. "Take it."

"Johnny . . ."

"One more peep, Mr. Ramey, and I'm going to start not liking you."

I slowed the car, turned the wheel. The shadow of the swaying, scraggly pines sent a shiver down my spine. We were on a sandy, rutted trail that led toward the distant swamplands, a little-used logging road. The narrow state highway fell behind. Now it was hidden from us by the piney woods. The world became very desolate, as if it were empty, deserted except for the two of us.

His breathing was thinning out, beginning to rasp slightly. "Stop the car, Mr. Ramey."

I braked, opened the door. He let the overnight case slide to the floor and moved across the seat behind me.

I timed the passing seconds with the sensitivity of raw nerves. There was a rustle of clothing as the gun came down, aiming at the back of my head.

I slipped to one side, lashing out with my foot, and dropping to the sandy carpeting of pine needles.

A meaningless sound caught in his throat. My heel had caught his kneecap. He thudded against the car.

Spinning and lunging toward him beneath the gun, I glimpsed his pain-contorted face. He forced the throbbing knee to support him, shifted his position, and the gun was swinging down again.

I slammed into his middle, grabbing for his wrist. I had it momentarily, but he was sweating. He slipped loose as we fell.

I tried to turn on him a second time. I had lost the advantage of surprise. He took a side step. A fresh look of viciousness was in his face. Halfway to my feet, I suddenly covered my head with my arms. The impact of the gun barrel made my right elbow feel as if it had dissolved.

I stumbled backward, concerned only with defense now. He danced in and out, in and out. The third or fourth blow with the gun knocked me cold. I'm not sure which. Johnny had ample time for a clean getaway.

I suppose an hour or more passed. The fog began to clear. I rolled over on the pine needles and sat up. The trees around me did a dizzy dance. I groaned, and cradled my throbbing elbow, lowered my aching head, and finally tried to brush away the swarm of sweat bees that made life right then even more hellish.

Another thirty minutes passed before I staggered onto the highway. I looked up and down the road, aching for the sight of a car, or a farmer in a truck. The road was devoid of all movement, except for the shimmering heat waves that made the road look like black water in the distance.

I started walking. A southbound car passed at last, but swooped by without even slowing for my frantic, waggling thumb.

I was on the point of passing out again when I reached the motel. I needed a doctor, but that could wait.

In an outside phone booth. I placed a call to Gervasi. He wasn't in his room. I guessed a faceless bellhop had to page him.

His cultured tones reached me at last, "Gervasi speaking."

"Nick Ramey here."

He took a breath. "You couldn't be anywhere near Dallas yet. What went wrong?"

"I lost the stuff."

He let the breath out. "Are you—confined?"

"No."

"Can you return under your own power?"

"Yes," I answered him bereftly.

"Then it wasn't the police?"

"No, Gervasi. It was a punk bellhop who followed me from the hotel."

"A *what?*"

"Look," I groaned, "I'm nearly dead. I'll give you the details later. He got the money. He got away. I did the best I could, and I won't apologize."

He gave himself a moment for it to sink in. When he spoke again, his voice was less strident. "I know you always do your best, Nick. Did he take the car?"

I looked across the motel parking lot where my car was still parked. "No, just the money. All of it. He didn't give me a chance to tell him, either. He kept shutting me up."

"Then you'd better get back here as fast as you can, Nick."

"You don't have to tell me," I was practically weeping. "Better start winding up things right now. That bellhop is going to have Federal men like a dog has fleas, when he hits the first bright spot and starts scattering two hundred grand of counterfeit dough. . . ."

When enough money is involved, there is more than one way to bend a will to one's desires. . . .

NINETEEN

A Way with a Will

I was very fond of my Uncle Dudley Gillam. Not for any singular reason. He was my only blood relation, but that didn't account entirely for my feeling. I've heard other people speak of their relatives with shuddering distaste, but my recollections of Uncle Dudley were pleasurable. He found joy in living; he was agreeable, kind, and thoughtful. He was an all-around likeable individual, and I liked him. That's all there was to it. And the regard was mutual. He never put it into words, but he left no doubt in my mind that I was at the top of his list of favorite people.

After he retired from the railroad we saw little of each other. He was an engineer until age forced him out of the big diesels. Not a strapping Casey Jones, but a wiry, tough little guy who ramrodded the long trains through the nights like a runty cowboy forking a dinosaur.

His years of motion had conditioned him to be restless. He was always on the go. He would wander down to Florida, up to big-game country in Wyoming, out to California. He would hit Vegas now and then for a splurge and, broke and hungover, amble down to Corpus Christi to dry out.

We always kept in touch. He pecked out letters on a portable typewriter with broken type and an always-grey ribbon, signing them with his bold flourish. The grammar was questionable but the details were colorful. When he wrote about the rupture of a radiator hose while he was driving across the Painted Desert you could hear the water sizzle.

He enjoyed sending picture postcards and wild greeting cards from various locales. On my birthday a zany card would enclose a twenty-dollar bill for the purpose of "oiling up a sweet patootie in a cozy bar, courtesy your Unc Dud."

I always responded, jazzing up the details of my dreary bachelor existence as much as possible. Each Christmas I would try to send

155

him something special—not expensive, necessarily, but something I had shopped carefully for. The kind of Wellington pipe he smoked or one of the baggy sweaters be favored.

Since he was a gregarious extrovert, it didn't surprise me he was a soft touch. He always had a dollar for the panhandling wino with the seared eyes and burning throat. He never passed up a Salvation Army kettle or the poor box on his infrequent trips to church. And now and then some down-and-outer would hang onto his shirttails for a while. A busted madam, a kid just out of jail, or an itinerant worker stranded in Salinas. Or someone like Odus Calhoun, dubbed "Hardtimes" by Uncle Dudley.

"A born loser," Uncle Dudley wrote. "One of those birds who gets all the frowns of fate—that's Odus Calhoun. Worked hard all his life, paid his taxes, and never broke a law. And what did it get Hardtimes? Flat busted in Dallas where I met him, for one thing. Wife dead, and three kids grown up and scattered who'd rather forget him.

"If Hardtimes crosses a street, the drivers nearly run him down. A stray dog follows him home and the first time Hardtimes lets the mutt out the dog catcher is cruising by. The last jalopy he managed to buy turned out to be stolen. He cashed a welfare check and was robbed in sight of a police station. I reckon if Hardtimes inherited a gold mine an earthquake would dump the vein to the boiling center of the earth."

From later letters I gathered that Hardtimes had settled into the role of handyman, cook, valet, friend, and confidant. "He more than earns his keep," Uncle Dudley wrote, "and it's nice to have a fellow critter around. He can't play checkers worth a damn, so I finally know the joy of winning."

It seemed to be a good arrangement. Uncle Dudley buffered Hardtimes Calhoun from the jaundiced eye of fate and at the same time escaped the loneliness of his wandering life.

But the fortunate circumstance was relatively short-lived. Three years ago Uncle Dudley wrote me the woeful news.

"Lost my pal. We was on the way to L.A. in my pickup with the camper cover. We stopped for the night at a campground near Yuma, and I couldn't wake up Hardtimes the next morning. The county coroner said he died peaceful in his sleep from a worn-out heart. I gave him a decent funeral and searched his duffel without finding the addresses of any of his kids. They may never know how their poor old pappy met his end."

He never referred to Hardtimes again and I respected his wish to leave a painful subject reverently closed.

A new wrinkle in our correspondence was added a couple of years ago. Instead of a twenty, a hundred-dollar bill dropped from one of his offbeat greeting cards. "I put some money where the profit is," he explained. "So simmer yourself a real high-class patootie this time."

And my last birthday turned up a blank check signed by Uncle Dudley. "Don't go wilder than a hog, nephew, but if you hanker to tootle around in a little sports car, do your shopping. Happy birthday, village cut-up."

His rapidly expanding affluence naturally tickled my curiosity, but he volunteered no details of his financial dealings, and I courteously cramped the urge to pry. I satisfied myself with a guess that he'd hit a run of beginner's luck in the stock market. His business hadn't pinned him down. He was still here and there on the map like a flea on a short-haired pup.

The most recent letter from him said: "Writing from the mugginess of a New Orleans August. Going up to Asheville, North Carolina, for a breath of summer-resort air. Drop me a note at the Great Smokies Chilton, Suite Charnot."

His plans offered me the chance to visit. I had vacation time coming, and the owner of the construction company where I worked had a Porsche he wanted delivered to his daughter, who was in an Atlanta college. With tin hat in hand I appeared in the boss's office and explained my proposition. He went for the idea, handed me the keys to the car, slapped my shoulder, and counted out more than enough cash to cover the expenses of delivering the car.

From Atlanta to Asheville by air is a matter of minutes, and I arrived on a deliciously cool Smoky Mountain day after I'd delivered the Porsche. I rented a car and drove a modest four-lane expressway ten miles north, took an exit ramp, moved westerly in a snarl of city traffic, and at last was wending up a coolly shaded macadam road. Valleys, rolling mountains, and the scanty skyline of Asheville spread in the distance. A final turn and the Great Smokies Chilton swam into view.

It was a Swiss architect's dream, worth a pursed-lip whistle. The huge main inn extended a warm invitation. Webbed from it were driveways winding to private chalets tucked into rolling, landscaped mountain greenery. People were sunning, swimming, and loafing at a crystalline lake scooped into the mountainside. At a long sweep of tennis courts, lazier players had knocked off to watch a smashing drive match between two lean, bronzed young giants. Beyond the courts I glimpsed a pair of horses and riders dipping into a steep mountain trail. I slowed for the passage of a golf cart as it chugged across the parking area with two elderly occupants, headed toward the green-velvet golf course that wandered across the plateau near the crest of the mountain.

A Mercedes SEL was gliding from a parking place near the can-opied entrance to the inn and I slipped my rented car into the vacated slot.

I got out, giving the surroundings an appreciative survey. A small plaque over the brass-studded door of the nearest private chalet caught my eye. AIN. I lifted my eyes to Ain's next-door neighbor. The sedate plaque there announced: BRAUN.

I figured out that the third chalet was Charnot, Uncle Dudley's domicile of the moment.

I was itching to know something about the late-in-life financial wiz-ardry that afforded Uncle Dudley spots like this in which to take the mountain air. But even that was secondary to the thought of seeing him. I was a little giddy as I hurried along the driveway and the feeling wasn't entirely due to the altitude.

I checked the plaque to make sure my guess was correct, and it was. I turned into the flower-bordered fieldstone walk bisecting the narrow lawn just as the door opened. It framed a blonde wearing a sleeveless white dress. She was young and tanned and so mistily lovely that I wavered to a halt, staring for a moment.

"Hi there," I said. That was certainly original.

She said nothing, looking at me with eyes of cool green. I was sure she'd spotted me during my brief walk to Charnot and was about to tell me to get lost.

"I'm Jeremy Fisher," I said. "I was looking for my uncle."

"Jake-o!" she said with a sudden flash of a smile, using Uncle Dud-ley's nickname for me. Her green eyes warmed. "I should have rec-ognized you from the pictures Dudley has of you." She reached out a hand. "Come in, Jeremy!"

I entered the cool of Charnot, where I got the impression of a well-heeled sportsman's lodge. A large living room panelled in wormy chestnut was furnished with huge tweedy couches and club chairs, tables and a bar of natural oak, and a fireplace fit for five-foot logs. The ceiling was vaulted and beamed. A heavy oaken stairway led to a gallery overlooking the living room, where bedrooms were tucked under the rear portion of the expansive roof. "Nice, isn't it?" she said.

"Very."

"Would you like a drink?"

"I wouldn't mind a wee Scotch."

The flash of her legs and movement of her hips was something to watch as she went around behind the bar. Leave it to Uncle Dudley to winnow out the best.

"I'm Amanda," she said.

"Well, hello, Amanda. Have you known Uncle Dudley long?"

She tipped a glance at me, probing, balancing my words and anything that might lurk behind them. "Almost a year. And the situation is something like you've guessed. I'm fond of Dudley and he's fond of me; we travel about and have fun."

"Lucky people."

"Also, I'm a very good secretary and manager. So it isn't altogether a case of a wealthy older man buying himself a dumb blonde toy."

"I can believe that—and I like your frankness."

"Just to get us off on the right foot, Jake-o."

I took the drink she held out to me and watched her make herself a small one. A social gesture, not the drink of a real drinker.

"I wish you'd warned us you were coming. Dudley will be so disappointed."

"Isn't he here?"

She shook her head. "He went off to Miami earlier today. He's seeing some people down there on business. He left me here to take care of some details and correspondence before I join him."

I felt a pang of disappointment.

She touched my hand and said softly, "I'm sorry, Jeremy."

"Well—" I lifted and dropped my shoulders "—I guess it was a childish notion when you get right down to it—the urge to surprise him." I tossed off the Scotch.

She took my glass and set it on the bar. "A very nice notion, I'd call it."

We drifted across the room to the door. She offered her hand in a farewell gesture. "I wish I had more time, Jake-o, but Dudley does have the habit of leaving me to pick up the last-minute bits and pieces. My schedule is tighter than strangulation."

"Tell him I came by, Amanda."

"Of course. He'll write you immediately, I know."

I plodded disconsolately to the car, got in, and was about to turn the ignition key when I realized I'd been ushered out so fast I hadn't found out where Uncle Dudley was staying in Miami. After all, I was on vacation—why not join him there?

I got out of the car and walked back to Charnot. I was about to press the bell when I heard Amanda's voice, sharply raised.

"Yes, you do owe me an explanation, Dudley! You've told me a dozen and one times that if Jeremy ever shows up in person to tell him you're away, get rid of him. You've literally ground it into my brain. Why? Those letters you write are so filled with warmth, I should think you'd want to—"

A male voice grunted something I didn't quite catch, but it was enough to break her off.

"Under the circumstances, it is too my business!" Amanda said.

The male voice inched up a grim level. "Amanda, I don't owe you an explanation or a damned thing else. You're beautiful, but that's a plentiful commodity. If you like the good life we lead together, get off my back!"

Her voice dropped to acquiescence while I stood dumb. What was going on? What did Uncle Dudley have to hide from me?

I grasped the doorknob, turned it, and after the barest hesitation, opened the door.

Amanda spun to face me so quickly her gossamer-blonde hair brushed about her cheeks and she almost tripped on the expensive luggage, old airline stubs dangling from their handles, that she—or Uncle Dudley—had taken from a nearby closet in the few minutes since I'd left.

"I should ask you—" I began.

I glimpsed a frightened flicker in her eyes as her gaze speared past my shoulder, then heard the rustle of his movement. He used a heavy brass lamp, scooped from the table beside the doorway. The blow almost jarred my eyes from their sockets.

I came out of it with a gremlin soldering my ears together and the taste of burned Scotch in my throat. I crawled, groaning, across the thick russet carpet, grappled with the edge of a chair, and pulled myself up.

I turned my head and studied the scene groggily. They'd closed the door on the way out. The baggage was gone. The brass lamp lay where it had fallen. I squinted at my watch—I'd been out for about an hour.

I thought of the old baggage checks on the suitcases and garment bags and it gave me a hunch.

The small but modern Asheville airport was briskly busy. People queued at the ticket counter, moved around the spacious waiting room, sat reading.

Through a rift in the crowd I caught the glint of sunlight on bright blonde hair. I moved aside, people off an incoming flight brushing past on their way to the baggage room.

Amanda and a strange man were standing on the further side of the waiting room near the tall windows that gave a view of the landing field and the jumble of mountains beyond.

Somewhat aloofly, Amanda was gazing at the scenery outside. The man kept glancing at the bank of time-zone clocks on the northern wall. He was clearly fidgeting for a flight due to be announced shortly.

He was tall, thin, and slightly stooped, with the look of a mournful hound dog. His hair was grey and thin on his narrow skull. He was wearing expensive blue slacks and a mottled sports jacket, but he looked a little like the boondocks despite the cut of the clothing.

He said something. Amanda nodded without looking at him. He moved across the lobby and I eased over to let the flow of people shield me from his sight. When he reached the open archway leading to the ticket booths, he turned right, out of sight.

I followed quickly. Around the ell, a door was swinging shut. It carried a simple message: MEN.

I pushed inside. He was alone, standing at one of the washbasins lifting a pellet from a pillbox and chasing it down with water from a paper cup.

As he lifted his head, my image spread across the mirror behind him. His movement stopped as if his chin had hit an abutment. He clutched the edge of the washbasin, his already grey face a shade more ashen.

"Hi," I said. "It's me—Jeremy. And since Amanda knows you as Dudley Gillam, you must be my uncle."

His head dropped.

"Who are you, actually?" I asked. "Could it be—" I caught my breath. "Who was buried in Yuma those years ago? Hardtimes Calhoun? Or Dudley Gillam, with a death certificate made out in the name of Calhoun?"

He turned to face me, his mouth twitching. "I swear to you, he died of natural causes, Jeremy. I wouldn't have harmed a hair on your uncle's head. He was the best friend I ever had."

There was a stretch of silence, broken only by the hiss of a leaky latrine.

"I guess it took some thinking about, that morning you found Dudley Gillam dead in the camper," I said. "First the idea, then wrestling with it, then giving in. You knew he had only one relative, a nephew named Jeremy Fisher. You knew all about Jeremy from Uncle Dudley. Dudley was a no-ties wanderer, and there didn't seem to be a single obstacle in your way. All you had to do was bury him as Hardtimes Calhoun in a town where no one knew either of you and take his place. Once you mastered his simple signature, his pension checks, his bank account, all his earthly possessions were yours. You could keep on writing the never-seen nephew the kind of letters Dudley had always written. Keep one jump ahead of the nephew and you were safe for life. Am I getting it fairly close?"

He raised bloodshot eyes. "Almost dead on the nailhead, Jeremy."

"What then, Hardtimes? Where did the money start coming from—the big money?"

"Piece of life, part of living," Hardtimes said. "I guess I buried the hard times right there in Yuma. I'd had nothing but hard times from my cradle until I dug that grave, but when I wheeled out of Yuma in that camper pickup I left it all behind. I felt like a new man—like a cocksure Dudley Gillam—and I acted like a new man."

He turned. It wasn't a suspicious movement. The single thing he dreaded, the only thing he had had to fear, had happened. He ran water, pulled down a paper towel, and wiped his grey face.

"In the old existence everything turned to mud," he said. "But once I had buried myself, I began encountering all the luck I'd missed in a lifetime."

He tossed the damp towel into a container. "Dudley had three thousand dollars in a savings account, his sole estate except for his pension checks and that camper. I ran the three to twenty thousand in a run at a craps table in Las Vegas. Drifted to Phoenix and won a hundred and fifty acres of land from a fellow in a stud game. It turned out to be worthless desert—but three months later a fellow from the government turned up. He had traced me, as Dudley Gillam, through my forwarding addresses. It scared the pants off me at first. But he was a purchasing agent, and Uncle Sam bought the desert land as a solar-energy pilot site."

"How much?"

"A thousand dollars an acre. He was tickled to get it so cheap."

"But even a hundred and fifty thousand doesn't guarantee a life-time at playgrounds like the Great Smokies Chilton and Miami."

"You're right about that. But I ran into a guy in Fort Worth, a wildcat oil man rigged up in Venezuela. Some minor civil troubles, guerrillas from the mountains, busted him up and he had run short of cash. He'd hopped up to the States to raise some. He needed a partner with a quick hundred thousand to see the drilling to comple-tion."

"And," I said mind-boggled, "you brought in the wells."

"Like water out of this faucet," Hardtimes Calhoun said.

"How much are you worth now?"

"I'm not sure. I guess I could sell out my interest for five or six million."

I drew in my breath.

"Now that you know—" His lank body began to pull itself to-gether. He was mastering the hangdog guilt in his eyes. His lips were thinning, hardening. "What next? I owe you three thousand plus the interest on it and some pension checks and the interest on them. The only law I broke was to bury the wrong man—who had died of natu-ral causes, as the Yuma coroner attested. Against my kind of money, you'd never make it in court if you tried to claim more than your just due."

The idea of trying to fight his amassed wealth inspired some hard thinking.

Only he and I knew the truth. He was Dudley Gillam, even to Amanda. He was Dudley Gillam—and I was his sole heir.

I had a deep-down certainty that he hadn't drawn a will cutting me out. His subconscious guilt would have forestalled that. And even if there should be a will, it could be destroyed, set aside. When there is enough money there is a way with a will.

I let a ruefully pleasant smile work to life on my lips. "It's a different reunion than I'd planned, Uncle Dudley."

"You mean—you're going to accept it?"

I nodded. "Why not? What good would it do to fight you? I take my hat off to you. In many ways, you're very much like the man you buried in Yuma."

And the man, I thought, I'll bury in Miami. A neat little accident. Maybe an overdose of some of his medication. Or a cramp when he went swimming in the ocean. Or an unfortunate fall down a stairway. Accidents are always happening to geezers his age.

"You don't have to duck me any longer, Uncle Dudley."

As we strolled out together, I dropped my arm across his shoulders. My touch was light, but he'd soon learn it was the returning touch of hard times—the hardest of all times.

When Berkmin figured out how Willard Ainsley had died, a most unusual opportunity was at hand. . . .

TWENTY

Money, Murder, or Love

The call came in shortly before I was due to go off duty at 7 A.M.

York stuck his head in the squadroom. "We got a job, Nick. A kid just found a stiff in an alley off Kilgo Street."

We went downstairs to the garage and got in one of the black, unmarked cars. As I drove across the city to Kilgo Street, York kept up a barrage of talk. He's been a cop almost as long as I have, twelve years, but he's never got used to the idea of death. He talks to cover his nervousness.

He talked about his wife and kid, as if really interested in selling me on the idea of marriage. He talked about the weather and of Sergeant Delaney's gall stone operation. He talked of anything except the violation of a human life.

The city was awakening, and for this brief moment it felt vital and clean, qualities that never extended to the street we were headed for.

By the time we reached Kilgo Street, York had run out of extraneous talk. "Well," he muttered, as I stopped in the mouth of the alley, "I guess he can't be much. Some bum. Who else would get himself killed in a Kilgo district alley?"

We got out of the car. The beat cop—a heavy, porcine guy intended by birth, reflexes and mentality never to rise far—came forward to meet us.

Hemmed in by scabby brick walls, a Kilgo Street alley is a particularly unpleasant place to die.

The beat cop grimaced. "He's back there."

"Touch anything?"

"No, sir."

"That kid find him?" I asked, pointing toward the skinny youth pressed against the wall.

"Yes, sir. He was short-cutting it through the alley, on his way to work at the produce market."

I saw York had that pale look about him. So I said, "Take over with the kid."

"Sure, Nick," he said quickly.

In our society, few people find their natural place. York should have been an insurance salesman. Instead, he'd needed a job years ago and the civil exams had been open. It's the little fates that put us where we are.

I walked back to the dead man and stood looking down at him. He was not big. He was slender, wiry, with a narrow, cruel face. I guessed that he had been arrogant and vicious when he hadn't had his way. He looked to be about thirty-five.

The strangest thing about him was the fact that he didn't belong in that alley. His clothing—suit, shoes, shirt, tie—had cost about what I draw for working a month.

I kneeled beside him. He'd been shot under the heart. Most of the bleeding had been internal. He hadn't lived long after the small bore bullet had struck him.

I touched his pockets, turned him slightly. His wallet had been jerked out of the hip pocket of his trousers. The wallet, soft, hand-tooled calfskin, was ripped. It had been cleaned of money. There was a driver's license, a club membership card, a diner's card, and a picture remaining in the wallet.

I had to look at the picture first. Even in that pocket-sized image, she was that kind of woman.

I stood up, holding the wallet. York had been wrong. This was a big one. The dead man was Willard Ainsley, according to the driver's license. And Willard Ainsley was a financier and playboy. Worth so much, if you believed the newspapers, that it was a remote, unreal figure to a man like me. Seven or eight million. No one knew for sure. In that category, it seemed to me that a million more or less wasn't terribly important.

The gun that had killed Willard Ainsley was nowhere around. There were two parallel lines in the cinders of the alley, marks his heels had made. He'd been killed elsewhere and dragged into the alley.

On the sidewalk, the beat cop was breaking up a gathering crowd. A siren growled the approach of the meat wagon and lab boys.

Ainsley had lived with his wife in the penthouse of the Cortez, the sumptuous apartment hotel overlooking the lake.

I was on overtime, but I wasn't sleepy. The doorman didn't want to admit me. The desk man endured the shock of having a policeman on the premises. I pocketed my identification, told him I was seeing Mrs. Ainsley, and asked him not to announce me. For York it would have been an ordeal. I didn't much care.

On the top floor, I crossed the wide, carpeted hall and knocked on Ainsley's door. It opened as I knocked a second time. I lowered my hand.

"Ramoth Ainsley?"

"Yes," the woman said.

"Mrs. Willard Ainsley."

"Yes. What is it?"

I pulled out my wallet and showed her my I.D. She gave me a cool look. "Nicholas Berkmin," she said. "Come in, Mr. Berkmin."

I followed her down a short, wide stairway to a large, sunken living room. Tall glass doors across the room opened on a terrace, as green as a landscaped park. The terrace offered a view of the lake, sparkling in the early sunlight.

Ramoth Ainsley paused near the concert grand and turned toward me. She wore a simple, silken dressing gown over her pajamas. It suggested the lines of a beautiful, supple body. There was strength in her face, and the wallet photo had failed to catch the texture and richness of her black hair.

She was lovely and fashionable, like many rich women. But she had an undefinable quality that money won't buy. Call it a sensuous vitality. You sense it on rare occasions when a woman, possessing it, enters a room or passes on the street.

"I assume," she said, "that something rather drastic has happened."

I nodded, and she said, "To Will?"

"I'm afraid so."

"Has he been hurt?"

"No," I said.

She continued to look at me. "He's dead."

"Yes."

"How?"

"It appears that someone killed him."

"I see," her lips framed the words, but didn't speak them.

I took her arm and guided her to a chair.

"Do you expect me to faint or have hysterics, Mr. Berkmin?"

"No," I said. "But I must say you are taking it very well."

"Is there any reason why I shouldn't?"

"I don't know."

"Well, there isn't," she said. "I'd like—Would you please hand me a cigarette from that box on the table?"

I opened the ivory box, extended it, and when she had the cigarette between her lips, I picked up the lighter and struck it for her.

"Thank you." She inhaled deeply. "When did it happen?"

"Last night, I think. We know very little yet. He was found by a boy on Kilgo Street."

"Not a very nice place to end up, is it, Mr. Berkmin?"

"Do you know what might have contributed to his ending up there?"

"No."

"It looks as if he was robbed. His wallet had been stripped of money. Did he carry much?"

"He considered five or six hundred dollars pocket change."

"There are a lot of people who wouldn't consider it that."

"I suppose."

"What time did he leave here last night?"

"Right after dinner. Seven-thirty or so."

"Did he say where he was going?"

She didn't answer right away. She smoked, then looked at the ash on the tip of her cigarette. "We'd had an argument. He slammed the door on the way out."

"Did you argue often?" I asked.

The cigarette ash broke and fell to the carpet. "You'll find out everything anyway," she said.

"We try to."

"We were on the point of splitting up, Will and I," she said. "You see, I come from one of those old families with a hallowed name and social connections. And for the last generation, we've been worse than on our uppers. How we've managed— Anyway, I let myself be talked into marrying Will. I believed that I could—well, develop some feeling for him in time. I didn't know then how domineering and cruel he could be." She rose and got herself a second cigarette. "I'm sure you understand these things, Mr. Berkmin."

"You've told me quite a bit," I said. "Do you remember what the fight last night started over?"

"He accused me of an indiscretion."

"Was he in the habit of storming out?"

"The cruelest thing that he could think of—at the moment—that's what he did."

"Did you expect him back later in the evening?"

"I didn't know. And I was certainly too angry to ask him what his plans were."

"And you heard nothing more from him?"

She shook her head.

"Did he have many enemies?"

"More than his share."

"Any who'd think of doing away with him?"

"I don't think so."

"I'll need the names of his business associates and his attorney," I said.

"I can supply those."

"I'll also need you downtown."

"Right now?"

"It would be better to get the identification over with," I said.

She nodded and started out of the room. Then she paused. "Murders like this—killing and robbing in an alley—are they always solved?"

"Not always."

She went out of the room, and I stood there with the feeling that her husband's murderer had a silent cheering section.

I slept for awhile and went back on duty at four-thirty. I wanted this case.

A list of facts was in. Willard Ainsley had been killed with a .32-caliber bullet. It had been removed from his body and turned over to ballistics. Death had occurred at about eleven the night before. Gumshoeing had turned up no one in the Kilgo district who admitted to having seen Ainsley around that time.

I checked the reports on Ainsley's business associates. None had seen him since late on the afternoon of his death.

His attorney, Bayard Isherwood, was possibly the last of his acquaintances to have seen Ainsley alive. They had met in the elevator of the building, where they both had offices. Each had been on his way home. They had exchanged greetings. Ainsley, Bayard Isherwood had stated, had seemed on the point of bringing up a business matter, but had said that he would see Isherwood the next day. Isherwood had dined alone in his bachelor apartment. He had then attended a concert, alone. And he had retired immediately upon returning to his apartment.

Bayard Isherwood was the senior member of the city's most sedate and respected law firm. There was no doubting his statement, nor the statements of any of Ainsley's associates.

I closed the file and went over to the Cortez.

There were several people, a dozen or so, in the Ainsley apartment. I supposed it had started as a sort of wake, people dropping in on a sympathy call. It now had the earmarks of a party, as the memory of good-old-Will was washed clean with drink.

Mrs. Ainsley led the way to a den off the main hallway and closed off the noise in the living room. She stood with her back against the door. "How are you progressing, Mr. Berkmin?"

"We're punching," I said. "Bayard Isherwood says your husband was concerned with a business matter, so much so that he made a compulsive mention of it during an elevator ride, without saying what it was. Do you know what it might have been?"

"No." She moved from the door and rested her hips against the edge of a desk, studying me.

"It probably isn't important," I said. "The case looks cut and dried. Robbery and murder. It may break if we pick up a punk spending beyond his means."

"Really?"

"Or liquor loosens him up and he starts bragging. Or he tells his girl and they have a fight and she makes an anonymous phone call out of spite."

Suddenly, a shiver crossed her shoulders. "You're a very good cop, aren't you?"

"I like promotions," I said, "and the bigger paychecks."

"But you don't like being a policeman?"

"Not particularly."

"You're a rather strange man."

Her words seemed to hang in the room, forming a quick, strange bond between us.

She looked away from me, found a cigarette on the desk, and lighted it.

"Thank you for coming," she said.

"Why don't you call me Nick?"

She ventured a look at me. "Okay, Nick. I hope you catch your punk and get a nice promotion."

The break came twenty-eight hours later. I was again on duty early. Fresh routine reports, masses of detail, were on my desk. Included was the fact that three phone calls had emanated from the Ainsley apartment the night of the murder. One had been to Bayard Isherwood, who'd been out at the time, ten o'clock. The others, between ten and eleven, had been to friends. In both instances, Ramoth Ainsley had asked if the friend had seen her husband that evening.

I pushed the reports back, wondering where we went from there. It was then that York came into my office, his breath short, his face very red.

"We got the gun, Nick!"

"Yeah?"

"Punk kid named Jim Norton hocked it this afternoon. Thirty-two revolver. The pawnbroker reported it. Ballistics checked the gun. It's the one that killed Willard Ainsley, all right."

I stood up. "Where's the kid?"

"That's the catch. When Simmons and Pickens went over to pick him up, he bolted. He's teetering on the roof of a six story tenement on Kilgo Street, threatening to jump."

I'd been through this kind of thing twice before in my years on the force. The youth looked like a skinny doll pinned against the night sky by spotlights. The fire department had roped off the block and unfolded the big net. Uniform-grade police had cleared out the rubberneckers.

I skidded the black car to a stop at the barricade. York hung back, needing all of a sudden to tie his shoe laces.

I knew most of the men on duty. I learned quickly that half a dozen men were inside the building, including a priest. They'd opened the skylight trap and reached the roof. Now they were stymied. Every time they moved a muscle, the kid got ready to jump.

A weeping girl was huddled in the shadows at the base of a building.

"Who's that?" I asked an assistant fire chief.

"Kilgo Street girl. Her name's Nancy Creaseman."

"Norton's girl?"

"Something like that."

"Why didn't you get her out of here?"

"Chief told Norton on the loud speaker she was down here. It may have kept him from going off. She's made no trouble."

I walked over to the girl. There are thousands like her in any large city. Thin, malnourished body. Mousy brown hair. Eyes shaded with long-continued anxiety. Wrong colored lipstick, attempting to hide the thinness of the pinched face.

"Nancy," I said.

"Yes, sir."

"My name is Nick Berkmin. I'm the homicide man in charge of the Ainsley case."

"Jimmy didn't kill him, Mr. Berkmin."

"How do you know?"

"He couldn't."

"Has he ever been in trouble before?"

"Not with the police. He's not the kind, I tell you."

"Willard Ainsley," I said, "was carrying a lot of money on him."

"Jimmy wouldn't, he wouldn't, he wouldn't!"

"Take it easy," I said. "I'm not saying he did it. But we don't want him doing anything foolish now, do we?"

Her anxious eyes lifted toward the spot of light in the night sky. A sob burst out of her.

"Where did he get the gun, Nancy?"

"He found it."

"Where?"

"In a gutter, around a corner off Kilgo Street. He didn't do anything with it at first. Then he went and pawned it."

"Why didn't he tell us that? Why did he break and run when the police came?"

"He's scared of the police, of everyone. He overheard them asking his mother where he was, if she'd seen him with a gun. Then he got scared, lost his head, and ran. Please help him, Mr. Berkmin!"

She grabbed my hand and clung to it with her sweaty, thin, sticky fingers. "I know it looks bad, but Jimmy didn't do it. You've got to help him. You see, he got hurt—"

"Hurt?"

"Weeks ago. He had a job, delivering for a drugstore. Some guys caught him one night, took his money, and beat him up. He's had these blind spells ever since. It's why he's so scared."

I got my hand loose from hers. "I'll tell you what, Nancy. You go up there, on the roof, and talk him down. I'll see that he gets a break."

Now it was her eyes clinging to me. Her weeping stopped. She squared her shoulders and started across the street.

I called Ramoth Ainsley from my office. She agreed to see me. I drove over, brought her down to my car, and we got in.

When she saw the direction I was taking, she said, "I was under the impression we were going to your office."

"Isn't this nicer?"

"I'm not at all sure," she said.

"I wanted a chance to talk to you in private."

She sat in cautious silence as I drove through the clean luxury of her neighborhood. I drove far down the lake shore to an undeveloped area. There, I picked a side road, turned off and parked.

"We might put the case on ice," I said.

"Really?"

"We've got a kid in a cell right now who was in possession of the murder gun. He says he found it, where someone had thrown it after wiping it clean. It isn't registered, but there are people who will sell unregistered guns—for a premium."

"Do you think he killed Will?"

"We have a case. We can make a monkey of him in court, with his statement about finding the gun. He had blackouts, and conceivably might not remember mugging somebody. There are ways of wrapping a thing like this up. Fact is, it probably would be best for the kid for me to wrap it up quick. A jury wouldn't go hard on him. He'd get needed hospitalization and treatment—and I promised his girl the best break for him."

She moved restlessly in the car seat. "You've got something on your mind, Nick."

"Yes, I have. You're a very beautiful woman."

"Thank you."

"One who'd do most anything for enough money."

"Now wait a—"

"I'm not being critical," I broke in. "Only analytical. By the way, why did you try to call Isherwood shortly before the time your husband was killed?"

"I didn't, Nick. Why are you asking me—"

"I thought so," I said. "You see, a call was placed from your apartment to Isherwood's residence. Only it was Will calling, wasn't it? You didn't know he'd made that call, did you? But now I can wise you up. He was in another room, using the phone a good two hours *after* the time you said he'd left the apartment. The call places him in the apartment very close to the time of his death. Why'd you want us to think he'd left earlier—unless he was in the apartment up to and including the time of his death?"

Her lips seemed to redden. The shift of color was actually in her face, not her lips. "Nick! What are you saying?"

"That you had motive. He was about to throw you out, separate you from all that nice money, wasn't he?"

"What makes you think I'd even considered killing—"

"First thing started me wondering was the matter of the car. Kilgo Street is a long way from your neighborhood. If Will had driven to Kilgo and got himself bumped off, why hasn't his car been found in that vicinity? The kid in jail hocked only an unregistered gun, he didn't peddle a hot car.

"When you've been a cop a long time, you get to wondering how a thing might have happened, if a detail strikes you wrong. You wonder if a beautiful woman gets herself a little gun as a last resort. You wonder if she, finally, feels she has to use it. You wonder if she has sneaked her dead husband down the service elevator from their swank apartment, driven him all the way to a crummy place like Kilgo Street. You wonder if she stripped him of money there to make it appear he'd been robbed. You wonder if she then drove herself home, her plan completed, satisfied that nothing could possibly connect her with a dump like Kilgo Street and the death of her husband."

"Nick, honestly, how could I, a woman—"

"Looked pretty good, didn't it, the whole plan? But you're strong, athletic, well-kept, and he was a small man. There was a service elevator to help get him downstairs. It was late at night. You envisioned little risk of being seen, and you weren't. The whole setup looked great and you saw no reason why you couldn't carry it off."

She hesitated a long time before she spoke. "Nick, you can't prove any of this. . . ."

"I'm in charge of the case. I can prove that kid guilty, if I want to. I got the power to close this case, but quick. On the other hand, there's a limited number of places where you can buy an unregistered gun. I know these places. I know how to make people talk. Believe me, baby, I can make them talk when I want to. If I took you to those places one by one, I'm sure I'd get an identification sooner or later. Of you. As the buyer of an unregistered gun."

"Nick—"

"Shall we start? Pay a call on one of those places?"

"Nick, please . . . ."

"You killed him," I said.

"No, Nick."

"Okay. Let's get started on this detail of a gun."

"Nick, you can't do this to me!"

"You killed him," I repeated.

She slid toward me. "Nick," she said, "it was self defense. I swear it!"

"Self defense—with the purchase of the gun a prior act?"

She put her arms around me. I felt her shiver. "Nick, will you give me a break?"

"I guess that'll do it," I said. I held her away briefly and reached under the seat. I clicked off the switch of the compact, portable, battery-powered tape recorder. Her eyes got large as she watched me put the tape carefully in my inside coat pocket.

"You tricked me," she said. "You didn't know—"

"I suspected," I said. "But I needed proof. Now I've got it. It's the finest insurance I can think of."

"Insurance, Nick?"

"Sure. I'll see that that tape's put in a safe place and fix things so it'll reach the right people—if anything ever happens to me."

She began to understand.

"You," I said, "are a beautiful woman worth six or seven million dollars. What's my future on the cops compared to that? You'll mourn, and I'll work awhile before I resign. For appearances sake."

Her eyes showed that her mind made a lightning fast survey of the situation. She saw no way out. And so, recognizing the inevitable, she accepted it.

She linked her arm in mine and rested her head on my shoulder. "You're right, Nick darling. We must think of appearances, mustn't we?"

When Rogers solved his own problem, he proved that bagging the wrong prey was a way of changing the hunt. . . .

TWENTY-ONE

The Ultimate Prey

You'll understand why I can't pinpoint the location of the Island. It's one of those hundreds of pieces broken from the mainland mass along the perimeter of the Gulf of Mexico from eastern Texas around to western Florida.

Countless such islands remain as they were created, semitropical mangrove jungles swarming with poisonous life, separated from the throes of civilization by narrow bays, sounds, bayous. These islands run to a type and therefore have much in common.

Developers have swarmed onto countless other Gulf Coast islands, bulldozing the jungle, pumping, dredging, filling, spreading lawns and domestic palms, laying out streets, marinas, golf courses, sites for homes, schools, and expensive condominiums. Dedicated to the Beautiful Life, these islands also have much in common.

The one I'm talking about, however, is used for a purpose that makes it unique among all islands.

I first viewed the Island from a low-flying helicopter on a hot, sultry day. It looked so peaceful and inviting, swimming toward us on a blue-green, sparkling Gulf. In shape, it was a finger lying on the serene sea, four or five miles long and a couple of miles wide.

The northern end had been plushly prepared for people. Amid acres of lawn and tropical gardens, a modernistic home of glass and redwood threw its three large, adjacent wings into the sunshine. The lawn sloped to a snowy white beach and marina where a seaworthy cruiser and a small schooner with furled sails bobbed.

South of the house were spread the huge kidney-shaped swimming pool, doubles tennis courts, a landing strip with parked Cessna, and, tucked to one side, a couple of small cement-block buildings that I guessed housed the pumps, generators and other necessities to keep the estate going.

The man-made paradise occupied only the northern quarter of the Island. Less than a mile south of the house the jungle crouched, a thick green tangle creating its own twilight; timeless and self-renewing, it seemed to brood with endless patience, awaiting the time when it would reclaim the small part that people had carved from it.

LaFarge, the sheriff, was flying the chopper, and so far he'd merely grunted every time I asked him where he was taking me and why.

Conscious of the weight of the handcuffs about my wrists, I studied his swarthy, big-boned, cruel profile. A flicker in his dark, heavy-browed eyes and gathering of muscle tension in his bullish body warned me that the Island was our destination.

LaFarge's town, Ogathalla, was an unimportant dot on the map, a crossroads cluster of weathered buildings in piney woods country, little more than a posted speed limit and main street traffic light to halt the big Kawasaki I was riding cross-country.

Before the light changed, a dusty red-and-white cruiser with constabulary markings and blue-flashing blinker quartered in front of the cycle. The big, indistinct image behind the steering wheel leaned in my direction and thumbed me toward the curb.

Obediently, I walked the wheels over, straddling the seat.

The man I was to know as LaFarge got out of the cruiser and padded toward me. He studied me closely, my rather skinny face and denim-clothed frame, the curl of sandy hair below the crash helmet, the eyes behind light amber glasses, the leather-strap sandals on dusty bare feet, the blanket roll secured behind the cycle's seat.

"What's your name, jimbo?"

"Rogers, Officer."

"Where you headed?"

"Down the coast."

"Where down the coast, jimbo?"

"Tampa, maybe. Sarasota. Fort Myers. Just someplace to work and spend the winter in the sun."

"Where you from?"

"El Paso," I said.

"Before that?"

"Phoenix. L.A. Vegas."

"You got people?" he asked, his dark, intent eyes making the question important.

"People?"

"Kinfolk," he snapped. "Someone who can vouch for you."

I slipped off the riding glasses and looked at him, frowning. "Why do I need someone to vouch for me?"

"The welcome mat ain't out for motorcycle bums in Ogathalla, jimbo."

"I'm not exactly a motorcycle bum, Officer. I've got money. I pay my way."

He kicked the front tire almost gently with his toe. "Just rambling around, seeing the country, enjoying your freedom, working when you have to?"

"Something like that." But it went deeper. It went back to hard questions that crystallized in my mind about the time I was one of the last of the soldier boys debarking from Vietnam. Simply framed questions without ready answers . . . who I am . . . where is truth among the falsehoods . . . what this business of living is all about . . . what to do with my life . . .

I was trying to settle a lot of things in my mind, but I doubted that the thug in uniform would understand, even if he were interested. So I said, "You've summed it up exactly, Officer."

"We'll see. We'll sure look into you." He moved with a short side step. "Now get off the wheels, jimbo. Our local pokey is just a short walk down the street."

I stood in dumb surprise. The look on my face gave him a short laugh. "Busting the speed limit as you rolled into town will do for a starter," he said. "You want to add a charge of resisting arrest?"

The urge flared in me to flatten him and kick the Kawa to life.

He read it in my eyes and dropped his hand to his gun. "Do it," he invited softly. "I step on your kind, with my heel. Do it—and I'll take you before the others even have a chance."

His reference to the others made no more sense than the rest of the situation, but I sensed clearly his sadism, and I hadn't survived to this point in time to give a prehistoric sheriff quick excuses to get his kicks.

The rest of the day was spent in a six-by-eight cell in the Ogathalla jail. The cells next to me in the decrepit old building were empty, leaving me suspended in sweltering heat and the aftersmells of ten thousand previous tenants.

I wasn't yet in the grip of real gut-fear. I figured LaFarge for a bored bully shoring up his tough, big-man self-image. He'd picked me up on a pretext, but he could only go so far. This was still the U.S. of A.

I couldn't see any other angle. I came from nowhere, was going nowhere. I had traveling bread; enough, I hoped, to satisfy LaFarge and a crooked magistrate in a kangaroo court.

I finally slept in a pool of soured sweat and the stink of the lumpy bunk.

After daybreak the next morning LaFarge came to the cell, grinned at me through the barred door, and slipped a tin plate through the slot at the bottom of the door. "Breakfast, Rogers."

I gripped the bars, white-knuckled. "I want a lawyer."

"Jimbo," he drawled, "you're old enough for your druthers not to hurt you. Relax and enjoy Ogathalla hospitality while you can."

He didn't seem to mind the things I yelled at him as he went away.

He returned in late afternoon with another tin plate of swill. After the vacuity of the day the sound of any other human footstep was welcome—almost.

"Can't we be reasonable, Sheriff?" I asked, ignoring the food.

"Sure. I'm the most reasonable man in the county."

"Then what's the charge against me?"

"Ain't decided yet, jimbo. I'm looking into you like you never been looked into before. I may be a hick sheriff, but I got a long-distance phone and a badge and a title, and before I'm through I can tell you if you've ever spit on Times Square."

I didn't have anything to say for a moment, and while I stood there looking at him through the space between the bars the first worms began crawling through my guts.

"Sheriff," I said, wetting my lips, "I do have some rights."

"Here, jimbo? Who says?"

"You can't keep me here forever."

"Who says? You got anybody to come fetch you out?"

The sun gradually slipped off in its habitual way, and nightfall came as a heavy and unwelcome shadow. The questions that had bothered me for so many months had a particular sharpness there in the darkness of LaFarge's jail, but I wouldn't let myself think too hard about anything, including the hours ahead and the idea of LaFarge having the last word.

I stood at the single small barred window listening to the nightly din of the nearby swamp. LaFarge couldn't have secured me more to his liking if he'd put me in a tomb, although I knew, bitterly, that stockade inmates I'd heard about in Vietnam could have cracked this cruddy, weather-rotten cell without much trouble.

I turned finally and sat down on the edge of the bunk, head in my hands. After a while, I stretched out on my back, feeling the sag of the bunk, listening to it creak every time I drew a breath. It seemed about ready to fall apart . . . and with that thought, my eyes snapped open.

I sat up quickly, whipped the grimy pad to the foot of the bunk. The springs and braces and framing stood out in the moonglow. My hands explored and tested the framework. A diagonal corner brace, a flat piece of old metal about an inch wide and twelve inches long, seemed to be hanging on only with the help of its rust. The rust showered off in grainy flecks as I took hold of the brace and twisted it back and forth.

The job was harder than it looked. The edges of metal rasped my palms to rawness. The effort and humid heat of the night oozed a sticky sweat out of my skin, but I had plenty of time. Patiently I twisted the brace back and forth, gripping it hard and putting muscle into it. At last, when the moon had shifted shadows about on the floor, I felt—or imagined—the brace yielding a little further.

Then the rivet at one end slipped out of its rust-eaten hole, and with the direct leverage that this gave me, I yanked the other end free. A pulse lifted through my chest as I gripped the end of the brace and took a couple of practice swings with it at an imaginary LaFarge hovering in the darkness.

He came to the cell two hours later than usual the next morning.

"We'll talk a little today before you have breakfast, jimbo." While he fitted the key in the lock, he looked in at me as if to note how I was making out. I was slightly ripe by this time, wrinkled, grimy, beardy, a few pounds having melted from a frame that couldn't afford the loss. LaFarge grinned with satisfaction at what he saw, and the metal weapon felt a few degrees warmer against my forearm where it was concealed by my sleeve.

LaFarge pushed the door open, and as he was wriggling the key from the balky old lock, the metal strap slipped down into my hand.

LaFarge glanced down at the lock, and I moved. He jerked about, glimpsing the metal strap slashing at him. Fear broke his knees and welded him to the door. The reflex saved him. The metal strap missed his head, glanced from his shoulder. Still clutching the door, he threw himself blindly away from me. The metal strap smashed against the edge of the moving door, and before I could balance and swing a third time, LaFarge was outside the cell, the lock snicking, the door a barrier between us.

A moment passed while we faced each other. LaFarge was rubbing his shoulder, but if it hurt, he didn't seem to mind.

"You've made it personal now, Rogers," he said softly. "I'm going to enjoy taking you to the others. Enjoy it real personal, believe it."

I looked at the piece of metal in my hand, useless now. I opened my fingers and watched the strap hit the dirty cement floor with a small explosion of grit.

Finally, I looked up and saw the bars banded over the image of LaFarge's face. "Who are these others? What's this all about? Why me, LaFarge?"

"Because you were in the right place at the right time, jimbo."

"This is crazy!"

"Can you think of many things in this world that ain't?" He slipped the handcuffs from his belt. "Cool it while you can, jimbo. I won't take any more chances with you. Now then, you just stick your hands out here . . . both hands through the same opening between bars so's I don't hook you to the door . . . and we'll fit the bracelets. Then the two of us will march the little distance to the helipad behind the jail and take a little trip in the Department chopper. You'd be surprised at the crime in this bayou country: poachers, moonshiners, thieves and killers. Chopper's the only way to chase some of them down."

The ride wasn't as short as LaFarge had promised. He flew us due south until the shoreline of the Gulf was below. Then we followed the coast eastward. We whirred over a traffic-clogged expressway, bisected the wake of a tanker steaming to the busy port just below the horizon to our rear.

Streaming along far beneath us were Gulf-front homes with private docks, pink-and-white resort hotels claiming miles of cake-icing beaches. little white sails cavorting offshore.

Then the interstate veered north through a wilderness of piney woods and cypress trees dripping Spanish moss, and we veered south with the curve of a shoreline that lost all traces of people.

In eight to ten minutes, LaFarge put the shoreline to our tail, and a scattering of small wilderness islands slid beneath the Plexiglas bubble. None of these interested LaFarge. Then the finger, one-quarter pure plush and three-quarters raw jungle, came into view, and the chopper began to drop.

As we whirred closer to the estate, three people came out of the west wing of the palatial home and started jogging southward across the lawn.

"On their way to meet us," LaFarge said.

"The others?"

"The others, jimbo." LaFarge gave a short laugh. "Ten grand to me every time I bring them a tiger, jimbo. Helps a poor country sheriff make ends meet, though I don't find a special nobody on a motorcycle every day who meets the purely rigid requirements. Make you feel any better, knowing you're worth ten thousand dollars?"

LaFarge had settled the copter a considerable distance from the house, not more than a hundred yards from where the jungle began.

As LaFarge prodded me out with his gun, the three men who'd trotted from the house came to a halt, semicircled about me and looked me over.

They were all young, very close to my own age, dressed in khaki shorts, bush jackets, and laced boots. Each carried a carbine, lightweight brush guns, in the crook of his right arm.

I had a vague feeling of having seen them before, of knowing them from some time or place, which seemed impossible.

The man on my right was very tall and thin, with muscles like wire, a gaunt face, a corrugated skull that was already totally bald, though he was only in his middle-twenties.

Facing me most directly was a heavyweight whose dark face and build reminded me of LaFarge. On his flank, the third member of the party was tall, broad-shouldered, round-faced, with ash-blond hair done in the wildest Alfro style I'd ever seen.

"Rogers," LaFarge said, "meet the Quixote Hunt Club. Hepperling the bald. McMurdy with the beef. And Convers, the panther here with the big blossom of white hair."

I knew, hearing the names, why they hadn't seemed total strangers. I—along with millions—had met them at a distance in newscasts and Sunday supplements.

Hepperling meant sugar millions; McMurdy, shipping; Convers, oil. The three were the latest stems on family trees that in all branches meant a good slice of a billion dollars in economic wealth and power. For each of them the coming of age had meant trust funds, allowances, and inheritances the rest of us wouldn't risk dreaming about. The three might have pooled their resources and bought themselves a small, undeveloped country rather than a mere island.

As Quixotes, they'd frequently made headlines; crashing a plane and disappearing in Alaska for a week after a Kodiak hunt, going after jaguar in restricted tribal grounds in South America, creating an international incident when Kenyan authorities had arrested them for poaching bull elephants, and they'd taken pains to insult the Kenyan government before a bank of international television news cameras.

LaFarge was saying, "Rogers is completely safe, fellows. No family ties, no close friends. Nobody to ask the first question about his disappearance."

"We know." McMurdy dismissed LaFarge as a human being. "We always make our own inquiries when you have a prospect in custody, and we've the agents and the means."

LaFarge endured McMurdy's insulting tone like a well-trained hound.

McMurdy studied me head to toe. "You seem to come from a tough-luck line, Rogers. Father walked out when you were six or seven—never seen or heard from him since. Mother remarried—a real stinker. Both of them killed in a car crash when you were hardly out of high school. Worked your way through a couple years of college, then the Army taps you. Off to Vietnam. Rough time over there. MIA for a while. Wounded once. Finally hung up dockside, one of the last to leave."

"I didn't have much to come back to," I said.

"But you survived," Hepperling said. "You seem to survive anything. That's a good omen. That should make it good."

"Let's hope so," Convers said. "We haven't had a good island hunt in months now."

I think I'd suspected the truth when they'd first ringed the grounded chopper with their carbines, but now as it was coming closer to me with every passing second, I still couldn't believe it. I wouldn't believe it. Then I looked at them, at the jungle, and back at them—and I had to believe it.

Convers bobbed his woolly white mane toward the jungle. "You'll be given a canteen of water and some field rations before you go in there, Rogers. How much life you buy for yourself is up to you, your wits and strength."

I was unable to move.

Hepperling said, "You do understand, Rogers?"

"Sure." The word was a husky whisper. "You guys have hunted everything, everywhere, until you've run all the way out of normal pleasure. So now, when you have the chance and can arrange it, here on this island . . . you hunt the prime game of all."

"How afraid are you, Rogers?" Convers asked as if the subject really interested him.

"If I wallowed on my knees would it help?"

"Last time the prey almost went nuts before dashing off into the jungle," Hepperling said, "screaming that we were crazy, not for real."

"Oh, you're for real," I said. "In twenty-seven years of living I've discovered that anything can be for real on this planet. Adolf Hitler. Scientists who talk about dedication, and devote their lives to thinking up bigger bombs and deadlier germs. Charles Manson. The Mafia. I don't doubt that you three are rather mildly real, compared to some of the things that go on."

I walked a few steps from the chopper and stood looking at the jungle. Then I sat down on the green coolness of the grass. "Only I'm for real, too, fellows. And you've left me just one thing. You've stripped me down to this one real thing. I won't do it. The hunt is off."

They came stalking toward me, their shadows flowing across me.

"That's the whole point of it," I said. "Without the point, there is nothing in it for you. Without fleeing prey trying to hang onto a few more hours of life there in the jungle, you've lost the point, and it's no dice. You've got the wrong tiger this time."

"LaFarge," McMurdy ordered in a quiet tone.

LaFarge came around to stand close in front of me. He pulled out his gun. "You want it right here, Rogers?"

"No," I said, "I don't want it anywhere for years and years yet. But you're betting against an enemy with nothing to lose, LaFarge. No matter what you do, the hunt is off. And I don't believe you'll be paid for this one or trusted in the future."

He fired the gun almost in my face. The flash blinded me. I felt the bullet nip the hair on my crown.

I pushed back the need to be sick all over the place. "You'll have to do better than that, LaFarge."

He put the gun to my temple and slowly eased back the hammer.

"That's the surest way of guaranteeing no hunt, LaFarge."

Taking a step back, he ventured a glance at the faces of his young employers. He didn't like the way they were looking at him. He didn't enjoy what he felt as they measured him. He wasn't liking any of it at all.

He coupled my name with a curse. "On your feet, Rogers. I'll make you run! Hit for the jungle!"

He exploded his booted foot directly at my face. He didn't have nearly the coordination or quickness of a Viet Cong. My handcuffed hands met the driving ankle. I flipped him hard, onto his back, and before he could catch the next breath, I'd wrung the gun from him and spun to face the others.

"Hold it!" I ordered.

Not a carbine moved. They had brains as well as loot. They knew they could have taken me—but not safely.

It was one of those crossroads moments in life for me, not because of anything outside myself, but because of the thought coming full-blown to my mind. I thought about the gig I'd had from the moment of birth. It seemed that the time was overdue for a putting of things in balance for a fellow named Rogers. The big, basic questions didn't bug me any longer. I was certain, right then, of the direction my life would take. I let a grin build on my lips.

In response, the first edge of tension eased from the Quixotes. They slipped glances from me to each other. Actually, there was a lot more rapport between the Quixotes and myself than between any of us and LaFarge.

"Fellows," I said, "being a country sheriff in mean bayou territory is risky business. If LaFarge turned up in some back bayou shot to death, no one would figure it any way except that he'd cornered one mean moonshiner or poacher too many."

I eased the snout of the gun in LaFarge's direction. "Into the jungle, big man."

"You're nuts, Rogers. . . . Fellows, you tell this character—" His words broke off as he looked at them. He couldn't take his eyes from their faces. He took a backward step . . . then another . . . and whatever it was that he'd substituted for nerve all of his life died inside of him. He broke and ran, disappearing quickly into the jungle.

McMurdy was standing closest to me. Carefully, I turned the police pistol around and handed it to him butt first.

"Gentlemen," I said, "I think the hunt resumes. And don't forget to get the keys to the handcuffs when you've tracked him down."

That's how my association with the Quixotes began. Now I draw seventy-five grand a year, plus expenses. I travel the plushiest resorts. I drive a thirty-five-thousand-dollar sports car. I buy the finest food and wines and wear a hand-tailored wardrobe.

Not surprisingly, I practically have to fight off the chicks. I usually pick the best-looking and healthiest of the crop of empty-headed dropouts and runaways from good, substantial homes. They're easiest to con, and once on the Island it's too late for them to come to their senses and realize they're facing something entirely different from the romantic and exciting weekend they've been promised. They're among the runaways who *every* year are simply not found. None is ever traceable to the Island. I see to that.

Girls . . . the ultimate prey. The Quixotes thought the suggestion was the greatest when I hit them with it. I coupled the idea with the offer to act as their agent, roaming the country, recruiting the prey, and bringing them to the Island. I've proven my absolute reliability, and the Quixotes respect my advice.

Summing up the brand-new life, I guess you could say I owe LaFarge a vote of thanks.

When Marilyn's attackers left her for dead, they never suspected that they left her with the tools of revenge. . . .

TWENTY-TWO

To Spare a Life

Marilyn speeded up, and so did the souped-up yellow and black striped hot rod behind her. Straining, she watched a lonely, twilight half mile sweep past. She took her sandaled foot from the gas pedal, slowing to a crawl. Her gaze inched to the rear-view mirror. Instead of swinging out to pass, the hot-rodder applied brakes, matching her own pace.

A shallow pulse of panic raced through Marilyn's throat. The steering wheel began to feel slimy beneath her long, tapering, hard-curled fingers. No doubt of it now, the cats in the hot rod had cast her in the role of mouse.

She looked at her surroundings for some sign of life. The emptiness of interior Florida threatened her, endless acres of greasy-green palmetto broken by patches of saw grass. Here and there reared a lonely, twisted pine tree or desolate, heat-blasted cypress in funereal shrouds of gray Spanish moss. The narrow state road was a vacant needle point in the grimly darkening distance, not a light in sight.

Marilyn drew a breath, clinging to calm. *Please,* she thought, *be a pair of harmless kooks getting bored with the game, ready to break it off . . .*

A college junior, Marilyn had worked most of the summer in her father's modest real estate and insurance company. Five days ago, his hearty, benign presence had loomed beside her desk.

"You're fired," he'd said, grinning. "Take that house guest invitation from your classmate in Sarasota. Go and get your water skis wet before you have to go back to school."

It had been a dreamy time, with an assortment of healthy young males vying for the attention of a glowing, lovely raven-haired girl with large, dark eyes and a sense of fun and humor.

Marilyn had stretched out the final day with the gang on the beach,

185

her packed bags stowed in her car. Shouted good-byes, an impromptu snake dance, promises of a reunion when the new semester opened in Gainesville had marked her departure.

She hadn't noticed the disappearance of the two shaggy youths who had loitered some distance away and watched the beach party disdainfully. She'd seen them again briefly in the parking area, lean, tanned, tawny-maned as young lions, their bell-bottoms garish splashes of color below open-fronted shirts. They'd lounged beside the zebra-striped rod. The taller had tossed a blue pill in the air, like a peanut, and dropped his head back to catch it in his open mouth. The action had caused an uncomfortable squirm of distaste in Marilyn. She'd got in her car and quickly driven away. By taking the short-cut on the state road she could be in her small home town in north-central Florida and having dinner with Mom and Dad in less than two hours.

With a sudden whine of racing cams and squeal of rubber, the hot rod was a yellow-black blur swinging out and roaring past. It snarled its twin chrome exhausts at her, catapulting half a mile ahead in a matter of seconds.

Marilyn drew her first deep breath since the rod had revealed itself a few miles back. They'd been very clever and deceptive following her through city traffic and deciding which road she would take. Now they had lost interest, and her fears—

She broke the thought with a gasp. In a grayish cloud from smoking tires the rod had slammed to a stop, reversed. It was a returning projectile.

Drenched with icy feeling, Marilyn saw the driver looking back over his shoulder as he steered. His companion was on his knees in the seat, facing rearward, half crouched on the turtleback of the open-topped rod. He seemed to be yowling something in wild excitement.

"Crazy pillheads . . . goofballs . . ." Marilyn choked. She twisted the wheel, taking to the outside lane, giving the rod room. In the rear-view mirror she saw it again screech to a stop, almost lifting the front wheels from the rough, graveled macadam.

She mashed the gas to the floor, gaining a bare quarter-mile lead while the rod was meshed into forward gear.

Spidery prickles swept over Marilyn as she heard it coming, a high keening in the turgid silence. Her thoughts tumbled desperately. *Can't outrun them . . . Narrow road . . . Tricky, sandy shoulders . . . Don't give them room!*

Her heart matched the laboring of the two-door's engine as it hurtled along the very middle of the road. She watched the intermittent white lines come slashing at the center of the windshield.

The rod rocked from one side to the other, the driver not quite taking the chance of trying to pass with two wheels on the shoulder.

An image of coiled tension, Marilyn flicked a glance in the rear-view as the rod beeped a horn that played a raucous how-dry-I-am.

The highway was surging at her with terrifying speed, but she kept those center-line marks streaking under the hood.

Then a hard thump and shattering of broken glass on the roof jarred the sedan. In the small mirror, Marilyn glimpsed the other car close on her rear bumper. The driver's companion was standing crouched, holding the top edge of the windshield, drawing his arm back to throw another empty beer bottle.

A wave of fear left Marilyn feeling faint at the thought of mangled wreckage, bloody human forms.

She shivered, fighting the faintness. Ahead, the road made a long bend through a lovely area of banyan trees and vine-trellised cabbage palms, and fifty yards to the left of the highway in the shady clearing stood one of those out-of-the-way country stores. It was an ugly, unpainted, rambling wooden building with a long ramshackle porch and rusty tin roof, but a dim light glowed from one of the dusty windows, warmly beautiful to Marilyn.

She did nothing to telegraph her intention to the other driver. When she was almost abreast of the store, she slammed down the brake and pulled the steering wheel over hard.

The sedan pitched and slewed in a sickening half-spin. She fed gas, and the tires took hold. The building and lacy banyan trees swam at Marilyn. She mashed the brake pedal and the sedan slithered to a stop in a shower of sand, dust, and dead pine needles.

She was out of the car before it stopped rocking. From the highway came the sounds of screaming rubber, the rise and fall of an angry engine, the crash of changing gears.

Marilyn raced across the gritty planking of the gallery and threw herself against the front door. The latch was an old-fashioned metal lever which rattled as she depressed it. The door yielded perhaps half an inch. She shook it and banged on it with her fist.

"Please . . . whoever's in there . . . open up!"

Her efforts created sepulchral echoes. She drew back a little. The iron hasp and heavy padlock securing the door loomed in her vision.

A soft whimper fell from Marilyn's lips. She slipped a glance over her shoulder. The zebra-stripe had skidded to rest near her sedan. Both youths had got out, a little hesitantly at first.

Marilyn was chilled to inaction for a moment. Then she forced herself to move. A glance through the iron-barred window beside the stout door revealed a gloomy interior of shelves cluttered with a few canned goods, a plank counter bearing a small glass showcase, a table near the rear stacked with work clothing. There was no movement, no sign of life. A single small naked bulb dangled over the rear counter, a night light, Marilyn realized dimly, required by the county sheriff's department.

Her cheek pressed against the rough planking, her nails dug in as voices rose behind her.

"The babe has found an empty pad, Rajah."

"How about that, Zeno?"

Footsteps softly crushed across the blanket of dry pine needles on the yard, voices in the dusk. . . .

"She sure turns me on, Rajah."

"From the sec I glom her on the beach, Zeno."

Marilyn broke free of her paralysis, peeling away from the wall and dashing toward the end of the porch.

"We got a hunt, Rajah."

"My bag, Zeno!"

Marilyn jumped from the open end of the porch, half stumbled, darted toward the rear corner of the building.

She heard them yelling instructions to each other. They were splitting up.

Beyond the store, the landscape was indistinct in the twilight pall but she had an impression of swampiness, tall grasses, and a tangle of trees in the distance. Her running feet were renewed with faint hope.

She angled away from the one who seemed nearer. She could hear his running feet directly behind her. Then she saw the shadow of the other one, flowing across the clearing to cut her off.

She tried to change directions. Her toe caught in a tough root. She pitched to her knees, flinging out her left hand to break her fall.

She was scrambling up when she felt his presence flowing over her. She heard his breathing, glimpsed the white savage mask of a face in its growth of heavy beard.

"No!" The word was a crazed mingle of snarl and scream. "You won't. . . . I won't let you. . . . Let me go!"

Her left arm felt as if it were being torn from the shoulder socket. She thrashed wildly in his grip. Her mind seemed to burst. Nothing was real. Nothing mattered right then, except the sanctity of her person.

She felt the hands of the second youth grabbing at her free arm, her shoulder, her throat. They grunted soft, vicious curses, almost no match for her transformation in this insane moment. She fought bitterly, clawing, kicking, biting.

Then her face exploded. One of them had struck hard with his fist. The back of her head struck the stone-like bole of a wild palm as she hurtled backward and down.

The pain lasted for a fiery fraction of a second. Then she seemed to float in a weird nothingness. She had the strangest sense of detachment, as if a stranger lay here with two sweaty, hard-breathing strangers standing over the limp body.

A soft breeze flapped the bell-bottoms and touched bearded faces marked by her raking nails. The two standing figures were quite still for a moment, immunized to real fright by pills but touched with caution.

"Glom the back of her head, Zeno."

"Yeah, all bloody."

"Is she dead?"

"Who cares?"

"Nobody saw it."

"That's right."

"But they'll see her car, some cruising county fuzz."

"So we'll park it out of sight behind the store."

"How about her? She comes to, busts a window in the store, finds a telephone before we've made miles."

"Not if she's in her car trunk."

"Hey, man! That's cool! If she ain't kaput already, she'll suffocate before anybody finds her."

"Go get her car. I'll drag her out of here."

Marilyn was vaguely aware of hands shoving under her armpits, of muscles straining against her weight. She sensed she was being half lifted and dragged, her heels bumping roots and grinding through sandy soil.

She floated away. Then the pain of twisted arms and legs came through as they lifted her and stuffed her callously in the car trunk. Somewhere in her mind despairing words formed, begging for mercy. The trunk lid slammed shut over her, locking automatically, the thud of a sealed coffin.

She was swaddled in blackness and silence for a long time. At last she choked a soft moan. Despite bleeding where the scalp had been scraped, her head wound was superficial. Her brain resumed its function with sparkles of pain.

She tried to move. She was wedged between the trunk lid and spare tire, and she thrashed wildly for a moment, in the grip of a nauseating claustrophobia.

She fainted in the midst of the useless, helpless effort. When she came to, she was weak, trembling, bathed in sweat.

She could move her left arm a little, and groped in the blackness. By straining, she reached the latch, but her fingers were powerless against the hard metal.

She fought down a fresh wave of panic. Her moving hand touched a tire tool. It was wedged under the spare. There was no way she could get it out.

Her muscles were cramping, but the growing fire in her lungs was the more real pain. She realized she was having to breathe very fast. Her heart was racing in its hunger for oxygen.

She tried to scream; then restrained herself. Very little oxygen was left in the sealed trunk. The faster she used it, the quicker she would die.

Everything in her collapsed. She closed her eyes and wept silently. The pain was mounting steadily. She felt as if her chest were being crushed with a two-ton weight.

She tried not to think of Mom, Dad, the nice young associate professor at school, the faces she would never see again.

The scene tomorrow morning built frightfully in her mind. The storekeeper would return, see her simple black sedan, look it over, call the sheriff finally. They would talk, search the car. At last the trunk would be opened, and they would fall back and ask, "What kind of beast could do this?"

They would lift out the cold, dead body and wish the stiff, unfeeling lips could answer the question. Perhaps in the light of day they would wish it almost as much as she wished it right now in her dying moment.

A strange warmth suffused her. Then the fire seemed to die as her lungs gave up the impossible fight for oxygen. Bright motes began showering through her brain.

Her face rolled limply against the spare tire. The tread roughness meant nothing at first. Then a final thought struggled—spare tire. Pounds and pounds of compressed air, loaded with life-giving oxygen; enough air, taken a sip at a time, to be alive when the storekeeper came a few hours from now.

The thought of the zebra-striped car gave her a final ounce of strength. Her fingers fumbled along the spare tire, found the valve stem. She unscrewed the cap, set her fingernail on the tip of the core, and pressed her lips about it. She depressed the core and the first squirt of air volleyed deep into her lungs.

Only a little at a time, Marilyn cautioned herself. It was going to be a long night, but a brand new morning would come—for her and, incidentally, for a pair of pillheads.

When Janet met her abrupt demise, it was only natural that she wanted to track down the person responsible. . . .

TWENTY-THREE

I Had a Hunch, And...

After a strangely timeless interval, Janet realized she was dead.

She experienced only a little shock, and no fear. Perhaps this was because of the carefree way she had conducted her past life.

She had never felt so free. A thought wave her propulsion, she zipped about the great house, then outside, toward the great, clean, open sky. Above, the stars were ever so bright and beautiful. Below, the lights of the suburban estate where she had been born and reared shone as if to answer the stars.

Janet was delighted with the whole experience. It confirmed some of the beliefs she had held, and it is always nice for one to have one's beliefs confirmed. It also excited the vivacious curiosity which had always been one of her major traits. And now there were ever so many more things about which to be curious.

She returned to the foyer of the house and looked at her lifeless physical self lying at the base of the wide sweeping stairway.

Whillikers, I was a very good looking hunk of female, she decided. *Really I was.*

The body at the foot of the stairway was slender, clad in a simple black dinner dress. The wavy mass of black hair had spilled to rest fanwise on the carpet. The soft lovely face was calm—as in innocent, dreamless sleep.

Only the awkward twist and weird angle of the slim neck revealed the true nature of the sleep.

A quick ache smote Janet. *I must accept things. This—this is really so wonderful, but I do wish I—she—could have had just a little more time. . . .*

The great house was silent. Lights blazing on death, on stillness.

Janet remembered. She had returned unexpectedly to change shoes.

191

Getting out of the car at the country club, she had snagged the heel of her left shoe and loosened it.

"I'll only be a little while," she had promised Cricket and Tom and Blake.

"We'll wait dinner," Blake had said, after she'd waved aside his insistence that he drive her home.

At home again, she had reached the head of the stairs when she heard someone in her bedroom.

She'd always possessed a cool nerve. She'd eased down the hallway. He'd been in there. Murgy. Dear old Murgy. Life hadn't begun without the memory of Murgy. He was ageless. He had worked for the family forever. Murgatroyd had been as much a part of Janet's life as the house, the giant oaks on the lawn, the car in the garage, over which Murgy lived in his little apartment.

She simply hadn't understood at first. Crouched in the hallway and peering through the crack of the partially-opened door, she had seen a brand new Murgy. This one had a chill face, but eyes that burned with determination. This one moved with much more deftness and decisiveness than the Murgy she'd always known.

He was stealing her jewelry. He was taking it from the small wall safe and replacing paste replicas. They were excellent replicas. They must have cost Murgy a great deal of money. But whatever the cost, it was pennies compared to the fortune he was slipping under his jacket.

She saw him compare a fake diamond bracelet with the real thing. The fakes were so good, she might have gone for years without knowing a large portion of her inheritance had been replaced by them.

As she saw the genuine diamond bracelet disappear into his pocket, she had gasped his name.

He had responded like a man jerking from a jolt of electricity. Frightened, she had turned, run. He had caught her at the head of the stairs.

She had tried to tell him how much his years of service meant, that she would have given him a chance to explain, a chance to straighten the thing out.

But he had given *her* no chance. He had pushed savagely at her with both arms. She had fallen, crying out, trying to grab something to break the fall.

She had struck hard. There had been one blinding flash, mingled with pain.

Murgy had followed her down. He had stood looking at her, wiping his hands on a handkerchief. He had listened, and heard no sound.

She had come alone. Everything was all right. Even the heel of her left shoe had come off during her fall.

Murgy's decision was plain in his face. He would go to his quarters. Let her be discovered. Let her death be considered an accident.

Janet broke away from the study of what had once been her body.

Murgy, you really shouldn't have done it. There is a balance in the order of things and you have upset it. There is only one way you can restore the balance, Murgy. You must pay for what you have done. Besides, my freedom won't be complete until you do.

Janet was aware of a presence in the foyer.

Cricket had entered. Cricket and Tom and Blake, wondering why she hadn't returned, beginning to worry, deciding to see what was keeping her.

A willowy blonde girl, not too intelligent, but kind and eager to please, Cricket saw the body at the base of the stairway. She put her fists to her temples and opened her mouth wide.

Janet rushed to her side. In her world of silence, she couldn't hear Cricket screaming, but she knew that was what she was doing. Cricket's merry blue eyes were not merry now. They strained against their sockets with a terrible intensity.

Poor Cricket. I'm not in pain, Cricket.

She tried to touch Cricket with the touch of compassion.

Cricket wasn't aware of this effort, Janet knew instantly. She wasn't here, as far as Cricket was concerned. She would never again be here for Cricket, or for any of the others.

Blake and Tom were beside Cricket now. Tom was helping her to a deep couch. Blake was taking slow, halting steps toward the body at the foot of the stairs.

Blake kneeled beside the young, dead body. He reached as if he would touch it. Then his hands fell to his sides. He rose, his dark, handsome face pained.

He turned, stumbled to Tom and Cricket. Cricket had subsided into broken sobs. Tom sat with his arms about her shoulders. Shock and fright made the freckles on Tom's lean, pale face stand out sharply.

They were discussing the discovery. Janet could feel their horror, their sorrow. She could sense it, almost touch it. It was as if she could almost reach the edges of their essence, of their being, with her own essence and being.

Blake was picking up the telephone now. This would be for the doctor.

Before the doctor arrived, Murgy came in. Janet strained toward him. Then she recoiled, as from a thing dark and slimy.

He was speaking. *Saying he had heard a scream, no doubt.*

Then Blake stepped from in front of Murgy. And Murgy looked toward the stairs.

Cosmic pulsations passed through Janet as she slipped along with Murgy to the body at the stairway.

She could feel the fine control deep within him, the crouching of the dark, slimy thing as, in its wanton determination to survive, it braced the flesh and ordered the brain and arranged the emotions.

The emotions were in such a storm that Janet drew back.

Murgy went to his knees beside the body and wept openly. *There was Blake now, helping Murgy to a chair. Everything was so dreadfully out of balance.*

She tried to get through to Blake. She strained with the effort. She succeeded only in causing Blake to look at Murgy a little strangely, as if something in Murgy's grief struck a small discord in Blake.

Blake went to fetch Murgy a glass of water. Janet turned her attention to Cricket and Tom. Tom's mind was resilient and strong. She battered at the edges of it, but it was too full of other things. Memories. Janet could vaguely sense them. Memories that somehow concerned her and the good times their young crowd had had.

Cricket was simply blank. Shocked beyond thinking.

Janet perched over the front doorway and beheld the scene in its entirety.

Look, people. He did it. Murgy's a murderer. He mustn't be allowed to get away with it.

Doctor Roberts came into the house. He spoke briefly with the living and turned toward the dead. He stood motionless for a moment. His grief spread like a black aura all about him. It spread until it had covered the whole room. He had delivered Janet, prescribed for her sniffles, set the arm she'd broken trying to jump a skittish horse during a summer vacation from college. He had sat by her all night the night he'd broken the news to her that her parents had been killed in a plane crash, that now she would have to live in the great house with Murgy and a housekeeper to look after her wants.

She flew to Doctor Roberts, remembering the way the big, square face and white goatee had always symbolized strength and intelligence to her.

You must understand, doctor. It was Murgy. He was ever so lucky; everything worked devilishly for him, my arrival alone, the broken shoe heel.

Then she fell back, appalled. It was as if she had bruisingly struck a solid black wall, the walls of a crypt where Doctor Roberts had shut away a part of himself. *She would never reach him, because he didn't believe. When a man died, he died as a dog or a monkey died. That's what Doctor Roberts maintained.*

Janet moved to a table holding an assortment of potted plants. She studied the activities before her.

She saw Doctor Roberts complete his examination. He talked with Blake. He looked at the broken shoe heel and nodded.

He put a professional eye on Cricket. He reopened his bag, took out a needle, and gave her a shot. Then he spoke with Tom, and Tom took Cricket out.

The doctor was explaining something to Blake. At last, Blake nodded his consent.

Janet felt herself perk up.

Of course, they'll phone the police. It's a routine, have-to measure when something like this happens.

She felt the dark, slimy thing in Murgy gather and strengthen itself, felt its evil smugness and confidence.

This was her last chance, Janet knew. The balance simply had to be restored. Otherwise, she was liable to be earth-bound until Murgy, finally, died and a higher justice thus restored the cosmic balance.

But what if they send someone like Doctor Roberts?

The policeman came at last.

He was a big man, had sandy hair and gray eyes and a jaw that looked as if it had been hacked from seasoned oak. His nose had been broken sometime in the past and reposed flagrantly misshapen on his face.

Janet hovered over him.

Look at Murgy!

For Pete's sake, one second there, when you walked in, it was naked in Murgy's eyes!

Intent on his job, the policeman walked to the stilled form at the foot of the stairway. He looked at the left shoe, then up the stairs.

After a moment, he walked up the stairs, examined the carpet, the railing. He measured the length of the stairs with his eyes.

Then he came slowly down the stairs.

He paused and looked at the beautiful girlish body.

His compassion came flooding out into the room. Janet felt as if she could ride the edges of it like a buoy.

It was a quiet, unguarded moment for him. Janet threw her will into the effort.

It was Murgy. Look at Murgy, the murderer!

He glanced at Murgy. But then, he glanced at the others too.

He began talking with Doctor Roberts.

Janet stayed close to the policeman.

If she could have met him in life, she knew they would have enjoyed a silent understanding.

I met a lot of people like that. Everybody meets people whom they like or distrust just by a meeting of the eyes.

You're feeling them out forming opinions right now, by looking into their eyes, talking with them, letting the edges of your senses reach out and explore the edges of theirs.

I feel your respect for the doctor.

I feel you recoil now as you talk with Murgy. The dark, slimy thing is deep down, well hidden, but somehow you sense it.

But for Pete's sake, feeling it isn't enough. You must pass beyond feeling to realization.

Murgy killed me.

The balance simply has to be restored.

The policeman broke off his talk with Murgy. More official people had arrived. They took photographs. Two of them in white finally carried the body away on a stretcher.

Except for the policeman, the official people went away.

Blake went out. The doctor departed. Murgy was standing with tears in his eyes. The policeman touched Murgy's shoulder, spoke.

Janet was in the doorway, barring it. But Murgy didn't know she was there. He went across the lawn, to his apartment over the garage.

Only the policeman was left. He stood with his hat in his hands looking at the spot at the base of the stairs with eyes heavy with sadness.

He was really younger than the rough face and broken nose made him appear.

Young and sad because he had seen beauty dead. Young and sad, and sensitive.

Janet pressed close to him. *It's all right, for me. You understand? There's no pain. It's beautiful here—except for the imbalance of Murgy's act.*

It wasn't an accident. You mustn't believe that. Murgy did it. You didn't like him. You sensed something about him.

Think of him! Think only of Murgy!

Don't leave yet. Ask yourself, are you giving up too easily. Shouldn't you look further?

He passed his hand through his hair. He seemed to be asking himself a question. He measured the stairway with his eyes.

She could sense the quiet, firm discipline that was in him, the result of training, of years of experience. The result of never ceasing to question, never stopping the mental probe for the unlikely, the one detail out of place.

Yes, yes! You feel something isn't quite right.

The shoe—if a girl came home to change it, would she go all the way upstairs and then start down again without changing it?

Oh, the question is clear and nettlesome in your mind.

It's a fine question.

Don't let it go. Follow it. Think about it.

He stood scratching his jaw. He walked all the way upstairs. Down the hallway. He looked in a couple of rooms, found hers.

In her room, he opened the closet. He looked at the shoes.

He stood troubled. Then he went back to the head of the stairs. Again he measured them with his eyes.

But finally, he shook his head and walked out of the house.

Come back! You must come back!

She couldn't reach him. She knew he wasn't coming back. So she perched on the roof of his speeding car as it turned a corner a block away.

He went downtown. He stopped the car in the parking lot at headquarters. He went into the building and entered his office.

Another man was there, an older man. The two talked together for a moment. The older man went out.

The policeman sat down at his desk. He picked up a pen and drew a printed form toward him.

Janet hovered over the desk.

You mustn't make out the form. You must not write it off as an accident.

Murgy did it.

He started writing.

It was murder.

He wrote a few lines and stopped.

Go get Murgy. He was the only one on the estate when it happened. Can't you see it had to be Murgy?

He nibbled at the end of the pen.

Think of the shoe. I went up, but I didn't change shoes.

He ran his finger down his crooked nose. He started writing again.

Okay, bub, if that's the way you want it, go ahead and finish the report. Call it an accident. But I'm not giving up. I'm sticking with you. I'll throw Murgy's name at you so many times you'll think you're suffering combat fatigue from being a cop too long.

Ready? Here we go, endlessly, my friend, endlessly. Murgy, Murgy, Murgy Murgymurgymurgy . . .

He drove home. He showered. He got in bed. He turned the light off.

After a time, he rolled over and punched the pillow. After another interval, he threw back the covers with an angry gesture, turned on the light, sat on the edge of the bed, and smoked a cigarette.

There was a telephone beside the bed and on the phone stand a pad of paper.

While he smoked, he doodled. He drew a spiked heel. He drew the outlines of a house. He wasn't a very good artist. He looked at the drawing of the house and under it he wrote: "No sign of forced entry. Only that servant around . . ."

He drew a pair of owlish eyes, and ringed them in black. He added some sharp lines for a face.

Then he ripped off the sheet of paper, wadded it and threw it toward the waste basket. He snubbed out his cigarette, turned off the light for a second time, punched his pillow with a gesture betokening finality, and threw his head against it.

He reached the curtain of sleep. He started through it. Cells relaxing, the barriers began to waver, weaken.

She pressed in close.

MurgymurgymurgyMURGY!

He tossed and pulled the covers snug about his shoulders. Then he threw them off, got out of bed, and snapped on the light.

He was still agitated as he dressed and went out.

He sat in the dark car for many long minutes, before starting it. He drove aimlessly for a couple of blocks, his mind a pair of millstones grating against themselves. He stopped before a bar and went in.

He sat down at the end of the bar, alone. He had one, two, three drinks. His face was still troubled by nagging questions.

Two more drinks. They didn't help. The creases deepened in his cheeks.

Janet balanced atop a cognac bottle. *Better give Murgy a little more thought. Why not follow him, shadow him? He isn't resting easy. He'll want to get rid of those jewels in a shady deal now and be ready to run if the fakes are spotted.*

The policeman raised his gaze and looked at the television set over the bar. He stopped thinking about the long stairway, the broken heel, Murgy, and various possibilities. His mind snapped to what he was seeing on the TV set.

A local newscaster with doleful face was talking about her, her death. He was only a two dimensional image and she could sense nothing about him from this point. He was taking considerable time, and she could only guess that he was talking about her background, her family. There were some old newspaper pictures, one taken when she'd been helping raise money for the crippled children's hospital. She hadn't wanted any publicity for that, and she wished the newscast were less thorough.

There was a sudden disturbance down the bar. A fat man with a bald head and drink-flushed face was giving the TV set the Bronx cheer.

Janet felt quick displeasure. *Really, I was never the rich, degener-ated hussy you're making me out, mister.*

The force of the mental explosion back down the bar caused Janet to rise to the ceiling. She saw that the fat man's exhibition had also disturbed her young policeman. He slammed out of the bar. And he was so mad he started across the street without looking.

Janet became a silent scream.

He looked up just in time to see the taxi hurtle around the corner. He tried to get out of the way. He'd had a drink too many.

Instantaneously, he became an empty shell of flesh and blood, shortly destined to become dust, lying broken in the middle of the street. A terrified but innocent cabbie was emerging from his taxi, and a small crowd was pouring out of the bar to join him.

This was defeat, Janet knew. Never had a defeat of the flesh been so agonizing. The stars could have been hers. Now the stars would have to wait, for a long, long time. For as long as Murgy lived. It wasn't the waiting that would be so hard. It was this entrapment in incompleteness, this torture, this unspeakable pain of being inescap-ably enmeshed in cosmic injustice.

She took her misery to the darkest shadow she could find and lurked there awhile, until the scene in the street had run its course, from arrival to departure of the police.

A bitter thought wave her propulsion, she returned to the estate. She filtered through the roof and hovered in the foyer.

While there had been hope, the foyer's full capacity for torture had not reached her. Now she felt it.

"Hello, Beautiful."

Where had the thought come from? She swirled like a miniature nebula.

"Take it easy I'm right here."

He swirled beside her. *Her policeman.*

"You!"

"Sure. I was so amazed at where I found myself I didn't get to you while you were hiding near the accident. You know, you *feel* even more beautiful than you looked."

"Why, thanks for the compliment. And your own homeliness, fel-low, was all of the flesh. But don't you concern yourself with me."

"Why not?"

"I'm stuck here. You didn't catch Murgy."

"I had a hunch about that guy. . . ."

"Hunch? Hah! It was me trying to get the guilt of the old boy across to you."

"Really? Well, I was going to keep an eye on him."

"I was after you to do that, too. See, I caught him stealing my jewels."

"I had to go and ruin everything!"

"But you didn't mean to barge in front of that cab."

"Just the same, I'll spend eternity being sorry. Sure you can't come with me?"

"Nope. Just go quickly."

He was gone. She felt his unwilling departure. It was the final straw of torture.

"Look, honey, my name's Joe."

He was back.

"I got this idea. It's worth a try at least."

It was so good having him back.

"My superior officer, Lieutenant Hal Dineen. He's the sharpest, most tenacious cop ever to carry a badge. That report of mine, to start with, is going to raise a question in his mind. The same facts you were trying to get over to me are there for him to find. I just bounced over to headquarters and back. Just a look told me my fray with that taxi has knocked his mental guards to smithereens. He was at his desk, reading that last report of mine. If you alone could do what you did, consider what the two of us trying real hard can do if we hit Dineen, in his present state, with full thought force."

Janet bounced to the rooftop. Joe was beside her.

"Janet, Dineen is razor sharp at playing hunches. He believes in them. All set to hit him with the grandfather of all hunches, the results of which he'll talk about for a lifetime?"

"Let's." *Let's, darling.*

Lieutenant Hal Dineen was talking to a fellow officer, "I dunno. Just one of those things. Comes from being a cop, I guess, from having the old subconscious recognize and classify information the eyes, ears, and hands miss. Just a hunch I had about this old family retainer. We all get 'em—these hunches. Me, especially, I'm a great one for 'em. And this one I couldn't shake and so I figured. . . ."

While it is easier to acquire a husband than to get rid of him, Janet found help in an unexpected place. . . .

TWENTY-FOUR

One Unnecessary Man

I remember how worried she was that night. Worried to the point of distraction. Yet for all the worry, so lovely.

She gave me only a brief kiss. Then she pulled away and the worry was naked in her eyes.

She walked to the sofa in the living room of her small, cozy house and sat down. She was looking at the window. I turned, half expecting to see something there because of the way she was looking. The window was a black, vacant eye framing the night outside. A street light, the lights of a passing car. There was nothing at the window.

She took my hand in hers and I yielded to the pressure of her cold fingers and sat on the sofa beside her.

"We'll have to wait, Roger."

"Why?" I said.

"Because of him."

"He has nothing more to do with it. With us. Or—or with you."

"He doesn't realize that," she said. She looked at the window again. "He says the divorce means nothing to him."

"Has he been bothering you?"

She nodded. A sensation of heat flowed over me as my muscles tightened. I kept feeling from my voice. "In what way?"

"Little ways," she said. "He calls me on the phone. He sends flowers and candy. Every night for a week—"

"He's been there at the window?"

"Yes," she said, the word a soft sigh.

I stood up and walked to the window, hands in my pockets.

"I've never seen him here," I said.

"He comes early in the evening, before you arrive. He raps on the window and pleads softly for me to let him in."

"Have you?"

"No."

"Not a single time?"

"Of course not! Why do you look at me like that, Roger?"

"I'm sorry," I said. "I was just trying to figure out why he would do it. Keep coming back. Calling you. With no encouragement—"

"I tell you I haven't encouraged him in the slightest way!" She was standing now. Framed in hair like pure gold mist, her face was white.

I crossed the room and put my arm about her. "This must be what he wants," I said, "to have us upset and at each other's throats."

"I don't know what he wants. There's no understanding him, Roger."

"He wants you back," I said. "It's easy enough to understand."

"He'll never have me," she said. "I stood between him and the world long enough. I acted as his shield until I couldn't take the bruises any longer."

"If he comes while I'm here," I said, "he won't come back again."

"You mustn't hurt him, Roger. He's so easily hurt."

I let my arm fall from her. "The habit of years," I murmured.

"What, Roger?"

"The habit of the years of taking care of him is not easily overcome, is it?"

Her eyes widened. "I'm still taking care of him, Roger."

"Trying. Wanting to. It won't work."

"I know that."

She stood a moment, deep in thought. Without awareness of her movement, she sat on the edge of the sofa. I waited and the room was silent. And the room wasn't real to her. She was thinking of days and months and years and little incidents of which I knew nothing. A hardness came to her face. Nothing changed, really. Yet she was different. She began cursing softly and steadily under her breath. I had never heard her use those words before.

"Janet!" I said.

She looked up at me. Her eyes cleared.

"You see what he's doing to me, Roger?" Her voice quivered. She was close to tears.

"Forget him," I said.

"How can I?"

"I don't know. But you'll have to."

"Will you help me, Roger?"

"If I was only sure—"

"Of me?"

"Yes."

"You can be. Kiss me, dear."

I kissed her. It was no good. Like kissing a lifeless image.

She laid her head against my chest. Her voice was muffled. "I'm sorry, Roger."

"It's all right," I said. But I didn't mean that. And she knew I didn't.

"I hate him, Roger."

"Of course," I said, the feeling of the kiss still stiff on my lips.

"I mean it. I do hate him. Hate the way he can make me feel like this, responsible for him and sorry for him and all."

"I understand, Janet."

"I'll mix us a drink," she said.

She drew out of my arms and walked toward the kitchen.

We'd planned the wedding for next month.

She'd get over him. She had to. A marriage is made by two people, not three.

She came back with the drinks, tall ginger ales spiced with a little bourbon. She set the tray on the cocktail table. Just as we started to pick up the glasses, the door chimes sounded.

She rose and went to the door. I saw her open it. Then she stepped back and I saw Harold come into the room.

He looked young, boyish. Except for the gun in his hand.

He glanced at the tray on the cocktail table. "Soft lights, a drink. What could be nicer?"

I was on my feet. I took a step toward him. "Ah . . ." he said, thrusting the gun. "Roger the big man. Roger the hero. Come and play hero, Roger."

I'd never seen such a light in human eyes before. I stopped. I willed myself to do something, but I remained where I was.

"Close the door, darling," he told Janet.

She closed the door. The living room became a gloomy, close world of its own.

"Harold," Janet said, "you shouldn't be here."

"Oh, I'm not afraid," he mocked her. "This is something I'm doing on my own. All by myself. And I'm not afraid. How do you like that, Janet?"

"I'm very glad. There was never any reason for you to be afraid of anything."

"I should have tried myself years ago, Janet. It's a wonderful feeling, to stand on your own feet."

"You and the gun," I said.

"Roger, please," Janet said.

"I'm not afraid of him," I said.

"That's not the question before us, is it?" Harold said. "But you are afraid of the gun, aren't you?"

"Yes," I said.

"I'm glad you have that much intelligence, Roger. I've wondered what Janet ever saw in you."

"She's the only one who can answer that," I said.

"Answer, Janet," he said. "Put your sublime feeling into words for me. I must hear it."

"Harold, you must go."

"Why? This is my house, too, you know."

"Was," I said.

He smiled. "Oh? And how do you like my favorite chair, Roger?"

"I'm not sure Janet ever told me which chair it is."

He glanced around the room. A livid ring formed about his lips. "Gone!" he said. "What have you done with my chair, darling?"

"I sold it, Harold."

"And my pipes?"

She bit her lips. "Please go."

"My pipes!" he said.

"I—gave them away."

"Gave my pipes away?" He passed his free hand over his forehead. "Who is smoking my pipes now, Janet?"

"The yard man," she said, as if she were all washed out inside.

"And the clothes I left here?"

"Packed in the closet, Harold. I sent them to you, but you—"

"I know, I know. I returned the package to the sender."

"You must take them, Harold."

"Oh, no. They belong here. With you. As I do. As I always will, Janet."

Janet sank into a wing chair. "What are we to do, Roger?"

"He can't stand and hold the gun forever," I said.

"Really, I don't intend to," Harold said.

"Then you are leaving?"

"Oh, no."

"Then you are planning to use the gun?"

"Certainly."

"What'll it get you?"

"Janet."

"You lost Janet a long time ago."

"I shall never lose Janet," he said. "Janet I shall have always."

I took a step toward him. The hammer of the gun eared back. Click! Loud and hard in the confines of the room's close, hot little world.

"Don't rush things, Roger," he said. His voice became very steady. "Nothing is enjoyable, if rushed. Don't you know that?"

"I know you'd better leave," I said. I was glad my own voice was steady; I was feeling anything but steady inside.

"When the little act is played out," Harold said, "I'll leave. Not a moment before. It must all be timed nicely, Roger. We don't want to kill the effect by hurrying things, do we? I want you to look at Janet, Roger."

I looked at Janet.

"See how beautiful she is?" he said. "The woman you wanted most in life. Doesn't it sadden you to know you'll never have her? Now you, Janet, look at Roger."

She raised her eyes to mine.

"See the nice face, Janet? The quiet way he carries himself? The strength of him? You like those things, Janet."

A sob came from her.

"Tell me!" he said, his voice faintly shrill. "Tell me how much you like him!"

"Harold. . . ."

"Dear, dear Janet," he said. "Shall I do the talking for you? You love him, need him. Yet you'll never have him, because I'm here. I'll always be here. You'll never forget this moment, Janet. You'll never forget that in order to get him you had to destroy me! Each time he touches you, whenever you hear his footsteps, you'll remember! Now look at me, Janet."

She looked towards him.

He looked straight into her eyes.

He laughed.

Then he put the gun at his temple and pulled the trigger.

The room was still slamming and tumbling with the explosion when I reached her side.

"He's gone, Roger," she said dazedly.

"Yes."

"He needed me. All those years that poor soul needed me."

I had to snap her out of it. "It's over!" I said.

"There's nothing I can do for him now."

I shook my head.

"He's not sad and miserable and longing for me, when he wants to call for help."

"Not any longer," I said, taking her hands in mine.

There was suddenly a look of great relief in her eyes, making her eyes sparkle.

And for the first time, I rather liked Harold.

Just when it appeared as if Henry Overby's best laid plans had been thwarted, he surprised everyone, including himself. . . .

TWENTY-FIVE

The Five Year Caper

The day was uneventful, except for the incident that occurred as Henry Overby was preparing to close his teller's cage at the end of the working day.

As he was totaling the cash in his drawer, Henry had the sensation of being watched. He glanced up, and there was Mr. Joshua Tipton, the bank president himself, standing in the doorway of his impressive, walnut-paneled office, studying Henry.

Mr. Tipton, a gray-maned old lion, a banker's banker in the ancient tradition, rarely showed concern for anything so low on the evolutionary ladder as mere tellers. Awareness of Mr. Tipton's drawn-out and minute appraisal of Henry Overby seeped through the bank, until just about all of his fellow workers were stealing glances in Henry's direction.

Despite the accelerating nature of his pulse rate, Henry gave no outward sign of dismay. With a properly respectful inclination of his head in Mr. Tipton's direction, Henry continued working with his normal quiet, deft efficiency.

Work in neighboring cages came almost to a halt as Mr. Tipton took it upon himself to stroll all the way across the bank to Henry's window and stood there.

"How are you, Overby?" The austere, craggy countenance nodded cordially.

"I'm fine, Mr. Tipton. And you, sir?"

The president glanced through the wicket. "Have a good day?"

"Very good, I'm glad to report."

"A number of our customers seem to prefer you, Overby. They like to have you wait on them."

"I try to serve with dispatch, Mr. Tipton."

"A commendable attitude." He glanced sharply away from Henry, and work behind the other wickets resumed with vigor. Less severely, Mr. Tipton's eyes returned to Henry. "You've been with us for some time now, haven't you, Overby?"

"Five years, sir."

"A mere breaking-in period in the business of banking," Mr. Tipton said.

"But time alone," Henry ventured bravely, "is only one yardstick. There remains the diligence with which an employee applies himself."

Mr. Tipton's bushy brows quirked to attention. "Quite true. Taken much sick leave, Overby?"

"Never missed a day, sir."

The president studied Henry a moment longer, then cleared his throat. "Yes, well . . . Nice chatting with you, Overby."

"The pleasure was mine, Mr. Tipton."

Henry was able to contain himself until he was alone in his neat, almost barren bachelor apartment. On his record player he put some very cool Brubeck and very torrid Rusty Warren and then, from the tenth which he'd purchased on the way home, poured himself a precise ounce of Scotch to celebrate the occasion. Unlike the slightly built, commonplace Overby of banking endeavors, Henry brazenly cracked back at Rusty, guffawing as he realized he'd topped the gag emitted by the tinny record player.

He danced his way to the kitchenette to stash the Scotch for future special occasions, a birthday ounce, a Christmas ounce, perhaps even two ounces at New Year's.

The usual covey of strutting and cooing pigeons were gathering on the window sill. Henry fed them generously with graham crackers, bran flakes, and bread crumbs.

"Eat hearty, pals," he told the fluttering flock, "toward the nearing day when it will be cake!"

Ah, yes, he thought as he began frying a thin hamburger for his dinner, Mr. Tipton's conversation today has but one meaning.

Mr. Darcy Featherstone, who was now cashier, was going to be made a vice-president of the bank. Everyone knew that. But until today there had been no indication of who might be elevated to the cashier's post.

As cashier, Henry thought, I'll enjoy complete trust, unquestioned access to that beautiful vault.

The culmination of five years of planning, working, and waiting was almost at hand. It made all Henry's past years seem remote and unreal. He could hardly remember the scrawny myopic little boy who, pushed from one unwilling relative to another after his parents had died, had long ago learned to keep his hungers, fears, and hopes to himself.

The day after he got his high school diploma, Henry had risen before dawn and crept from the house of the final relative, an uncle named Hiram. Henry had never turned back.

For the next couple of years, Henry had sampled the world, drifting and working odd jobs. A neat, polite, unobtrusive young man, he had been employed as a hardware clerk when he'd heard of the opening at the bank.

Applying for the job, he'd known he had impressed Mr. Joshua Tipton, then a vice president, as a fellow whose wants and needs were simple and few.

Little did he know, Henry chuckled as he flipped his dinner patty of ground beef.

After his loveless and vitamin deficient childhood, Henry had a secret yearning for prestige so powerful that it occasionally boiled out of his subconscious in the form of dreams. Slumber might transform him briefly into a renowned statesman, or a famous philanthropist planning an Alice-in-wonderland community for orphaned children, or an eminent explorer pushing far up the Amazon.

But the fiber of Henry's agile mind was far too strong to be satisfied by mere dreams. Prestige, he analyzed, was possible to him only through material things, since he had little prospect of becoming a statesman, philanthropist, or explorer.

He lined his secret sights on four specific prestige symbols: an imposing home; membership in an exclusive country club; a big expensive automobile, and an expensive and somewhat snobbish wife with a family tree, even if she should turn out to be a bit plain.

It was not through choice that he placed the wife at the bottom of the list. He was simply realistic, accepting the natural order of things.

The prerequisite to Henry's needs was, of course, commonplace. Money, money, money; enough to take him far away, to a new name, to a beginning of life.

He'd had no hope of ever coming into so much money, even when he had gone to work at the bank. The position, at the outset, had attracted him for two reasons. A bank teller enjoyed more prestige than a hardware clerk. And he liked the feel of money, the thought of being surrounded daily by so much of it.

Then one day, he'd watched Mr. Darcy Featherstone go into the bank vault where fortunes, plural, were stacked. And the thought had come quite naturally to Henry's mind: If I were in Mr. Featherstone's position, I'd disappear one day, and when they started checking up they'd find I'd become a very rich man. In Mr. Featherstone's position, I could easily alter the record of the serial numbers of the large bills. With free run of the vault I could secrete the bills in my clothing, if I prepared the garments beforehand with hidden pockets and pouches, slip into my topcoat, bid everyone the usual goodbye for the day, and walk out of the bank as a veritable animated gold mine. I could break down the bills later in one part of the country, take the hoard to some nice little town in, say, Vermont.

Who would think ever of looking for the boldest of bank robbers around a snooty Vermont country club?

Henry had been jarred out of his trance, a few beads of sweat on his forehead, by the impatient clearing of a customer's throat.

The idea hadn't frightened Henry for very long. It became a part of him, another facet in that unknown portion of his personality. The bank vault, only a few yards from where he worked each day, became something more to Henry than mere case-hardened steel and flame-resistant alloys. With the passage of time, the vault assumed the aspects of a hiding place for Henry's own secret treasure trove; a personal depository just waiting the day when he could claim his fortune.

He was young. He had plenty of time. Eventually, efficient worker that he was, he had to be taken into the inner circle, from which he would have intimate and unsuspected association with the treasure. It was his one hope. It was surely worth waiting for.

Meanwhile, he had more than his salary to sustain him. Each day, he would be near his treasure. In a way, he would be watching over it.

With a start, Henry came out of his money-spangled fog. Greasy black smoke was rising from the hard lump of scorched hamburger. Not only that, someone was knocking on the door of his apartment.

He grabbed the frying pan, blistered his fingers, yelped, reached for a pot holder, and removed the pan to the sink. Then, sucking his burned fingers, he dashed for the door.

With a vacuous smile on her large, damp mouth, Miss Mavis Birdsong was standing in the corridor. She had moved into the building a few weeks previously. Ripened to the point of generosity in face and figure, she was a blonde with large, round blue eyes. There was just a little too much of her for Henry's taste, although he had accepted her friendship from the day she had moved in and crossed the hall to borrow a cup of sugar.

"Hi, Henry."

"Hello, Miss Birdsong."

She gave him a little pinch on the cheek. "Come on over. I made spaghetti like even the Italians wish they could make, more than I can handle by myself."

Henry thought of the charred mess in his frying pan. "Well, I. . . ."

"Fine." She linked her arm with his, precluding any further hesitation on his part. "I even have wine to go with it."

"If you're sure it won't inconvenience you, if none of your other gentlemen callers. . . ."

"Just a couple guys I know, Henry. But you're the only real gentleman in my life!"

In her apartment, Mavis hummed in a throaty voice as she prepared his plate. "How goes it at the bank, Henry?"

"Okay. Well, excellent, really."

"That's great. You get a promotion or something?"

"I think I'm going to. I—I'm sure they're going to make me cashier. It's been a long time coming, five years, but I'm certain I'll be more than amply rewarded." He gave a beatific sigh.

"Wonderful!"

Henry gave her a glance. For some reason or other, Miss Birdsong seemed slightly strained this evening.

"I'm afraid," Henry said, "I've bored you with nothing but talk of the bank."

"Not a bit. I've enjoyed every minute."

Henry woke bushy-tailed the next morning. He bounced out of bed, did his knee bends and twenty-five daily pushups with no more effort than bending a finger.

In the preparation of his breakfast, he grasped the skillet handle and flipped the eggs in a manner that would have brought the envy of a first-rate short order cook.

Even the date didn't bother him today, first day of the month, the day for cashing those endless payroll checks from textile and food processing plants in the area.

Henry made his customary prompt arrival at the bank. The blinds were still drawn on the double front doors, but he knew that Mr. Darcy Featherstone would have already arrived, met the guard, and unlocked.

Henry stepped inside. He promptly ceased all motion as a small, round object was jammed against his back.

"It's a gun, pal." A gritty voice behind Henry imparted the information.

Henry's gaze made a wild sweep of the bank. Judkins, the guard, with a lump on his head and no gun in his holster, was bending over a leather couch where Mr. Darcy Featherstone was recovering from a faint. Against the far wall, the bank's small complement of employees were lined up under the gun of a squat man who wore coveralls and a rubber monkey mask that covered his entire head.

In a similar overall-mask disguise, the man behind Henry herded him forward. "You can fill the sacks, chum."

"We're vegetarians," the second monkey face said. "We like lettuce. All that lettuce you got on hand to meet the payroll checks."

"Save it," the man behind Henry said. "Just be sure to watch them jerks so nothing goes wrong until we get the lettuce into her car."

Her? Henry had a queerly detached feeling. *Her!* Driving the getaway car. Waiting behind the wheel right now, engine at the ready, for her male partners to emerge from the bank loaded with loot.

Mavis Birdsong. Yes. It had to be. The men in coveralls and masks were the exact size and shape of the pair who had visited her. Her choice of apartments had been by design, as well as her friendship for Henry. She wanted him to tell her about the bank so that she and these two hoodlums could plan a despicable act.

"Come on, come on," one of the robbers was snarling at Judkins, the guard. "Get the cashier on his feet and about the business of opening the vault!"

"Right with you." Mr. Darcy Featherstone's voice was that of a whimpering child caught in a sepulchre.

Pressed forward by the man behind him, Henry watched the teller's cages swimming toward him. From the corner of his vision, he saw Mr. Featherstone cravenly rushing toward the vault.

Mr. Featherstone was going to open the vault. And these unspeakable usurpers, the greedy pigs in monkey faces, were going to take, in a matter of minutes, the treasure to which he, Henry Overby, had been willing to devote years of his very life.

A wild shriek came from Henry's throat. He felt the hard pressure of the alarm button behind the teller's cages under his toe.

A bell began to clang. A gun blasted. A female employee screamed. Mr. Darcy Featherstone made a dull noise as he fainted and keeled over again.

Henry was vaguely aware of being in motion, the shrill yells still coming from his lips. He had a strange object in his hand which he'd scooped up from the shelf below and inside a teller's cage. He curled his forefinger, pointing the object, and the bank resounded with the blast of gunfire.

Then half the building seemed to fall on Henry's right shoulder. The process was instant. He blacked out.

Henry returned to the realm of consciousness with a wince, a groan, a slow opening of his eyes. A doctor, a nurse, and Mr. Joshua Tipton, bank president, were hovering beside his hospital bed.

"Welcome back, Henry," Mr. Tipton said as if speaking to a son.

"Did they. . . ."

"They didn't, Henry," Mr. Tipton said. "When their deal soured, they broke and ran. Both got caught. Unfortunately for them, they were stranded on foot. When she heard the commotion, the blonde woman bolted in the get-away car. In her panic, she ran into a bridge abutment. But she was the only fatality."

"Better let him rest now," the doctor said.

"I'll give him something to rest on," Mr. Tipton said. "When you come back, Henry, you're through as a teller."

"I am?"

"The most miserable showing of Darcy Featherstone in a crisis has convinced me that he's not quite the man for the v-p post. Your experience and length of service, along with proof that still waters do run deep, qualify you for the job, I think."

"They do?"

"Welcome to our ranks, fellow executive. Mr. Vice-President!"

"Hmmm," said Henry. He squinted one eye in deep thought. In five years, he realized, he had come to like the bank. Except for that shrimp Darcy, the other employees were pretty nice. And Mr. Tipton . . . why, the old man had unsuspected emotions behind that leonine exterior!

"You have the personal interest we all must share in the great responsibility intrusted to us," Mr. Tipton was saying. "Even I, Overby, must take a lesson from your courage and intense personal devotion to our fine bank."

"You must?" Henry inquired. His thoughts skittered briefly on a tangent. After all, bank vice-presidents do belong to country clubs. They do buy imposing homes, being in a position to ferret out a bargain. A v-p can invest, handle his money wisely, even purchase a fine car, and court a slightly snobbish fruit off a fine old family tree, although she may be a bit plain.

Henry's ambition began to leap and dance. The mere thought of filching from the vault seemed puerile. Certainly it was unworthy of Henry Overby, vice-president, who in a few more years would very likely occupy the very office in which now Mr. Tipton reigned.

"Yes, Overby," Mr. Tipton's tone was an oratorical flourish. "We are proud to have a man with your sense of duty, your very personal regard for our noble institution. You expressed it fervently, Judkins reported, even if somewhat abstrusely."

"I did?" Henry said cautiously.

"Certainly, man! Don't you remember? As you went down under the gunman's bullet, you were yelling it at the top of your lungs. Overby, the heroic words you uttered were, precisely, 'You can't have the treasure out of my vault . . . my vault . . . my vault. . . .'"

Talmage Powell sold his first story when he was barely out of his teens. The author of more than twenty books and numerous screen plays, Powell especially enjoys writing Hitchcock-type short stories that reflect on that "nothing is certain" quality of life. Powell and his wife live in Asheville, North Carolina, after residences in Florida, New York, California, and various Mexican border locales.